ELMORE LEONARD

KILLSHOT

"One of his most ambitious . . . Leonard has written an Elmore Leonard crime fiction thriller, but it's a novel, too. Not a pretentious or 'literary' novel, of course, but a novel that only Elmore Leonard could write. . . . While there is plenty of the physical tension erupting into violence you expect, the real menace is psychological. . . . Leonard tops himself every time."
Boston Globe

"Terrifically enjoyable . . . takes your breath away . . . the suspense hardly lets up . . . Leonard's well-known virtues are all on display: the ripe, funny dialogue; a final scene so masterfully crafted you want to applaud; an array of secondary characters that stay with you the way secondary characters do in Dickens."
Washington Post Book World

"A master of narrative . . . A poet of the vernacular . . . Leonard paints an intimate, precise, funny, frightening, and irresistible mural of the American underworld."
The New Yorker

"Classic Leonard . . . *Killshot* is probably his best."
Newsweek

Books by Elmore Leonard

And in Hardcover

When the Women Come Out to Dance

ELMORE LEONARD

KILLSHOT

HarperTorch
An Imprint of HarperCollins*Publishers*

This is a work of fiction. Names, characters, places, and incidents are products of the author's imagination or are used fictitiously and are not to be construed as real. Any resemblance to actual events, locales, organizations, or persons, living or dead, is entirely coincidental.

HARPERTORCH
An Imprint of HarperCollins*Publishers*
10 East 53rd Street
New York, New York 10022-5299

First HarperTorch paperback printing: February 2003
First William Morrow trade paperback printing: March 1999
First William Morrow hardcover printing: April 1989

HarperCollins ®, HarperTorch™, and ♥™ are trademarks of Harper-Collins Publishers Inc.

Printed in the United States of America

Visit HarperTorch on the World Wide Web at www.harpercollins.com

10 9 8 7 6 5 4 3 2 1

For Gregg Sutter

_____

1

THE BLACKBIRD TOLD HIMSELF he was drinking too much because he lived in this hotel and the Silver Dollar was close by, right downstairs. Try to walk out the door past it. Try to come along Spadina Avenue, see that goddamn Silver Dollar sign, hundreds of light bulbs in your face, and not be drawn in there. Have a few drinks before coming up to this room with a ceiling that looked like a road map, all the cracks in it. Or it was the people in the Silver Dollar talking about the Blue Jays all the time that made him drink too much. He didn't give a shit about the Blue Jays. He believed it was time to get away from here, leave Toronto and the Waverley Hotel for good and he wouldn't drink so much and be sick in the morning. Follow one of those cracks in the ceiling.

The phone rang. He listened to several rings before picking up the receiver, wanting it to be a sign. He liked signs. The Blackbird said, "Yes?" and a voice he recognized asked would he like to go to Detroit. See a man at a hotel Friday morning. It would take him maybe two minutes.

In the moment the voice on the phone said "Detroi-it" the Blackbird thought of his grandmother, who lived near there, and began to see himself and his brothers with her when they were young boys and thought, This could be a sign. The voice on the phone said, "What do you say, Chief?"

"How much?"

"Out of town, I'll go fifteen."

The Blackbird lay in his bed staring at the ceiling, at the cracks making highways and rivers. The stains were lakes, big ones.

"I can't hear you, Chief."

"I'm thinking you're low."

"All right, gimme a number."

"I like twenty thousand."

"You're drunk. I'll call you back."

"I'm thinking this guy staying at a hotel, he's from here, no?"

"What difference is it where he's from?"

"You mean what difference is it to *me*. I think it's somebody you don't want to look in the face."

The voice on the phone said, "Hey, Chief? Fuck you. I'll get somebody else."

This guy was a punk, he had to talk like that. It was okay. The Blackbird knew what this guy and his people thought of him. Half-breed tough guy one time from Montreal, maybe a little crazy, they gave the dirty jobs to. If you took the jobs, you took the way they spoke to you. You spoke back if you could get away with it, if they needed you. It wasn't social, it was business.

He said, "You don't have no somebody else. You call me when your people won't do it. I'm thinking that tells me the guy in the hotel—I wonder if it's the old guy you line up to kiss his hand. Guy past his time, he don't like how you do things."

There was a silence on the line before the voice said, "Forget it. We never had this conversation."

See? He was a punk. The Blackbird said, "I never kiss his hand or any part of him. What do I care?"

"So, you want it?"

"I'm thinking," the Blackbird said, staring at the ceiling, "you have a Cadillac, that blue one." It was the same vivid light-blue color as his grandmother's cottage on Walpole Island. "What is it, about a year old?"

"About that."

So it was two years old, or three. That was okay, it looked good and it was the right color.

"All right, you give me that car, we have a deal."

"Plus the twenty?"

"Keep it. Just the car."

This guy would be telling his people, see, he's crazy. You can give him trading beads, a Mickey Mouse watch. But said over the phone, "If that's what you want, Chief." The voice gave him the name of the hotel in Detroit and the room number, a suite on the sixty-fourth floor, and told him it would have to be done the day after tomorrow, Friday around nine-thirty, give or take a few minutes. The old man would be getting dressed or reading the sports, he was in town for the ball game, Jays and the Tigers. Walk in and walk out.

"I know how to walk out. How do I get in?"

"He has a girl with him, the one he sees when he's there. It's arranged for her to let you in."

"Yeah? What do I do with her?"

The voice on the phone said, "Whatever your custom allows, Chief." Confident now; listen to him. "What else can I tell you?"

The Blackbird hung up the phone and stared at the ceiling again, picking out a crack that could be the Detroit River among stains he narrowed his eyes to see as the Great Lakes. Ontario, Erie, Lake Huron . . .

His name was Armand Degas, born in Montreal. His mother was Ojibway, his father he didn't remember, French-Canadian. Both were dead. Until eight years ago he had lived and worked with his two brothers. The younger one was dead and the older one was in prison forever. Armand Degas was fifty years old. He had lived in Toronto most of his life, but didn't know if he should stay here. He could go downstairs to the Silver Dollar and after a while feel pretty good. There was a bunch of Ojibway that hung out there. Maybe he looked like some of them with his thick body and his thick black hair lacquered back hard with hair spray. They'd talk, but he could tell they were afraid of him. Also there were more punks coming in there, crazy ones who colored their hair pink and green; he didn't like the way they called him the Blackbird, the way they said it. The Italians, most of the time, called him Chief. It was like they could call him anything they wanted, the guineas posing in their expensive clothes, talking with their hands. Even if they said he could be a made guy, one of them, he wouldn't ever belong to them. When the phone rang he had been trying to figure out why he drank so much. He was thinking now, as he began to picture a young girl in the the hotel room in Detroit, he drank because he needed to drink.

The girl would be young and very pretty. It was the kind they found for the old man. She'd be scared. Even if they told her, you open the door, that's all you have to do, and gave her some money, she'd be scared to death. He wondered if the old man would notice it. You didn't become old in his business missing signs. He wondered if he should wear his suit to go into that hotel. It was tight on him when he buttoned the coat. He'd drive to Detroit in the Cadillac . . . and began to think about his grandmother, trying to picture her now, older than the old man he was going to see. They called him Papa, a guy who'd had his way a long time, but no more. The Blackbird saw himself drive up to the blue cottage in the matching Cadillac and saw his grandmother come out . . . Then saw a young girl in a hotel room again, scared to death.

But when the girl opened the door she didn't seem scared at all. She was about eighteen maybe, wearing a robe, with long blond hair down over her shoulders like a little girl. Except her expression wasn't a little girl's. She looked him over and walked away and was going into the bedroom as he entered the suite and saw the room-service table and what was left of breakfast. The bedroom door was open. He could hear her voice saying something— that nice-looking young girl, not the kind he had expected. The Blackbird glanced at the bedroom but didn't see either of them. He walked past the room-service table to the room's wide expanse of windows filled with an overcast sky. Now he was looking at Canada from six hundred feet in the air; Windsor, Ontario, across the river, Toronto two hundred and fifty miles beyond. Not straight across but more east, that way, where the Detroit River turned into Lake St. Clair. Keep going and you come to Walpole Island. Staring in that direction he squinted into the distance. A sound behind him made him turn.

The old man they called Papa, head bent, showing the straight part in his white hair combed flat, was pouring himself a cup of coffee. He stood at the room-service table with a bath towel wrapped high around his waist, white against tan skin, almost to his chest: this man who always dressed in style, a gold pin fixed to his shirt collar, always with a tan. But look how frail he was, dried up, aged in the sun. A bird could perch on his shoulder blades, hop to his collarbone.

Now a shower was turned on. In there beyond the open bedroom door. The girl giving him privacy.

"Papa?"

The old man looked up. Surprised and then frowning with the windows in his eyes: the same way he had looked when a government commission, the one investigating organized crime in Canada, asked him what he did for a living and the old man said he was in the pepperoni business, he sold it to places they made pizza.

He said with his heavy accent and a note of hope, "You got something for me?"

"From your son-in-law."

The old man's hope left him as he said, "Oh, Christ," sounding tired. He looked down at the room-service table but seemed to have forgotten what he wanted. He stared for several moments before looking up. "I told my daughter don't marry that guy, he's a punk. She don't listen. I'll give him six months, they gonna be another funeral."

The Blackbird said, "You want him done sooner than that, tell me." He saw the old man staring at him, frowning again, and he said, "You don't know who I am?"

"I can't see you," the old man said, coming around the table, one hand gripping the towel, the fingers of his other hand touching the edge of the table. He seemed so small, his bones showing, his eyes, as they looked up, tired and moist. He said, "Yes, of course," and seemed to shrug as he moved close to the window.

The Blackbird watched the old man staring at the beginning of Ontario reaching out beyond the city and across open land to the sky.

"You know Walpole Island, Papa?" The Blackbird pointed upriver. "It's that way past the lake, on the Canadian side of the channel. The big ships go by there, up the St. Clair River to Lake Huron and around through Lake Superior, go to places over there, and back again till the ice comes. Walpole Island, it's an Indian reserve where my grandmother lives."

The old man took his time to look up at him, patient, not going anywhere, making these moments last.

"She's Ojibway, same as me. You know what else? She's a medicine woman. She was going to turn me into an owl one time, I said to her, 'I don't want to be no owl, I want to be a blackbird,' and that's how I got this name. From my brothers, when we were boys and we visited there."

The old man was staring out again and seemed off in his mind.

"You remember us, the Degas brothers? One dead working for you, shot dead by the police. One in Kingston doing life for you. Papa, you listening to me? And I'm here."

"Can she do that," the old man said, "turn you into an owl?"

"If she wants to. Listen, when we went there in the summer when we were boys, we had a twenty-two rifle, a single-shot we used, go in the marsh and hunt for muskrats. See, but we hardly ever found any, so on the way home to her house we'd shoot at dogs, you know, cats, birds. Man, it got people mad, but they wouldn't say nothing. You know why? They were afraid the grandmother would do something to them."

The old man was listening. He said, "Turn them into something they don't want. How does she do that?"

"She has a drum she beats on and sings in Ojibway, so I don't know what she saying," the Blackbird said. "Imagine a day you don't even see the trees move. She beats on the drum and sings and a wind comes in under the door and stirs the fire in the fireplace. She wants to, she can burn a house down. Or like if you do something to her and she gets mad? She can get a bird to shit on your car. She does it best with seagulls. A seagull flies over, she beats on the drum, points to the car. That one. The seagull shits on the hood, on the windshield. Or she can get a whole flock of them to do it, all over the car. I'm going to go see her. Drive up there, you take the ferry over from Algonac, a half-mile across the St. Clair River from the U.S. side to Walpole Island."

The old man's head was nodding as he thought of something and said, "I could use a woman like that. Have her turn me into a blue jay." He smiled, showing his perfect dentures. "Those fucking Jays, they gonna do it this year, go all the way to the World Series. I'll give you five to three. I don't care who they play. We going tonight, see them beat the Tigers." The old man paused. He turned and looked up with his tired eyes. "No, I'm gonna go in there, put on my robe . . ." He paused again. "No, I think I like to be dressed. Is that okay with you?"

"Whatever you want."

The old man walked toward the bedroom saying, "That fucking son-in-law, I never like that guy."

The Blackbird gave him time. He stepped to the room-service table and poured a cup of coffee. It was barely warm. He ate a croissant with it and two strips of cold bacon he believed the girl had ordered and didn't eat. What did she care, she wasn't paying for it. She had taken one bite out of each half piece of toast. He could hear the shower running. There was a Coca-Cola bottle on the table and a glass half full she had left, wasting it, not caring.

It was warm in here and he was uncomfortable in his wool suit, a black one, double-breasted, he wore with a white shirt and green-blue tie that had little green fish on it. A Browning 380 automatic, stuck in his waist at the small of his back, dug into his spine. It was a relief to pull it out. The Blackbird worked the slide to rack a cartridge into the chamber. The pistol was ready to fire and he believed he was ready. But now his pants felt loose and he had to adjust them to stick his shirt in good and straighten his tie and button his coat before going into the bedroom. He had to feel presentable. It was something he did for himself; no one else would think about how he looked, notice the suit was too tight for him and needed to be pressed. The old man wouldn't care.

The old man wouldn't even see him. He was lying on the unmade bed in a starched white shirt and tan trousers, brown shoes and socks, hands folded on his chest, his eyes closed.

The shower was running in the bathroom, the door open a few inches.

The Blackbird brought the sheet up over the old man's body all the way, covering his face. Now he was looking at the outline of the face and saw the sheet move as the old man breathed in, sucking the white cloth flat against his mouth. That was where the Blackbird placed the muzzle of the Browning and shot him. He fired once. The sound filled the room and maybe it was heard on the other side of the wall in another room, or maybe not. It was sudden; if anyone heard it and said what was that and stopped to listen, there was nothing else to hear.

Only the shower running in the bathroom.

When he pulled the shower curtain aside the girl with long blond hair, the hair darker now, her face and body glistening wet, looked at him and said, "Are you through?"

The Blackbird said, "Not yet," raising the pistol, and watched the girl's expression finally change.

*   *   *

The last time he came to Walpole Island was nine years ago, with his two brothers. They had finished some business in Sarnia for the Italians and drove down through Wallaceburg and across the bridge. That way, it wasn't like coming to an island.

This time he came from Algonac, Michigan, on the U.S. side, drove over the metal plates from the nine-car ferry to the dock and pulled up in the Cadillac to tell the customs guy he used to live here when he was a boy and had come back. He followed the road south along the ship channel where he and his brothers used to throw stones at the freighters going by. They had seemed so close in the channel, those ore carriers sliding past forever without a sound. This was when their mother would send them here from Toronto, in the summer. Once they swam the channel to Harsens Island on the U.S. side, maybe a quarter of a mile, and his brother now in Kingston for life had almost drowned.

Then he and his brothers didn't come again till they were grown men: came to visit because they were nearby, that time in Sarnia, and stayed to repaint the blue cottage and fix some leaks in the roof. The cottage was damp and smelled, full of mice the Degas brothers caught in glue traps they got at the A & P in Algonac. The traps held the mice by their feet in a sticky substance; or sometimes the mouse's face would be stuck in it. The brothers would carry the traps outside, the mice still alive, and shoot them with their high-caliber pistols. *Bam*, that mouse would be gone, disappear, and the Degas brothers would look at each other and grin like they were young boys again shooting at dogs and cats. The grandmother, getting old, had watched them but didn't say much or work any kind of medicine.

This time, when he came to the cottage, it seemed deeper in the trees, its blue paint faded and peeling, its plywood storm shutters down covering the windows, the yard overgrown with weeds.

The woman at Island Variety, across the road from the ferry dock, said yes, the grandmother was in the cemetery, buried last winter. The woman said the Band office didn't know what to do about the house or the furniture, all the grandmother's things. Armand Degas told her he'd take care of it and turned away, not wanting to talk to this woman in the noise of kids playing video games, Breakout and Zaxxon. There were other people too. Some duck hunters in the store were buying candy bars and potato chips, talking loud to each other. Their cars with Michigan plates were parked outside where Walpole guides waited smoking cigarettes. They had stopped talking as Armand walked by them, coming in. They knew who he was.

Pretty soon the duck hunters in their camouflage outfits and two-tone rubber boots, still talking loud and taking forever, moved out the door and Armand saw a guy he recognized, toward the back of the store.

Lionel something. Coming away from the cooler with two cans of Pepsi. Sure, Lionel, walking with that limp. He was a kid when the Degas brothers came here as kids. They beat him up the first time they met; Lionel came after them with a live snake and they got to be friends. Then nine years ago they saw him in the bar at Sans Souci on Harsens Island where the Indians went to get drunk and he was using a cane to walk. They had some beers and he told them how he fell off a building, "into the hole" as he called it, and broke his legs pretty good. He was an ironworker then. Lionel Adam, that was his name. He was still limping, swinging one leg way around, but didn't have the cane—taking the Pepsis over to a guy leaning against the craft counter, where they sold handmade Indian stuff.

The guy was taller than Lionel, maybe younger, with light-colored hair. He wasn't Indian. He was thin but looked strong. Now he straightened up, turning away from the counter as Lionel handed him a Pepsi, and Armand saw something written on the back of the guy's blue jacket. In white letters it said IRONWORKERS, and under it, smaller, BUILD

AMERICA. So he was another one of them, probably an old buddy of Lionel's.

Armand went to the cooler and got himself a Pepsi. He popped it open edging closer to Lionel and the ironworker, looking at a poster that announced BINGO TONIGHT at the Sports Center. VISIT THE CANTEEN FOR ALL YOUR REFRESHMENT NEEDS! Lionel didn't seem to notice him. They were talking about hunting whitetail.

It sounded strange, the ironworker telling the Indian he was going to make sure Lionel got a buck to hang on his meat pole. Saying he bought a salt lick to put out in the woods. Lionel was saying they should take a sweat bath and not eat any meat for a week. A whitetail could smell it if you had a hamburger and tell if you had mustard or ketchup on it. The ironworker said you had to take time beforehand to read the deer, think like them and you'd get your shot.

"Pretend you're a buck," Lionel said, "with a big rack."

"Sixteen points," the ironworker said.

"You see a doe, her tail standing up in the air waving at you," Lionel said, "you won't know whether to shoot it or hump it."

"Or both, and then eat it," the ironworker said. "I fill the freezer every November and it's gone by May."

They walked toward the door, Lionel telling the

ironworker he could make it tomorrow afternoon about four o'clock. Armand came to the front of the store with his Pepsi. Through the window he saw them standing by a tan Dodge pickup. When the ironworker backed around and drove off toward the ferry dock, Armand saw a tool box in the pickup bed and a Michigan license plate. He waited for Lionel to come back into the store, but saw him walking away, limping past the window. Armand had to go after him.

"Hey, where's your cane?"

Lionel stopped and half-turned to look back, standing behind Armand's blue Cadillac. He said, "I thought maybe it was you," sounding different than when he was talking to the ironworker, not much life in his voice now. "You go by the Band office?"

"For what?"

"About your grandmother. We been trying to get hold of somebody, a relative, find out what to do with her house."

"I don't know," Armand said, "I been thinking, I could fix the place up." His gaze moved to the trees along the road, then over to the tip of Russell Island, where the freighter channel joined the St. Clair River. He saw gulls out there, specks against the afternoon sky. Lionel was telling him he could sell the house the way it was. Why spend money on it?

"No, I mean fix it up and live there," Armand said, turning enough to look down the river road. You couldn't see any houses, only trees changing color. This island was all woods and marsh, and some cornfields. He couldn't imagine staying here for more than a few weeks. Still, he wanted Lionel to say sure, that's a good idea, live here, become part of it.

But Lionel said, "What would you do? You know, a guy use to living in the city. That place, all it has is a wood stove."

Armand's gaze returned to Lionel in his wool shirt and jeans, rubber hunting boots, Lionel still half-turned like he wanted this to be over and walk away.

"What are you, a guide for those big-shot duck hunters come here from the States? I could do that, be a guide," Armand said. "I know how to shoot. In the winter trap muskrats." He wanted Lionel to say sure, why not?

"We do it in the spring," Lionel said, "burn off the marsh. You get all dirty out there, filthy. You wear a nice suit of clothes. . . . You wouldn't like it."

Armand watched Lionel shift his weight from one leg to the other, careful about it, as though he might be in pain.

"How long were you an ironworker?"

Lionel shrugged. "Ten years."

"Now you work for those big-shot hunters come here, think everything's funny. You live here but have to go across the river to get drunk in a bar. Or you stay here and play bingo, visit the canteen for all your refreshment needs. But I can't live here, 'ey? That what you telling me?"

Lionel stared back at him like he was getting up courage to answer and Armand looked away, giving him time, Armand's gaze following the ferry on its way to Algonac, Michigan, another world over there. He heard Lionel say:

"There's no life for you here. There's nothing for you."

Armand wanted to ask him, Then tell me where there is. But when he looked at Lionel again he said, "You ever ride in a Cadillac? Come on, we'll drive over there, have some drinks."

"You have some," Lionel said. "I'm going home."

He walked over to his pickup truck swinging one leg, leaving Armand standing there in his suit of clothes by his blue Cadillac.

2

RICHIE NIX BOUGHT A T-SHIRT at Henry's restaurant in Algonac that had IT'S NICE TO BE NICE written across the front. He changed in the men's room: took off his old T-shirt and threw it away, put on the new one looking at himself in the mirror, but then didn't know what to do with his gun. If he put his denim jacket back on to hide the nickel-plate .38 revolver stuck in his jeans, you couldn't read the T-shirt. What he did was roll the .38 up inside the jacket and carried it into the dining area.

There was a big IT'S NICE TO BE NICE wood-carved sign on the shellacked knotty-pine wall in the main room, over past the salad bar. It had been the restaurant's slogan for fifty years. Most people who came to Henry's liked a table by the front windows, so they could watch the freighters go by while they ate their dinner. Richie Nix took a table off to the side where he could look at freighters and ore carriers if he wanted, though he was more interested this evening in keeping an eye on the restaurant parking lot. He needed a car for a new business he was getting into.

The waitress brought him a beer. He looked up, taking a drink from the can, and there was a big goddamn ore carrier a thousand feet long passing from the river into the channel. Richie grinned at the sight. It was neat the way the boat looked like it was going right through the woods. It went by the point of Russell Island, a narrow neck of land, and you saw the boat through the trees without seeing the channel. It could be going to Ford Rouge or one of the mills downriver from Detroit.

For the past few weeks Richie had been staying with a woman he'd gotten to know at Huron Valley when he was doing time there a couple of years back and she was a corrections officer in charge of food services. Her name was Donna, Donna Mulry. She was retired now, actually forced out, after twenty-five years working in corrections, and didn't like the way they'd treated her. Richie Nix believed she was close to fifty, old enough to be his foster mom (he never knew his real one), but she was a little thing with a nice shape, a big butt on her for her size and not too bad-looking. Donna had retired to Marine City, the next town up the river, and spent four hours a day driving a school bus for the East China Township system. She'd come home ready to play Yahtzee, which she loved, or watch TV, have some drinks. Donna introduced him to her favorite, Southern Comfort and 7-Up. It was pretty good. After a while she'd ask him what kind of Campbell soup and frozen gourmet dinner he wanted, Donna never having learned to prepare a meal for less than twelve hundred people at a time. She'd have on her sparkly cat-lady glasses and her orange hair a pile of curls trying to look young and sexy for him. She was always fussing over him. He let her pierce his ear and stick a little diamond in it. He let her wash his hair with a special conditioner to take out the oil and bring back its natural luster, but drew the line at letting her cut it. Long hair made you feel you could do what you wanted. Short hair was what you had entering prison life. She'd say, "Honey, don't you want to look nice for your Donna?"

Richie *knew* he could do better than her and her frozen dinners. He was being nice to Donna in return for her being nice to him in the joint. Otherwise she was not in his class. Hell, he had an NCIC sheet that printed out of that national crime computer as tall as he was: six feet in his curl-toed cowboy boots with three inner soles inside. His ambition was to rob a bank in every state of the union—or maybe just forty-nine, fuck Alaska—which he believed would be some kind of record, get him in that book as the All-American Bank Robber. He had thirty-seven states to go but was young.

Right now Richie was considering a score he'd lined up that was way different than robbery. It was higher class and took some thought.

Meanwhile he spent his leisure time drinking Southern and Sevens and watching TV with Donna pawing him or listening to her tell him how, after devoting her life to corrections, they had treated her like dirt. Richie's opinion was that if you liked corrections it meant you wanted to live with colored, because that's what it amounted to. He'd tell her from experience. The first place he was sent, the Wayne County Youth Home, stuck in Unit Five North with twenty guys, all colored. In Georgia, when he got the six-to-eight for intent to rob and kidnap, he did three and a half at Reidsville, most of it stoop labor, all day in the pea fields with them. Hell, he'd been eligible to serve time in some of the most famous prisons of the south, Huntsville, Angola, Parchman, and Raiford, all of them full of colored, but had lucked out down there and only drew the conviction in Georgia. Okay, then the two years in the federal joint at Terre Haute, they were mostly white where he was. But then the transfer to Huron Valley put him back in with the colored again. How could she like living among guys, white or colored, that would tear your ass out for the least reason? Donna said, "Women are good for a prison. They have a calming effect on the inmates and make their life seem more normal." Richie said, "Hey, Donna? Bull shit."

He'd get tired of lying around and go for a drive in Donna's little Honda kiddycar, go over to Harsens Island on the ferry and wonder about those summer homes boarded up, nobody in them. Stop at a bar on the island where retired guys in plaid shirts came in the afternoon to drink beer, waiting out their time. It was depressing. Donna told him to stay out of the bar at Sans Souci, Indians from Walpole Island drank there and got ugly. Oh, was that right? Richie dropped by one evening and glared for an hour at different ones and nobody made a move. Shit, Indians weren't nothing to handle. Go in a colored joint and glare you'd bleed all the way to the hospital.

The score he had a line on had come about sort of by accident. One night bored to death listening to Donna and watching TV, Richie slipped out to hold up a store or a gas station and couldn't find anything open that looked good. So he broke into a house, a big one all dark, on Anchor Bay; got inside and started creeping through rooms—shit, the place was empty. He hadn't noticed the FOR SALE sign in the front yard. It got Richie so mad he tore out light fixtures, pissed on the carpeting, stopped up the sink and turned the water on and was thinking what else he could do, break some windows, when the idea came to him all at once. He thought about it a few minutes there in the dark, went out and got the name and number off the FOR SALE sign.

Nelson Davies Realty.

Richie had seen the company's green-and-gold signs all over the Anchor Bay area from Mount Clemens to Algonac and had heard their radio ads in the car: sound effects like a gust of wind whistling by, gone, and a voice says, "Nelson Davies just sold another one!" He seemed to recall they had a new subdivision they were selling too, built on a marsh landfill they called Wildwood, a whole mess of cute homes, twenty or thirty of them.

Pretty soon after, while Donna was out driving her school bus, Richie called up Nelson Davies, got his cheerful voice on the line and said, "Them Wildwood homes are going fast, huh?" Nelson Davies said they sure were and began telling him why, listing features like your choice of decorator colors, till Richie cut him off saying, "I bet they'd go even faster if they caught fire."

Nelson Davies asked who this was, no longer cheerful.

Richie said, "Accidents can happen in an empty house, can't they?"

Nelson Davies kept asking who this was.

"I understand you already have one messed up," Richie said. "It can happen anytime. Call the police, they'll keep a lookout for a while, but how long? They get tired and quit it could happen again, huh? Or you can pay so it won't, like insurance. You get ten thousand in cash ready and I'll come pick it up sometime. If you don't have it when I come, you're dead. If I see police cruising around that subdivision you're also dead. You understand? You get ready, 'cause you don't know when I'm gonna walk in the door. Or which one that comes in I'm gonna be." Richie paused to think about what he'd just said. He believed it made sense. "I'll tell you something else. You remember a guy working in a Amoco station, one up in Port Huron, was shot dead last year during a holdup? Not last summer but the one before?"

The real estate man said he wasn't sure, he might've read about it.

"Well, that was me. The guy had this big roll of bills in his pocket. I knew it was there, I saw it, but he didn't want to take it out. I said, 'Okay, I'll give you three seconds.' By the time he started to reach in his pocket I was at three and it was too late. So I blew him away. You understand? I won't hesitate to blow you away you give me any trouble. Or I find out you have cops in your office pretending to be real estate salesmen. Shit, I know a cop when I see one. Look him in the eye I can tell in a minute. See, you won't know me from any other home buyer that comes in, but I'll know who you got there in the office and if any're cops. If I see any I won't do nothing *then*, I will later on, some other time. Say you come out of your house to go to work, I could hit you with a scope-sight rifle. You understand? There's no way you can fuck with me. Ten thousand when I come to collect or you're a dead real estate man."

That was how he'd set it up four days ago.

The guy should have the money by now, ten thousand, a figure Richard had used in estimating how much he could make robbing a bank in every state of the union, a half million dollars minus Alaska. Except that robbing a bank by yourself you only had time to hit one teller and the most he'd ever scored was $2,720 from a bank in Norwood, Ohio. Another thing different about this one, besides the score, you had to look the part of who you were supposed to be, walk in that office as a young home buyer. The other day he'd swiped a sport coat at Sears, a gray herringbone, the sleeves a little too long but it was okay. Donna got excited and bought him some shirts and ties, thinking he was dressing to look for a job.

So here he was sitting in Henry's drinking beer, wondering if he might go semicasual and wear the IT'S NICE TO BE NICE T-shirt under the sport coat. Thinking of that but mostly thinking about getting a car for tomorrow. He couldn't use Donna's. Once he drove away from the real estate office

with all that money he was gone. If somebody read
the license number they could I.D. him through
her. Or if he took her car Miss Corrections would
turn him in for walking out on her. So he'd have to
steal one. Go out in the parking lot after it got
dark, see if any fool left their key in the car. People
did that, rings of keys they didn't want to carry—
stick it under the seat. Otherwise, since he didn't
have a tool to punch out the ignition, he'd have to
wait for people to come out after they finished
their dinner and get in the car with them. Or him
or her. That meant taking the person on a one-way
trip in the country. But shit happens, if that's the
way it had to be. At least he could pick and choose.

He watched an '86 Cadillac pull into the lot and
park. Baby blue with an Ontario plate. Richie
liked it right away. He watched the guy get out of
the car, short and stocky, his hair slicked back, ad-
justing his coat, Jesus, getting ready to make his
entrance. Richie waited. There he was, the hostess
taking him to a table by the front windows. Shit,
the guy looked like an Indian. Most likely got paid
today. Got all dressed up in his suit and tie to come
in here for the dinner.

Richie liked the car and liked the guy more and
more the way he sat there all alone ordering one
drink after another, still drinking as he ate his dinner and the river and the trees outside turned dark.
The guy would look up at the running lights of a

freighter going by or stare across toward Walpole Island where he probably lived—look at him—had a job up at the oil refinery for good money, got paid and came over here to spend it, the only Indian in the whole place. It's nice to be nice, Richie thought, staring at the guy and working himself up to what he was going to do. But I got news for you . . .

Armand drank Canadian Club, doubles, good ones. He told himself it was to keep his mind alive, thoughts coming, as he had a conversation with himself and made some decisions. He asked himself, Why would you want to live here? Answered, I don't. Asked himself, Why do you want Lionel or anybody to want you to live here? That one, facing it, was harder. He took a drink and answered, I don't. I don't care or want to live here or ever come back. He knew that but had to hear it. No more Ojibway, no more the Blackbird. He knew that too. What was he losing? Nothing. You can't lose something you don't know you have. What would he get out of being Ojibway? He watched a downbound ocean freighter, its lights sliding through the trees, and thought, Learn to do the medicine and turn yourself into a fucking lion, man, or anything you want. That ship, tomorrow sometime it would be going by Toronto, then going by Kingston, and imagined his brother seeing the ship from a window in the prison. Armand had never visited his brother; he didn't know if you could see the lake or the St. Lawrence River from the prison; but the ship had made him think of his brother and that life they were in, beginning from the time they were young tough guys and liked having people afraid of them. He raised his glass to the waitress for another drink and looked around at people eating, nobody alone, nobody afraid of him. There was *one* person alone over there, a guy with long hair staring at him, a guy making muscles, it looked like, the way his bare arms were on the table, something written on his shirt, a guy who'd be at home at the Silver Dollar. He's trying to tell you something, Armand thought, and turned to look at the river again, through his own reflection on the glass, not interested in anything the guy had to tell him. The guy was a punk. The ship was gone, down in the channel now through the flats, all that marsh and wetlands for the big-shot duck hunters from Detroit. He could go back that way tonight, keep going fifteen hundred miles south and spend the winter in Miami, Florida. There were Italian guys there if he needed something to do for money. Finding work was easy. And thought in that moment, *You didn't get rid of the gun.* Anxious to come here and see the grandmother. It was under the front seat as he came

through the tunnel from Windsor to Detroit and
told the customs guy he was visiting and got waved
on. If the customs guy had wanted to look in the
car for any reason and found the gun, it would
have been a problem, yes, but the car was still registered to the son-in-law and the gun was registered to no one. The Browning with two shots
fired. Throw it in the river when you leave. It was
on his mind now to do that. Still, he took his time
and had two more drinks with his deep-fried pickerel and ate every bite of the fish and French fries
with a big plate of salad. It was good and he was
feeling good as he left the restaurant, looking over
at the punk's table but the punk wasn't there.

He was outside standing by the Cadillac, wearing a work jacket now over the T-shirt with the
words on it. Waiting to give you some shit about
Indians, Armand thought. But could he be that
kind of punk? He wasn't big enough. He said, "I'm
looking for a ride." Starting to grin.

"Good luck."

"No, you say, 'What way you going?' And I say,
'Any way I want.' Look it here." He held open his
jacket to show the grip of a revolver sticking out
of his pants. A checkered-wood grip on a nickelplate Armand believed was a .38 Special made
by Smith & Wesson. He saw the gun and saw IT'S
NICE TO BE NICE on the guy's T-shirt, beneath the
jacket held open. The guy was older than he had

appeared in the restaurant, maybe thirty years old or more, with that tough-guy stare and a diamond pinned to his ear, things that told you he was a punk. Armand walked past him to get in the car and the guy went around to the other side.

When they were both in the car and Armand looked at him again, the guy was holding the nickelplate on his thigh. It was a Model 27 Smith & Wesson with a four-inch barrel. Armand had used a blue-steel one like that one time and liked it, it was a good gun. The guy held it with his hand resting on his crotch. Armand dropped his left hand from the wheel to push a button. The front seat moved back with the hum of the electric motor and the guy said, "What're you doing?"

Armand looked at him again as he turned on the ignition. "What's the matter, you nervous? You gonna hold that thing pointing at me, I hope you not nervous. You want this car? Take it."

The guy said, "I'll tell you what I want. I'll tell you my name too, in case you ever heard of me, Richie Nix, N-i-x, not like Stevie Nicks spells hers."

Armand shook his head. He'd never heard of either one.

They drove through Algonac away from the river, the guy, Richie Nix, saying turn here, turn there, like he knew where he was going and maybe wasn't so nervous, though he could still be a punk.

They passed lights in windows of houses, then pretty soon there were only trees, once in a while a house. They were going toward a road that would take them to the freeway. Armand began to think the guy wanted to go to Detroit. They'd get there and the guy would get out. That would be okay, it was the way you had to go to get to Florida. It was strange the way the guy said the word as Armand was thinking of it.

"I was driving up from Florida one time," Richie said. "I picked up this hitchhiker coming onto Seventy-five from Valdosta. I'd spent the night there. The guy was kind of dark-skinned like you only he was Mexican, I think. You're an Indian, right?"

Armand glanced at him. "No, I'm not Indian."

"What are you then?"

"Quebecois," Armand said, "French Canadien," giving it an accent. Why not? Half of him was.

Richie said, "Don't you wish. Anyway we're driving along the interstate, this Mex tells me how he's been picking oranges half the year and how he's going up to Michigan to pick sugarbeets. We're getting along pretty good, I bought him a Co'Cola we stopped for gas, so then pretty soon he's telling me how much money he made picking oranges and how he saved a thousand bucks and is gonna send it home once he gets to Michigan and sees there's work there. You believe it, telling a stranger he's got all this money on him? Shit, I start looking for the next exit sign, get the guy off someplace on a back road. We're moving along about eighty, I see this Georgia state trooper parked at the side of the road. Shit, it wasn't even my car, I picked it up in West Palm . . . a Buick Riviera, if I remember correctly. Anyway I go, 'Hey, you want to drive?' to the Mex, and got him to trade places with me while we're moving, the guy laughing, having a good time. Till he looks at the rearview and goes, 'Uh-oh,' seeing that state trooper coming up on us with his gumballs flashing. We get pulled over, the guy tells the trooper it's not his car, it's mine. I go, '*My* car? This fella picked me up, Officer. I don't even know him.' It was funny there for a while and I almost made it, but we both got taken in. Shit, they find out there's a detainer out on me and I'm fucked. Next thing, I get charged with attempted robbery and kidnapping. I go, '*Kid*napping, you think I was gonna hold this fucking migrant for *ran*som?' Here's this Mex, he don't even know what's going on. Had no idea, or prob'ly even to this day, I was gonna take him out'n the woods and shoot a hole in him, it hadn't been for that trooper sitting there at the side of the road. That's what you call one lucky Mexican, huh?" Richie stared through the windshield and said, "This road coming up looks good. Take a left."

So they weren't going to Detroit, Armand decided. They turned onto a gravel road, white in the headlight beams, and could hear stones hitting under the car, no houses in sight. They'd be stopping pretty soon.

Armand said, "So you been to prison."

"Three different ones," Richie said. "After I got out of Reidsville they sent me back to Florida on the warrant, but I beat that one, an armed robbery, on account of they couldn't locate any their witnesses. Then I got sent to a federal joint for one of the banks I did. That was where I killed a guy and then some guys tried to kill *me*, so I was put in this federal protection program where you change your name and was transferred to Huron Valley. But, shit, I still got made, even with a different name. Some guys I was working with in the kitchen tried to poison me to death, so I was taken out of the population till I got my release. That was about two years ago. . . . Hey, this's good. See? Where that road is, less it's somebody's drive. No, it's an old wore-out dirt road. Pull in there a ways and stop."

Armand slowed and made the turn, headlights

sweeping the corner of a plowed field and coming to rest in a tunnel of trees.

"Okay, now lemme have your wallet."

Armand leaned against the steering wheel to dig it out of his hip pocket, brought the wallet along his thigh and let it drop on the floor. He reached for it with his head turned, seeing the guy past his shoulder. The guy wasn't even looking. The guy was hunched over trying to get the glove compartment open.

"This thing locked?"

"Push the button," Armand said, his hand finding the grip of the Browning automatic, right there with the seat pushed back. He brought the pistol up between his legs and was reaching down again when the guy looked at him.

"The hell you doing?"

"You want my wallet?" Armand came up with it. "Here."

But Richie was holding the car registration in one hand and his revolver in the other. The glove compartment was open now, a light showing inside. He said, "Shit, this isn't even your car. What's L and M Distributing, Limited?"

"They sell pepperoni," Armand said, "to places they make pizza."

"Yeah? You work for them?"

"Sometimes, when I feel like it."

"And they let you use this car?"

"They gave it to me. It's mine."

"Gave you a Cadillac, huh?"

Armand watched the guy take the wallet and try to open it with one hand. He watched the guy lay the revolver on his lap and hold the wallet with one hand and take the currency out with the other and then hunch over, holding the money close to the glove-compartment light, to look at it.

"What's this, all Cannuck?"

"Most of it."

"It's pretty but, shit, what's it worth?"

Armand laid both hands on his lap as he watched the guy riffle through the currency, counting numbers, getting an idea of how much was in the wad.

"Man, you got about a thousand here."

"Same as that lucky Mexican, 'ey?"

The guy, still hunched over, said, "The hell you do they pay you this kind of dough?"

Armand felt himself changing back, no longer Armand Degas, dumb guy taken for a ride. He was the old pro again as he came up with the Browning auto and touched the muzzle to the side of the punk's head.

"I shoot people," the Blackbird said. "Sometimes for money, sometimes for nothing."

Without moving his head or even his eyes, staring at that wad of cash, Richie Nix said, "Can I tell you something?"

"What?"

"You're just the guy I'm looking for."

3

THE DAY THE REAL ESTATE SALESMAN showed the Colsons the house, five years ago, he told them it was built in 1907 but was like new. It had vinyl siding you never had to paint covering the original tulipwood. You had your own well, you had a Cyclone fence dog-run there, if the Colsons happened to have a dog.

Carmen Colson said, "No, but we have a car and a pickup truck and I don't see a garage anywhere."

They were standing on the side porch off the kitchen, toward the rear of the two-story Dutch Colonial. The real estate man said, well, it didn't have a garage, but there was a marvelous old chickenhouse out there. See it? Carmen's husband, Wayne, said, "Jesus, look at that!" Not meaning the chickenhouse. There was a whitetail doe standing way back against the tree line, off beyond a field growing wild. As soon as he said it Carmen knew they were going to buy the place. It didn't matter the front hall was bigger than the sitting room, the closets were tiny and wasps were living upstairs in the bedrooms. There were deer on the property. Twenty acres counting the field that ran nearly a quarter of a mile from the house to the tree line and all the rest woods connecting to other woods the real estate man said, you bet, were full of deer.

Carmen said to her husband, after, "Hon, I was *born* in a house newer than that one." At this time five years ago they'd been living in one a lot newer, too, a crackerbox ranch in Sterling Heights, ever since they got married.

Wayne said sure, it was old, but look at its possibilities. Knock out a wall here and there, do a little remodeling, the kind of work he could handle, no problem. Wayne said, "You sit in that back bedroom window upstairs. It's like looking out a deer blind."

Their only child, Matthew Colson, transferred to Algonac High, where he starred three years as a wide receiver, power forward and third baseman for the Muskrats, won nine varsity letters, graduated, joined the U.S. Navy and was now serving aboard a nuclear carrier, the U.S.S. *Carl Vinson*, in the Pacific. The front hall was still bigger than the sitting room and the closets tiny; but the wasps were gone from upstairs, Carmen had removed all the paint from the woodwork and they now had a two-car garage. In one half of it was Wayne's sixteen-foot aluminum fishing boat on a trailer. Their Oldsmobile Cutlass went in the other half, because Carmen got home from work a good hour before Wayne's Dodge Ram pickup would pull into the drive. Wayne was an ironworker and ironworkers stopped to have a few once they came down off the structure.

Carmen's dad, now retired and living in Florida, had been an ironworker. Her parents were divorced when she was seventeen, the same year she graduated from high school a straight-A student and her dad took her to the Ironworkers Local 25 picnic. This was where she met Wayne Colson, a young apprentice they called Cowboy, blond-haired and tan wearing just athletic shorts and work shoes, and she couldn't keep her eyes off him. She watched him look over his bare shoulder at her as he put on his gloves, getting ready for the column-climbing contest. It was where they used just their hands and feet to go straight up a ten-inch flanged beam staked to the ground and held in place by a crane. Carmen watched Wayne Colson climb that thirty-five-foot beam like it was a stepladder and fell in love as he came sliding down the flange in seven seconds flat, muscles tensed in his arms and back, and looked over at her again.

That summer Carmen would borrow the car, drop her mom off at Michigan Bell, where she worked as a telephone operator, then drive forty

miles to happen by the building site where Wayne
was working. She could pick him out—standing
up there on that skeleton of red iron, shirt off, hard
hat on backward, God, maybe nine or ten stories
in the air—because once he spotted the car he'd
wave. Then he'd stand on one foot on that narrow
beam, the other foot out behind him, his hand flat
above his eyes in kind of an Indian pose and she'd
just about have a heart attack. Sundays they'd go
for a ride and he'd show her office buildings in
Southfield he'd bolted up, Carmen imagining him
climbing columns, walking beams, fooling around
way up there in the air. Wasn't he ever scared?
Wayne told her there was no difference between
being up forty feet or four hundred; go off from either height it would kill you. If you had to fall, he
told her, try to do it inside the structure, because
they decked in every other floor as they bolted up.
But either way, falling inside or out, it was called
"going in the hole." Wayne let seventeen-year-old
Carmen heft his tools, his spud wrench, his sleever
bar, his bull pin, the sledge he called a beater they
used for driving the bull pin to line up bolt holes
that weren't centered. He buckled his tool belt
around her slim hips and she could barely move
with the weight of it. He handed her a yo-yo, the
thirty-five-pound impact wrench they used for
bolting up, and Carmen had to tense her muscles
to hold it. He told her, hey, she was pretty strong,

and said, "Don't ever get hit on the head with one of these, some Joe happens to drop it." He told her a Joe was an ironworker who couldn't hack it. If you were in the trade and your name was Joe you'd better change it. He told her an apprentice was referred to as a punk. If a journeyman called you that, it wasn't anything to get uptight about. He told her she was the best-looking girl he'd ever met in his entire life. She smelled so good, he loved to stick his nose in her dark-brown hair. He'd tell her he wanted to marry her, the sooner the better, and Carmen would get goose bumps.

Her mom, Lenore, said, "You're crazy to even think about marrying an ironworker." Carmen said, well, you did. Her mom said, "And I got rid of him, too, soon as you were of age. Ironworkers drink. They don't come home from work, they stop off. Don't you remember anything growing up? Us two eating alone? Doesn't Wayne drink? If he doesn't, they'll throw him out of the local."

Wayne said to Carmen, "Well, sure ironworkers drink. So do painters, glaziers, electricians, any trade I know of the guys drink. What's wrong with that?"

Lenore said, "You are a lovely young girl with your whole life ahead of you. You're smart as a whip, you got all A's in school. You could go on to college and become a computer programmer. You keep seeing that ironworker he'll talk you into doing things you'll be sorry for. You'll get pregnant sure as hell and then you'll *have* to get married."

Wayne said, "I would never make you do anything you don't want to," giving Carmen a wink.

Lenore said, "A girl as attractive as you, with your cute figure, can do better than an ironworker, believe me. You know what's going to happen? You'll be stuck in a house full of babies while he's out having a good time with the boys. Once you're married you'll never see him."

Wayne said, "What do I do? I go fishing once in a while, deer hunting in November. I'm in a softball league but you come to the games, and I bowl, yeah, but that's all. No more than what other guys do."

Lenore said, "At least live in Port Huron, so I can be nearby when you need company, 'cause you're gonna."

Carmen had taken a course in handwriting analysis, A Guide to Character and Personality, at the Y when she was a senior in high school. One evening in a bar, just to double-check her own judgment, she asked Wayne to write something, for instance about the job he was working on, and she'd analyze it. He didn't even hesitate. She watched as he wrote fairly fast with a moderate right-handed slant, forming large letters of uniform size. Carmen was relieved to tell him his writing showed he was reliable, enthusiastic and sociable—Wayne nodding—and that his big middle zone indicated the size of his ego, but was probably necessary for anyone who did structural work. She told him she liked his upper-zone dynamics, the way he crossed his *t*, putting the bar above the stem, pretty sure it meant he was witty in a satirical kind of way. The even pressure of his writing showed he had a strong will and that when he was told what to do it had better make sense. She said uneven pressure meant emotional instability. Wayne said, "Or your pen's running out of ink."

Carmen told her mom, see? He was not only reliable, he was funny. Lenore said, "How come I keep asking, but you never do my handwriting?" The reason was because Carmen knew her mom's hand and had not seen anything good to say about it. Her uneven spaces and lack of style values showed indecision plus an inability to think clearly. She couldn't tell her mom that, because her wide-spaced *t* stem showed she was easily hurt and would take offense.

Carmen and Wayne were married in Port Huron at St. Joseph's Catholic Church in May 1968. They moved into a two-bedroom ranch in Sterling Heights and Matthew was born the following March.

Within the next few years Carmen had a series of miscarriages due to what the doctor called endometriosis and finally had to have a hysterectomy. She was quiet for months, let her housework slip and watched TV thinking about the two boys and two girls she and Wayne had talked about having. Wayne told her Matthew was a handful and a half, that boy was plenty. Twice during her depression Wayne drove the three of them to Florida to see Carmen's dad. Maybe getting out helped a little.

But Carmen brought herself back to life. She remembered her book on handwriting analysis saying that if you weren't happy or lacked confidence in yourself you should examine your handwriting, paying particular attention to the way you wrote the personal pronoun *I*. As soon as Carmen got into it she said, "Holy shit." Her handwriting was okay for the most part, but there was more of a backward slant to it now, it was light, weak, and look at the way she was making her *I*, like a small 2. That became the starting point, changing her capital *I* to a printed letter with no frills, like an *l*; that showed insight, an ability to analyze her own feelings. She devised a clear, straight up-and-down script, one that said she lived in the present, was self-reliant, somewhat reserved, a person whose intellect and reasoning power influenced emotions. It seemed so natural to write this way, making that *I* a bit taller as she practiced, keeping her letters squarely in the center of her Emotional Expression chart, that finally she had the confidence to write in her new script, "What are you moping around for? Get up off your butt and do something."

Her mom retired from Michigan Bell but couldn't stay away from the telephone. She'd call Carmen every day to give her recipes Carmen never used, or to talk about the weather in detail, the arrogance of doctors who made her wait knowing she was suffering excruciating back pain, eventually getting around to Wayne. "What time did the man of the house get home last night? If it was before seven you're lucky, depending how you look at it. If you don't mind that booze on his breath when he comes in and gives you a kiss then you're different than I am, I won't say another word."

Wayne said, "You'd have to wire her jaw shut."

He knew Lenore was talkative without ever having seen the way she left her vowels open at the top when she wrote. Her small *d* and *g* also.

Wayne would list different reasons why ironworkers stopped off after. It was too goddamn noisy to talk on the job and it sure wasn't anyplace to get in an argument. Raising iron, it was best to extend a certain amount of courtesy to others and settle any differences you have on the ground. Also, structural work was stressful; you come down off a job you needed to unwind. Like walking a horse after a race.

Yeah, but why couldn't he unwind at home? Carmen said she'd walk with him. Then sit down and have a beer and he could help Matthew with his homework for a change. Wayne said what was wrong with eating a little later? Carmen said yeah, eight or nine being the fashionable hour to dine in Sterling Heights.

She didn't pout, whine or nag him. What Carmen did, once Matthew was in junior high, busy with sports after school, she got a job at Warren Truck Assembly on the chassis line. Wayne said if it was what she felt like doing, fine. What he said when she got home later than he did, Wayne in the kitchen frying hamburger for their starving boy, was, "What happened, you have car trouble?"

Carmen said, "I work a whole shift with that air wrench, eight hours bolting on drag links and steering arms in all that noise, I need to unwind after."

Wayne said, "See? If you feel that way working on the line, imagine coming off a structure after ten hours."

Carmen said, "I like to be *with* you." She did, he was a nice guy and she loved him. What he drank never changed his personality, it made him horny if anything. "Isn't there something we can do together?"

Wayne said, "Outside of visit your mom and pretend we're as dumb as she is?"

"I mean some kind of work or business we

could both get into," Carmen said, "and be together more."

"Wear matching outfits," Wayne said, "and enter ballroom-dancing contests. Tell me what you
want."

"I don't *know*, but it isn't doing laundry and
dusting and making pies. I don't even know how to
make pies."

"I noticed that."

"And I don't care to learn, either."

"You're sorry now you didn't become a computer programmer."

"That must be it," Carmen said. "I love machines that talk back to you, cars that tell you the
door isn't closed or you don't have your seat belt
on."

"You want to be independent. Like me."

Carmen said, "You guys are individualists all
doing the same thing. Remember hippies? You're
like hippies only you work." Wayne had to think
about that one. She said, "I could stay at Warren
Truck and work on the line. I think I can do anything I put my mind to. I could even go to apprentice school and become an ironworker." She said,
"You have women now—how does that sound to
you?" knowing it would embarrass him, just the
idea of it.

"We have one woman journeyman, I mean
journey-person, and a half dozen apprentices out

of twenty-two hundred in the local." He told her
you had to be a certain type to be an ironworker,
man or woman. "You're too sweet and nice
and . . . girlish."

She said, "Thanks a lot."

They moved into the farmhouse and it kept her
busy, Carmen doing more of the fixing up than
Wayne, who was handier with a thirty-five-pound
impact wrench than a hammer and saw. He bor-
rowed a tractor with a brush-hog twice a year to
keep the field cut and have a clear view of the tree
line. Carmen, thinking of moneymaking ideas, got
him to clean out the chickenhouse, believing some-
day it could be made into a bed-and-breakfast
place; cater to duck hunters and boaters who came
up from Detroit and got too smashed to drive
home. Wayne said, "We'll call it the Chickenshit
Inn. I never seen so much chickenshit in my life as
out there." Carmen planted a vegetable garden in
the backyard. Every spring Wayne put in a row of
corn out by the woods and let the deer help themselves to it in August.

It wasn't until Matthew left for the navy in January, their fifth year in the farmhouse, that Carmen
took the real estate course at Macomb County
Community College and went to work for Nelson
Davies Realty. Wayne said if it made her happy,
fine. She sold her first house in April. Wayne took
her to Henry's for dinner and listened to her tell

how she'd closed the deal, Carmen glowing, excited, telling him what a wonderful feeling it was, like being your own boss. By June Carmen was offering the idea that real estate was the kind of thing they could maybe even do together, work as a team; it'd be fun. Wayne said he could see himself going back to school, Jesus. By August Carmen had him looking into the future, playing with the idea of eventually starting their own company. Wayne said, paperwork being so much fun. Now it was October and Carmen had Wayne at least agreeing to talk to Nelson Davies, a man who'd made millions in the business and wasn't much older than Wayne. Wayne said he could hardly wait.

Carmen got home first and parked in the garage. A few minutes later, in the kitchen putting groceries away, she looked outside and saw Wayne's pickup in the drive. It was half past six, getting dark. Wayne had been coming home earlier since Matthew left. Carmen went out to the porch. She was wearing her "closing suit," a tailored navy; it was lightweight and she folded her arms against the evening chill in the air. Wayne was lifting fat paper sacks from the pickup bed, bringing four of them over to the porch steps.

"Sweet Feed," Wayne said, looking up at Carmen on the porch. "It's corn and oats, but that's what they call it."

"I thought you meant me."

"You're tastier'n corn and oats. How'd it go?"

"I closed on a three-bedroom in Wildwood."

"That's the way."

Wayne was wearing his IRONWORKERS BUILD AMERICA jacket. Carmen watched him turn to the truck, lift out a twenty-five-pound block of salt and place it on the grass next to the gravel drive. As Wayne straightened he said, "I saw Walter out on the road. He showed me whitetail tracks going all the way across his seeding to the state land."

Walter, their neighbor, grew sod for suburban lawns. Carmen would think it was a strange way to make a living, watching grass grow.

Wayne came over to the steps with two more bags of Sweet Feed. "They love this stuff."

"They think what a nice guy you are," Carmen said. "Then you shoot them."

"You don't want to eat live venison," Wayne said. "They're hard to hold, and it's not good for your digestion." He stepped over to the truck, reached into the cab window and came out with paper sacks he handed up to Carmen. "This goes in the house." She could tell from the weight what was inside. Boxes of 12-gauge hollow-point slugs.

"I don't see how you can shoot them."

"I can't, less I get within fifty yards. Not with a slug barrel."

"You know what I mean."

"I don't see them as little Walt Disney creatures," Wayne said, rolling up the cab window. "That's the difference. You shoot some in the fall or they starve in the winter. Look at it that way."

This was an annual exchange, Carmen giving her view without making a moral issue of it; Wayne seeing deer as meat, now and then citing a fact of ecology. Carmen raised her face as he came up on the porch. They kissed on the mouth, taking their time, and let their eyes hold a moment or so after. Twenty years and it was still good. She asked him how his job was going.

"I'm finished at Standard Federal. They want to put me on the detail gang, plumbing up, I said no way, I'm a connector, I'm not doing any tit work."

"You didn't."

"I told 'em that—I want to take a few days off."

"Good."

"I'm gonna look at another job next week." He told her there was a new basketball arena going up in Auburn Hills, fairly close by, except it was all precast, so he'd most likely go to work on the One-Fifty Jefferson project in Detroit, he believed was to be a hotel, thirty-two levels. He said he'd rather drive all the way downtown to a story job than work precast across the street. He said, "Lionel's coming by tomorrow, we're gonna look for antler scrapings."

Carmen said, "Wayne?"

He moved past her and was holding the door open. "Let's have a cold one. What do you say?"

"You promised you'd see Nelson tomorrow."

"I did?"

"Come on, now don't pull that."

"I forgot, that's all. What time?"

"Two o'clock."

"That's fine, Lionel's not coming till four. He's gonna take a look, see if there's any white oak out there. I read that deer eat white-oak acorns like potato chips. They can't stop eating them. I know there's plenty of red oak."

Carmen placed the sack of shells on the kitchen counter. Wayne got two cans of beer from the refrigerator, popped them open and handed her one. "You look nice. I'd buy a house off you even if I already had one."

Carmen said, "You're really going to talk to Nelson?"

"I can't wait. You know how I love working for assholes."

"Wayne, try. Okay?"

"You're gonna be there, aren't you?"

"I'll be in the office. What're you going to wear?"

"I don't know—I have to get dressed up?"

"I think you should wear a suit."

Wayne stepped to the counter, put his beer down and opened the sack. "I could. Or my sport coat."

"And a tie?"

Wayne said, "I'll wear a tie if you want," taking the boxes of shotgun slugs from the sack. "I'm trying three-inch magnums this year. Lionel says they'll 'bull the brush,' nothing like it out to fifty yards. Hit a buck you hear it slap home."

Carmen said, "Wayne?"

"What?"

"How you look is important. The impression you make."

He paused. She could see his mind still out in the woods for a moment. He took a sip of beer, the can almost hidden in his big hand, his wedding band, a speck of gold, catching light from the window. She would see him in the bathroom shaving, a pair of skimpy briefs low on his hard body and would think, *My God, he's mine*. She wished she could take back what she'd said. He didn't have to try to impress anybody.

"Wear what you want," Carmen said, "be comfortable."

"I wear my blue suit," Wayne said, "and you wear yours, will that impress him?"

"Forget I said that, okay?"

Wayne sipped his beer, staring at her. He seemed

to grin. "I like that short skirt on you. I bet Nelson does too."

"If he does," Carmen said, "it's because when hemlines go up, so does the stock market. Nobody knows why. Then interest rates go down and we sell more homes."

"Like the moon and the tides," Wayne said, "is that it? Or the seasons of the year. Did you know hunting season comes when the does are in heat?" He reached into the sack again and took out a small plastic bottle fixed to a display card. "The bucks know it. They're ready, so you use some of this. Foggy Mountain 'Hot' Doe Buck Lure." He held it for Carmen to see, then read from the card. " 'A secret blend with pure urine collected from live doe deer during the hottest hours of the estrus cycle.' "

"You're kidding," Carmen said. "You put that on you?"

"You can, or sprinkle it around your blind. The buck smells it, he goes, 'Man, I'm gonna get laid,' and comes tearing through the woods. . . . I was thinking," Wayne said, "if we could invent something like this for the real estate business . . . You know what I mean? Something you sprinkle on a house and all these buyers come running? What do you think?"

"I think you're right," Carmen said. "Wear the blue suit."

"And my hard hat? It's blue, it'd match nice."

"Yeah, put it on backwards," Carmen said.

"Just be myself, huh?"

"You can do whatever you want," Carmen said, turning to look out the window at Wayne's pickup and dead vines in the vegetable garden and the chickenhouse that would be a chickenhouse till it rotted and fell apart.

"What're you mad at?"

"I'm not mad."

"What are you, then?"

"I don't know," Carmen said. "If I find out I'll tell you."

4

IT WAS AFTER THEY CAME to Donna's house in Marine City, Armand invited to spend the night, Richie started calling him the Bird. First, introducing him to this woman Donna as Mr. Blackbird, then right away saying, "Yeah, I ran into the Bird at Henry's." And a couple of minutes later, "Get me and the Bird a drink, will you?" Making it sound like they were old buddies and he'd always called him by that name. The funny thing was, Armand didn't mind it.

The Bird. New name for the beginning of a new time in his life. Different, not so Indian-sounding as he played with it in his mind. Who are you? I'm the Bird. Not a blackbird or a seagull, but his own special kind. He liked the way Richie Nix said it, the guy sounding proud to know him, wanting to show him off. Donna came in from the kitchen with a dark drink in each hand. Richie said, "The Bird's from Toronto," and Donna said, "Oh? I was there one time, it's real nice."

Armand the Bird took a sip of the drink and wanted to spit it out. Jesus Christ, it was the worst thing he ever tasted. Richie said, "What's wrong, Bird?"

The Bird becoming just Bird now.

"What is it?"

"That's a Southern and Seven," Donna said. "It's our favorite."

Armand, or whoever he was this moment, went out to the car, where he had four quarts of Canadian Club in the trunk, for the stay at his grandmother's, and brought one of them inside. He said to Donna, "I don't drink that. I only drink real whiskey."

Once he made this known, Donna stuck close to Richie and didn't say much, peering out through her big shiny glasses like some kind of bird herself, pointy face and a nest of red-gold curls sitting on her head. Hair fixed and face painted like she was going to the ball—except for her tennis shoes and the lint and hair all over her black sweater. Coming here after they'd stopped for drinks and had a talk, Richie Nix had said, "Wait till you meet Donna. She was a hack in the joint where I met her and got fired for fucking inmates, man, if you can believe it."

The Bird didn't care for what he saw of Donna, a woman who had to get it off convicts, or this dump she lived in, a little frame house he could tell in the dark coming here needed to be painted and was overgrown with bushes. He couldn't see how two bedrooms would fit in here and how Richie Nix could sleep with that woman, if he did.

He didn't care too much for Richie either, except the guy had nerve. With a gun against his head saying, "You're just the guy I'm looking for." To pull that off, get the Bird to believe it, took something that couldn't be faked. Telling him, "No shit, I mean it. I'm glad this happened." Telling him, "Man, you have to be somebody, drive a car like this, a piece under the seat." Respect in his tone of voice. Then telling in detail about the deal he had going. The Bird listened and came to realize this punk actually had something, wasn't making it up. It could even work. The Bird had seen enough variations of it in Toronto, all kinds of shakedowns and protection deals; he knew how to convince a slow pay to come up with what was owed. This one was different, a one-shot deal, but based on the same idea: scare the guy enough and he'll pay every time.

There was one part of the deal that bothered him. He had to concentrate to think about it in this living room decorated with prison photographs on the walls: Donna in groups of officials and corrections officers; Donna with groups of inmates, one of them signed "To Donna 'Big Red' Mulry from the boys in E Block." Pictures of Donna's life behind walls, not wearing glasses in any of them. She and Richie were on the sofa watching television, a cop show with fast, expensive cars and Latin rock music. Richie saying now, "Look at that, Bird. I don't believe it." The Bird looked and didn't believe it either, the cop acting emotional, broken up about something. Cops didn't do that, they were cold fucking guys that never showed what they felt—if they felt anything. Here or across the river in Canada cops were the same. There were cops in Detroit right now investigating a homicide that happened this morning in a hotel and would not be broken up about the old guy or about the girl either. This guy Richie Nix, this punk, was grinning with a dreamy stupid look, the woman Donna moving her hand underneath his T-shirt that said it was nice to be nice. She had looked at it when they came in and said, "Oh, is that ever cute." What was she trying to be, his mother or what? The Bird had asked what people called him and he said Richie, that was his name, Richie Nix. "Donna likes Dick," he said, "if you know what I mean, but it isn't my name." There was an Elvis Presley doll in a white jumpsuit standing next to the stereo. There were stuffed animals on the sofa and chairs, little furry things, bears, a puppy dog, a kitty, there was a turtle, a Mr. Froggy . . . This woman who used to be a hack, with her pile of hair and her glasses, was going to stuff Richie and use him as a pillow if she could. That was what it looked like.

The Bird got up out of his chair, walked over to the TV and turned it off. He heard the woman say, "Hey, what're you doing?" When he looked at her she was sitting upright with her back arched, one leg underneath her.

"Time for you to go to bed."

"I got news for you," Donna said. "This is my house."

"Yeah, and it's a dump."

She said, "Well, you certainly have your nerve."

He said, "You want me to take you in there?"

Donna turned her head to look at Richie sitting next to her with his mouth open. Richie looked up at the Bird who waited, not saying anything. Now Donna was looking at him again. Still the Bird waited. After a moment she got up and walked out of the room. Richie called after her, "And close the door." He grinned as they heard it slam.

"You phone the guy tomorrow morning," the Bird said.

"What guy?"

The Bird moved to the sofa, taking his time, and sat down. "The real estate guy. You call him and say to bring the money out to one of the model homes, four o'clock in the afternoon. We'll go out there before and take a look, decide which one."

"Sounds good."

"You know why we do it this way?"

"We'll be out closer to the interstate."

The Bird shook his head. "We do it because if there are cops, he tells them and that's where they gonna be."

Richie waited. "Yeah?"

"We go to his office before he leaves for the model home. Watch his place, we don't see any cops around, or ones that could be cops, we go in. Say about two."

5

NELSON DAVIES REALTY was in a big white Victorian home on St. Clair River Drive that Wayne thought looked like a funeral parlor. It must have belonged to somebody important at one time, probably a guy in shipping or lumber. Nelson Davies had added on a first-floor lobby in front with glass doors. But this house had so many wings and angles as it was, added on over the years, Wayne didn't believe the modern front entrance made it look any worse.

Carmen had told him to park in back. Her car was there with two others. She seemed nervous the way she smiled, looking him over in his dark-blue suit, asking what happened to the handkerchief she'd put in the breast pocket. Nothing, he'd taken it out, that's all. Then losing the smile as her gaze reached his tan scuffed work shoes.

She said, "Wayne . . ." disappointed, but that was all.

One of the things he liked most about Carmen—

besides her brown eyes and the way she could give him a certain look after twenty years—was the fact she would never moan or wring her hands over something that couldn't be changed. She might kick the lawnmower when it didn't start; but something like this, she'd never go on about his work shoes. He followed her legs up the stairs, the skirt stretching around her neat fanny. Wayne loved Carmen's legs in those skirts that came a few inches above her knees. He'd see her when he got home from work and have an urge to pull the skirt up around her hips. There were times he could tell she wanted him to and he did, the two of them alone in the house with Matthew gone.

Nelson Davies had the front office, a good size one. The first thing Wayne saw was the trophy-class buck mounted up on the striped wallpaper. Jesus, a twelve-point rack on it and the guy sold real estate.

"You never told me he was a hunter."

"Nelson goes duck hunting," Carmen said. "See the decoys?" There was an entire shelf of them behind the reddish-brown desk the size of a dining-room table. Mallards, greenheads, susies, one or two Wayne couldn't identify right away. It didn't matter, he was more interested in that trophy buck.

"He didn't get that around here. He might've, but I doubt it."

"He tells everybody he only went deer hunting that one time."

"I bet he hit it with his car."

Wayne looked around some more as Carmen told him Nelson was never late for his appointments and should be back any minute. Wayne asked how he would know what time it was from that thing. The clock on the wall didn't have any numbers on it. Then saw another one between the ceramic lamp and the computer on the desk, a gold-plated alarm clock that looked like some kind of an award. Carmen told him to sit in Nelson's chair, soft black leather with chrome trim, see what being the boss felt like. She left saying she'd get him a cup of coffee.

When she came back with it Wayne was sitting in the chair, his feet up on the desk, scuffed cowhide on polished teak.

"I think I like it."

Carmen said, "See?" and left him there to go do some work.

Fool with papers, fill out different forms—what Wayne believed the real estate business was all about. Writing in numbers. There was a pile of forms on the desk. Escrow Closing Instructions. Seller's Proceeds Net Out Work Sheet. Jesus. Mortgage Payoff/Assumption Request and Authorization. Wayne thinking, I can't do it. He could read blueprints but not this shit. A Limited Service Agreement that was all fine print. A person could ruin their eyes selling real estate. Wayne looked at

the computer, pressed a couple keys: it made click-
ing sounds but nothing happened. He got up and
walked over to the big picture window, to sunlight
and a clear blue sky, the river and the dark edge of
Walpole Island over there. He thought of Lionel,
coming to the house at four. He looked down at
the roof of the lobby, with a little decorative slat
fence around it, that stuck out a few feet below the
window. What good was putting up that fence if
there was no reason to go out on the roof? He
would see this kind of bullshit ornamentation and
be thankful he worked up on the iron.

A blue Cadillac pulled up to the house and
parked on the street.

Wayne watched a guy come out of the car and
toss his head, getting his hair out of his face as he
looked up at the house; the guy wearing a sport
coat that seemed too big for him in the shoulders,
the sleeves too long. Another guy came around the
back of the car buttoning his suit coat; this one
older with a stocky build, his hair slicked back and
shining in the sun. They reminded Wayne of
the couple of guys who'd been given a bath and
secondhand clothes at a street mission. As dressed
up as they'd ever be. Not used to a residential
neighborhood either, the way they looked up and
down the street. Coming up the driveway they
looked toward the back of the house, then turned
into the walk and Wayne lost sight of them.

He returned to the desk, sat down and picked up a color brochure that described "Wildwood, modern living in a back-to-nature setting." It showed model homes on a bare tract of land, some of it fill, some of it cleared, where they'd bulldozed out the existing trees. Why did they do that? Carmen said this way you could plant your own trees, sit out on the patio and watch them grow for the next fifty years. Saying it with a straight face. She'd do that and he'd have to think about how she meant it.

He looked up, hearing the door close.

The two guys from the Cadillac were standing in the office: the older, stocky one turning from the door as the skinny one, wearing sunglasses now, brushed his hair out of his face and looked around coming over to the desk. He opened his loose sport coat and put his hands on his hips. Now the older one was looking around the office. Both of them right at home. The skinny one grinned at Wayne as he said, "I told you you wouldn't know which one I'm gonna be when I come in? Remember? Well, here I am."

Wayne said, "What?"

"On the phone. Four days ago."

"I think you want to talk to somebody downstairs," Wayne said. "They'll help you."

The skinny one looked over at the older guy, who was studying the trophy buck now and didn't seem to be paying attention. "You hear that? He's playing dumb."

"He's fucking with you," the stocky older guy said, still looking at the buck.

It caught Wayne by surprise. He eased up a little straighter in the leather chair, already feeling irritated, not caring much for their attitude. Now he was curious as well as irritated; but careful. He watched the skinny one come over and plant his hands on the desk to hunch in closer and stare at him through his sunglasses.

"Are you gonna give me a hard time? You know what I want. Where's it at?"

He had a little diamond stuck to his ear.

Wayne said, "Where's what at?" Staring back at the guy, barely able to see his eyes behind the glasses. Wayne wondered if the idea was not to be the first one to blink, then wondered if the guy had some kind of disease. He looked sickly, hardly any color in his face.

"You gonna try and tell me I never spoke to you?"

"No, I think what he saying," the older guy said, coming over to the desk, "he don't believe what you told him on the telephone. What could happen to him. So he's fucking with you."

The guy was Indian.

Wayne realized it for the first time. At least he

was pretty sure, looking at the guy's face now, close, the hair, the thick body in the tight suit. Indian or part Indian and something else familiar about him that made Wayne think of Walpole Island right away and Lionel, though Lionel didn't sound like this guy. This guy had just the trace of an accent. Wayne didn't know what kind, maybe French-Canadian. He began to see the Indian as the one to watch, though the skinny guy irritated him more.

"Show him you mean it," the Indian said, standing close to the desk now, "how you can hurt his business." He reached out, still looking at Wayne, and brushed the coffee mug with the back of his hand, tipping it over on Nelson Davies's real estate papers. "Like a sign, 'ey? What can happen."

The skinny one said, "Hey, yeah," coming alive.

Wayne watched him grab the gold-plated alarm clock from the desk, look around for a target and throw it at the numberless clock on the wall. He missed, said, "Goddamn it," picked up the coffee mug, threw it and missed again. He said, "Shit," and now he looked mad, picked up the ceramic lamp and shattered it against the wall. It seemed to make him feel better. Now he was looking around for something else, the Indian patient, watching.

Wayne thought about getting up and walking out. What would they do? But he sat there, watching now as the skinny guy went over to the trophy buck, tossing his hair as he looked up at it, then jumped, grabbing hold of the antlers. He hung up there for a moment struggling with it, kicking against the wall, came down all of a sudden with the deer head, that beautiful twelve-point rack, and threw it across the room. Wayne saw him breathing hard, out of shape for a young guy, looking around for something else. Maybe the decoys, all of Nelson's wooden ducks in a row. These guys could mess up the office, but there weren't enough things to break. Unless they threw the decoys through that big picture window. Wayne thinking he could put the skinny one through it, no problem. The Indian might be more to handle.

The skinny one said to Wayne, "Am I making my point?"

The Indian shook his head. "You wasting your time."

"Well, he's gonna be a dead fucking real estate man he don't give us the cash, I already promised him that."

"Yeah, but he don't believe you."

"Then I'm gonna show him."

Wayne said, "Okay, you win," and pushed up from the chair. "I'll get it for you. It's downstairs." He walked around the desk and the Indian stepped in front of him.

"I've seen you someplace."

They were close enough that Wayne could see

the guy's eyes, a deep dark brown, calm but worn out, bloodshot. He smelled of after-shave. Wayne couldn't name the brand, something cheap. For some reason it helped him remember where he had seen the Indian, the same place the Indian had seen *him*. Yesterday, in the variety store on Walpole Island.

"Where was that I saw you?"

There was the trace of an accent. *Where was dat* . . . Wayne shrugged. He heard the skinny one say, "Let him by. I want to show him something."

The Indian kept staring at him. He was a few inches shorter than Wayne but a good thirty pounds heavier. The skinny one was saying it again, "Will you let him by?" The Indian took his time, none of his moves hurried, and the skinny one was waiting, anxious to have his turn. He moved in to stand even closer than the Indian, his sunglasses about level with Wayne's eyes, right there, like he was a big-league manager and Wayne was an umpire about to get chewed out.

The skinny guy said, "Remember me telling you I've killed people? I want to be sure you believe it."

Wayne didn't. Not from what he saw of this skinny guy's face, imperfections all over it, lack of character hiding behind the sunglasses. Even if he'd been told, he wouldn't believe it. Till the guy's hand came up from somewhere with a big nickelplate revolver and stuck the barrel under

Wayne's nose, giving it a nudge. Wayne tried to raise his head believing now, yes, it was possible.

Very gently he pushed aside the gun barrel with the tips of his fingers, still looking at the guy's sunglasses, and said, "I never doubted for a minute."

"I want you to be sure," the skinny guy said to him. "So you know what can happen to you."

Wayne felt himself shoved from behind, the Indian saying, "He believes you, okay? Let's go."

They went downstairs, Wayne leading. He paused in the foyer to say, "It's this way," and took them along the remodeled hall past rows of office cubicles partitioned in panels of knotty pine and frosted glass, most of them empty. Carmen's desk was at the end of the row, on the right. He didn't want her to be there. But she was, talking on the phone. Wayne saw her look up, saw her eyes, her surprised expression, as they walked past and came to a glass door in the rear of the house. Wayne was pulling the door open when the Indian placed his hand against the glass. He held it, looking out at the gravel parking area in the backyard.

"It's in your car?"

The skinny one, anxious, said, "Where else would it be? He's taking it out to that house I told him."

The Indian said, "Okay, let's go."

Wayne pulled the door open. He was stepping outside when he heard Carmen's voice behind him, raised, coming from the hall, "Wayne?" but didn't turn or even pause. He kept going, hearing the Indian say, "Who's Wayne?" and the skinny one, closer to him, say, "Who cares? Somebody works there." Then saying, "You drive a truck?" as Wayne approached the side of the pickup bed and reached over to work the combination on the metal tool box. Wayne said, "When I go out on the job, yeah," slipping the lock off, lifting the lid and reaching in with his right hand. He heard the Indian say, "There's a woman there, watching us," Wayne's hand touching cold metal now, a spud wrench, a bull pin next to it—too short—his hand groping until it found the sleever bar, thirty slender inches of solid metal, about three pounds worth, one end flat for prying. Wayne gripped it hearing the skinny guy say, "What're you doing?" The Indian saying, "She still watching us." The skinny one, closer to him, saying, "Come on, will you?" His hand still in the tool box, Wayne turned his head enough to see the skinny one right there and the Indian a few feet behind him, looking toward the office.

"I found it."

The skinny one said, "Well, gimme it."

And Wayne said, "Here."

* * *

Carmen saw it through the glass door, the heavy-set man in the way at first because he was watching her and looked as though he might come back inside.

She saw Wayne come around from the truck with the sleever bar a flash of metal, knew what it was and saw the one with the hair twisting away, sunglasses flying and the metal bar raking him across the shoulders. He stumbled, yelling at Wayne, but didn't fall down, not that time, not until Wayne swung at his legs, going for his knees. The guy was jumping back as Wayne connected, hitting him low in the thighs, and his legs went out from under him. Carmen saw the heavyset man hurrying to get his suit coat unbuttoned, Wayne after him now, raising the bar to swing it at him, the heavyset man reaching into his coat, but had to bring his hands out fast to protect himself, hunching, and Wayne hit him twice across the arms, high, around the shoulders, the man trying to cover his head, and that was when Wayne swung the metal bar with both hands, like a baseball bat, and slammed it into the man's stomach, hard. The man doubled over, bringing his arms down, and Wayne hit him across the back two-handed, coming down with the bar, twice, and the man dropped to his hands and knees in the gravel, then onto his elbows and knees, covering his head again with his big hands. But it wasn't finished. Carmen saw the other one, the one with the hair, getting to his feet with his head down, trying, it looked like, to get his belt undone and shove one hand into his pants. She saw him look up as Wayne came at him swinging and this time he dodged out of the way and went into a crouch facing Wayne, Wayne circling him, it looked as though to keep him in the yard, backing him this way toward the house, Wayne stalking him with the sleever bar. It amazed her, she had never seen that cold, intent look on her husband's face before. She saw the heavyset man still on the ground. Then got a shock to see the one with the hair coming right to the door, one hand holding his groin, his face close for a moment through the glass, white and drawn, then ugly, turning into some kind of wildman, as he banged against the door. She tried to hold it shut but he pushed through, knocking her against the wall and ran past her toward the front. Carmen hung on to the door, holding it open for Wayne, and yelled after him running up the hall, "Wayne, he's got a gun!" Wayne yelled something back over his shoulder but she didn't know what it was he said, he was moving away from her fast, intent on getting the one with the hair.

* * *

Carmen would tell later that she saw the gun, or what she thought was a gun, when Wayne came downstairs and walked by her office followed by the two men and the one with the hair had hesitated for a moment to look at her. She saw what she believed was a gun in his belt. When Wayne hit him the gun must've slipped down and he was holding it against his groin as he ran into the office, so it wouldn't fall down his pants leg. Carmen said she didn't find out until later that what Wayne had yelled at her was to call the police.

What she did was run after them, up the hall and the stairs to the second floor, where she saw Wayne going into Nelson's office. By the time she got there . . .

Carmen would tell what happened next in a quiet voice, looking off, separating it step by step in her mind, seeing it, she said, almost in slow motion.

"I saw Wayne from behind. He was in the middle of the room. The one with the hair was by the window, with his pants open in front. He was wearing cowboy boots. As Wayne moved toward him he pulled the gun—it had a bright metal finish—out of his pants. He was raising it when Wayne threw the sleever bar at him. But it missed. The man ducked, twisting around, and the sleever bar went through that big window in front, smashing the glass. But because the man turned away as he ducked, it gave

Wayne time to grab him. That was when the gun fired. It fired again, it fired three times altogether. Wayne had hold of his arm with one hand and his clothes, the front of his coat, with the other and was shoving him toward the window. Somehow Wayne had a good enough grip to pick him up, not much but I saw the cowboy boots off the floor, his legs kicking as Wayne gave him a shove and he went out through the broken window. I ran into the room thinking for sure Wayne had been shot, but he was all right, he was looking out the window as I reached him and looked out, expecting to see the man lying on the roof that was just below the window, but he wasn't. It was all covered with broken glass. Then I noticed the little fence around the roof was broken off and hanging down where he had fallen through it to land on the ground. I didn't see him though. That is, not right away. The one I saw first was the heavyset older man, going toward a car parked on the street and looking this way. Not at us, he was looking at the other one, with the hair. We both saw him then, running across the front lawn away from the office, running but limping. When he got to the car he turned around and fired his gun twice, but I don't think he hit the house even. The heavyset one pushed him and it looked like they started to argue with each other, the younger one pointing this way. I think there was blood on his face and the front of his

jacket. The heavyset one gave him another shove
and got him in the car. Then he went around to the
driver's side and got in. They made a U-turn and
drove away, north."

Carmen noticed the police called her Carmen and
Wayne Wayne, but they called Nelson Davies Mr.
Davies. He had arrived with the police, Nelson
wearing a suit and tie as always, a matching hanky
in the breast pocket.

The questioning was done in the office lobby,
Carmen telling her story several times: to the local Algonac officers, both of them who were on
duty, to investigators from the Michigan State Police, an officer from the Township Police and four
deputies from the St. Clair County Sheriff's office.
All those different uniforms. She could see Wayne
was irritated. First, because he was supposed to
meet Lionel and had to stay here and second, because of the way they asked him questions, almost as though what happened was his fault.
Beginning with, What was he doing in Mr.
Davies's office?

Did he tell the two guys he was Mr. Davies?

Did he let them think it?

Did he try to get tough, antagonize them?

Did he realize he could have endangered the
lives of the other people in the office?

Wayne said that was why he got the two guys out of there. They were so sure he had the money, he didn't see any choice but let them think it.

They wanted to know if he was trying to kill them with that crowbar.

Wayne said it was a sleever bar, or some guys called it a connecting bar or rod, they used it in their work to pry the ends of iron beams, get them to fit snug. He said if his intention was to kill those two guys he would've gone for their heads. He said, "What I don't understand, why don't you go over to Walpole and find out who drives an '86 Cadillac? That shouldn't be too hard."

Some of the police didn't care for this kind of talk. One of the sheriff's deputies asked Wayne if he had an attitude problem. Wayne, who'd walk off a job if the raising-gang foreman showed poor judgment, said, "No, sir, I'm just curious why you're sitting around here with your finger up your butt."

Carmen didn't blame him for being arrogant. Especially when the deputy told Wayne if the guy he'd thrown out the window was seriously injured, the guy could take him to court. Wayne said, "It might be the only way you'll ever see him."

They were the ones with the attitude. Carmen saw them as either very serious and impersonal, not showing any kind of sympathy except to Nelson, or they were condescending and treated her like a child. "Now, Carmen, you think you can tell us again exactly what you saw?" And she'd hear Wayne say, "Jesus Christ." At one point Nelson asked *her* to make a fresh pot of coffee for the officers. She didn't dare look at Wayne.

He showed his irritation while she managed to keep hers inside. Until, listening to Nelson and the police talking, it sounded as though they'd known about the two guys all along. When Carmen asked Nelson about it he said, "Well, of course. One of them called me."

"But you didn't tell anybody," Carmen said.

"I told the police."

"I mean any of *us*, my husband."

"Because the guy called again and changed the arrangement," Nelson said. "If he was coming to Wildwood then we had to, well, the police had to set up a surveillance. We had to think of the safety of the homeowners out there."

Carmen listened to Nelson saying he wished the two guys *had* come out to Wildwood. They sure would never have suspected those people raking leaves were police officers.

"You could've called Wayne, told him not to come."

Nelson said, "What?" He said, "To tell you the truth I didn't think he was coming anyway. Or if he did it would only be, well, as a courtesy."

"To humor me?" Carmen said.

Nelson grinned. "You said it, I didn't." He looked over at Wayne. "Am I right? Don't answer if it'll get you in trouble."

Wayne said, "Are we through?"

It was after six by the time they got home. Wayne popped open beers. He handed one to Carmen sitting at the kitchen counter. She took a sip and looked up at him.

"When Nelson mentioned the cops out at Wildwood raking leaves, I thought of saying, 'You must've had leaves hauled in, 'cause there sure aren't any trees out there.'"

"You should've."

After a minute Carmen said, "All those guys acted so . . . sure of themselves."

"Like they know what they're doing."

After another minute she said, "What an asshole."

"Which one?"

"Nelson, who else? I should've figured him out before this, just from the way he makes his lower loops."

Wayne said, "His lower loops, uh?"

"In his writing. The way he makes them, you know, very elaborate, ornate, it means he's preoccupied with himself. His upper loops are okay, they show mental alertness."

"What's that prove?" Wayne said. "You have to be mentally alert to be a good bullshitter?"

"Well, I know one thing," Carmen said, "I'm not gonna work for that jerk anymore."

Wayne raised his beer can to her.

"Some good has come of this after all."

6

ARMAND HAD THOUGHT he liked being called Bird, but now he wasn't so sure. Not the way Richie, bleeding all over himself, kept moaning, saying to him, "Bird, you have a hanky? Man, I'm cut bad. Bird, get me to Donna's." Saying Donna knew first aid. Richie had a cut on his chin where he went through the window and landed on the broken glass. That's all was wrong with him, a cut and sore knees he kept rubbing, getting blood on his pants. Armand had a sore back and ribs where the guy had worked him over with the iron bar, a tough guy. They had to run into one of those, not only a tough guy but the wrong guy. Armand believed the blood on Richie made the injury look worse than it was.

He said, "Let me see," and looked over as Richie raised his chin. "You could use a few stitches, that's all."

They drove through Marine City, passed the

street that went to Donna's street and Richie got excited. "Stop. Where you going?"

"Over to Sarnia."

"That's in *Can*ada."

"We can't drive around in this car," Armand said. "The guy saw it."

The guy who was no real estate man and also the woman. They had both gotten a good look at the car. Armand remembered who the guy was now, with that same pickup truck as yesterday. The guy with IRONWORKERS on the back of his jacket talking to Lionel Adam in Island Variety.

He was pretty sure the woman worked at the real estate office. He could see her now, looking out the back door at them, getting a good look. She was the one that had called out a guy's name, probably the ironworker's, but Armand couldn't think of it now.

He was too busy seeing what could happen to him. If he was picked up, the ironworker and the real estate woman would say, yeah, he's the guy. Pretty soon the police would find out where he's from and that he's driving a car owned by the son-in-law of a guy, also from Toronto, who was shot and killed yesterday in Detroit. Armand knew one thing for sure: he couldn't let this get to where they looked him up on their computer machine.

Now Richie was saying that he was going to get the son of a bitch. "I promised him and I will."

"Which son of a bitch?" Armand asked him.

"The real estate guy. Why didn't you shoot? They're standing right there in the window, Bird. There's the guy big as life. Why didn't you fucking shoot?"

"That's the guy you want, 'ey?"

"Man, you had him."

There was so much this punk didn't know.

"Let me tell you something, okay?"

"What?"

"That wasn't the real estate guy."

"What're you talking about?"

"I'll explain it to you sometime. What I want to tell you now, the only time you take out your gun and aim at somebody is when you gonna kill them."

"You could've back there."

"No, no could've. Only when you know you can do it. Then all it takes is one shot. It's the same as with a hunter, a guy that knows what he's doing. He don't take the shot if he thinks he could miss, or might only wound it. See, then he has to go find the animal to finish it. Okay, what if it's a kind of animal that could eat him up? Like a lion that's mad now 'cause it's shot and waits to jump out at the guy. You understand? That's why you always make sure. One shot, one kill."

"Man, I'm bleeding something fierce."

"Don't get it on the seat. What I'm saying, you don't want to have to shoot anything more than once."

"I'm in fucking *pain*."

This guy was not only a punk, he was a baby.

"We gonna take you to a hospital," Armand said.

"In Sarnia?"

"I think it's St. Joseph's. I'll know it when I see it. Me and my brothers went there one time to kill a guy."

Richie said, "No shit," quieter.

This was how you got his attention, tell him how the big boys did it.

"None of that bullshit," Armand said, "like in the movie you see the guy who's gonna do it come in the hospital? Then you see him go in a room and close the door. He comes out, he has a white coat on and everybody's suppose to think he's a doctor. This guy nobody in the hospital ever saw before."

"Or the janitor," Richie said. "I've seen it where the guy's suppose to be a janitor. With a mop, you know, and a bucket? Yeah, nobody says, 'Hey, who the fuck are you?' "

"Listen, okay? You want to learn something?"

"Yeah, go ahead."

"We get to the floor, one of my brothers holds the elevator. My other brother, this kind of setup, watches for anybody that might come along." Armand thinking, Like a nurse. But didn't say it. He paused, still thinking of a nurse and what happened after, months later . . .

Until Richie said, "This's at night?"

It brought Armand back. "Yes, it's at night. I go in the room where the sick guy is—I think he had a heart attack. I mean why he was there. I pull the sheet up over his face and pop him. Once." Armand took his hand from the steering wheel and pointed to his mouth. "Right here. One shot."

"One shot, one kill," Richie said. "What'd the guy do?"

"He died."

"I mean what'd he do you had to blow him away?"

"I don't know. I didn't ask."

"Why not?"

"It's not any of my business, it was a job."

"You blow a guy away, it's none of your business?"

"Whatever he did isn't, no."

"Were you pissed off at him?"

"I didn't *know* him. Don't you understand nothing?"

"To me, that doesn't make sense," Richie said. "Me, I have to be pissed off at the guy. Like you know, he doesn't do what I tell him."

Driving along the river road toward Port Huron

Armand turned to look at Richie, blood all over him, holding the bloody handkerchief to his chin. Some things maybe you couldn't explain to a guy like this.

They crossed into Canada over the Blue Water Bridge. It was midafternoon. The customs officer in his uniform checked the Ontario license plate and asked where they lived. Armand said, Toronto; they were here looking for work at the oil refinery. The customs officer hunched over to stare through the window at Richie, at the dark stains on his coat. He asked where they'd been. Armand said they went to Port Huron, to fool around, and his friend cut himself trying to open a beer bottle with his mouth. The customs officer said, "That's kind of stupid, isn't it?" Armand told him his friend was a stupid guy. It was the only thing he said that was true. The customs man shook his head and waved them on.

Armand parked by the hospital emergency entrance. He let Richie go in alone and waited in the car so he could take this time to think, plan ahead.

They would return south along the Canadian side of the river. Take Vidal Street out of Sarnia, he remembered that from nine years ago with his brothers. Go down past miles of petroleum and chemical works, Ontario Hydro, another name he remembered. Go all the way to Wallaceburg, yeah, and then cross that swing bridge over the Snye River and you were on Walpole Island. Like coming in the back door.

He didn't believe Richie had ever killed anybody. Okay, maybe with a shiv one time in prison. But he would be surprised if Richie had ever used a gun, as he said to blow a guy away. That was something he picked up at the movies, that blowing away. Armand tried to think how his brothers used to say it. They would say they were going to *do* a guy. Or they might say so-and-so got popped. Maybe because when you used a suppressor it made a popping sound, like an air rifle. The old man's son-in-law would ask if he'd go see somebody. Go see a guy. No one Armand could think of ever used the word *kill*. Maybe because it was a mortal sin.

Wait a minute. Armand remembered now that Richie had used the word *kill.* . . . No, that was when he was in prison and killed a guy and some other guys had tried to kill him. The migrant worker, the hitchhiker he picked up, he said he would have robbed the guy and shot a hole in him if the cop hadn't been there. But that one, and Richie saying he had blown people away during holdups, robbing a store one time and a gas station, didn't make sense. Killing a person without a good reason. Or, as he said, because he was pissed off. That was how a punk would imagine it and make up a story.

He did shoot at the guy in the real estate office.

Yeah, because he was scared to death. He had to.

One thing for sure, if Richie had never shot anybody he was anxious to try it. See what it was like to use a gun.

Armand thinking, Yes, you could help him out there. Show him where to point it. This guy had to be good for *some*thing.

The ten stitches in his chin didn't keep Richie from talking. Only now he barely opened his mouth when he spoke and was hard to understand. Armand was getting tired of saying "What?" every time Richie asked him something. Now he wanted to know where they were going. Wasn't that the guy Lionel's house they went by?

"That's right," Armand said, "and his wife was there. We got enough people already have seen this car."

"I told you, take it to Detroit and let it get stolen," Richie said. "*Now* where we going?"

They were crossing a short span of bridge over one of the many channels in these flats. "Now we're on Squirrel Island," Armand said. "It's like part of Walpole. I want to see if it's a good place."

"I think down in the marsh is better," Richie said.

He was probably right. Armand, letting the Cadillac coast to a stop in the dirt road, remembered this island green with corn in the summer. Now it was all dead, rows of withered stalks as far as you could see, reaching way over to that freighter in the ship channel. It got Richie excited.

"Look at that. Like it's going through the cornfield. Over at Henry's you see them, it's like they're in the woods. *Now* where we going?"

"Back," Armand said.

Back across Walpole, following roads through deep woods to the other side, to Lionel's house on the Snye River. Richie saying, "Now let me get this straight. This guy's Indian, but used to be an ironworker. Same as the guy you're trying to tell me isn't the real estate man."

"Believe me," Armand said.

"Well, what was he doing there?"

"I don't care," Armand said, "long as you know what we have to do. There's the house. Good, his wife's gone."

"How do you know?"

"Because he's right there—you see him? And the truck's gone that was there."

"That's him, huh? Not a bad-looking house—I mean for an Indian. Shit. What's he doing?"

It was a little white-frame place set among willows: a window, a door, a window. A bike in the yard. Lionel was on the front stoop, taking the screen out of the aluminum door and putting in the storm pane for winter. Armand didn't see anyone else around. Lionel had a couple of grown kids, gone, and one that was a baby when Armand was here last. He turned into the worn tire tracks that extended past the house to a shed where Lionel kept his muskrat traps and decoys, fishnets hanging from the roof. Lionel was looking this way now. Hands on his hips, not very anxious to see company. Beyond the house was the wooden dock on the river, where Lionel's outboard was tied. Lionel was coming across the yard now, swinging his leg.

"What's wrong with him?"

"Get him to tell you."

"He looks more Indian than you, Bird."

They got out of the car. Armand said, "Lionel, this guy wants to do some duck hunting." He didn't bother to introduce them. Lionel had stopped, hands beneath his folded arms in a sweat shirt, not ready to shake hands anyway. Not too happy to see them.

Though he said, "Wants to knock down some ducks, 'ey?"

Armand said, "You see this guy's chin? He was putting up his storm windows and fell off the ladder, cut himself up so he can't work. I said, 'Well, let's go duck hunting.' How does it look? You free tomorrow?"

Lionel acted as if he had to think about it. "I don't know, maybe. I can go out later, see if it's gonna be any good, any ducks landing."

"Where, down the marsh?"

Lionel turned, looking off at layers of clouds with dark undersides. "I go down by St. Anne's, see how it is. Maybe, I don't know."

"We could go now," Armand said, "take a ride in your boat. Richie hasn't ever seen a marsh."

"I've seen one. Shit, I've even seen this one." Armand gave him a look, staring hard, and Richie said, "But I've never been like *in* one. In a boat."

"You guys," Lionel said, smiling a little, "you want to go like that?"

Armand buttoned his suit coat and held his hands out. "What's the matter? I always wear this when I go duck hunting. How about him?" Armand hooked a thumb at Richie, blood all over his sport coat. "Couple of dudes, 'ey?" He moved toward Lionel saying, "Come on, let's go," extending his hand to touch Lionel's arm. Lionel turned away, swinging his leg out to walk off. Following him around back and along a path to the river, Armand said, "Tell this guy—Lionel? Tell him how you fell and hurt yourself."

"That's what happened," Lionel said.

"Tell him how high up you were."

"Seventy feet."

Richie, following Armand, said, "Shit, and it didn't kill him?"

"Tell him what you landed on. What do you call those things? They stick out of concrete."

"Retaining rods," Lionel said.

"Retaining rods," Armand said over his shoulder, "they put in concrete. He landed on one of those things, sticking straight up."

"Jesus Christ," Richie said.

"Like he sat down in it."

"Jesus Christ—it went up his ass?"

"It hit him under his butt," Armand said over his shoulder as they came to the boat dock: a plank walk that extended out into the river, Lionel's aluminum boat with its forty-horse Johnson tied alongside.

Lionel turned to them, saying, "The rod went through me and came out my back here, at my kidney. Where it used to be."

"Jesus Christ," Richie said.

"He only has one kidney," Armand said.

"I lost the kidney, I broke both my feet and my legs and had to get a new plastic kneecap, this one," Lionel said. "But I was lucky, 'cause if I didn't land on that retaining rod I'd be dead. It slowed me down." He moved toward the boat saying, "What else you want to know?" and began to free the line.

Armand said, "Ten, twelve years ago, 'ey?"

"More than that. It was when we were building the Renaissance Center, over in Detroit. More like fourteen years now." He was holding the boat for them, offering a hand. Armand, stepping aboard, gripped Lionel's hand. Richie ignored it.

"You were talking to a guy yesterday," Armand said, "I notice was an ironworker."

"Yeah, he was on that job too," Lionel said. "I think it was the first time I met him. He was a punk then."

"But not now, 'ey?"

"A punk," Lionel said, coiling the line, "is what ironworkers call an apprentice. No, believe me, he's no punk now."

"What's his name?"

Armand waited. Lionel was looking toward the house and was thinking about something or maybe didn't hear him.

"I should have left my wife a note," Lionel said. "She drove our girl to go ice-skating, over the sports arena."

Armand looked toward the house, then up at Lionel on the dock. "This won't take long."

A lake freighter appeared, a small one but towering over them as it passed, Lionel saying it was going up to Hazzard Grain in Wallaceburg, Lionel now telling them things without being asked.

At first it was like any river with land on both sides, tree lines and thickets Lionel called "the bush." But as they moved south the banks of the Snye changed to marshland, reeds and cattails as far as Armand could see from low in the boat. Now it was like a river that ran through weeds growing out of the water. He said, "Where's the land? There's no place you can get out."

Lionel seemed to smile. He was not so serious now guiding his boat, the forty-horse Johnson grumbling in the water. Pointing then to an opening in the marsh bank he said, "That swale there—when the water's up you punch your boat through there, find some muskrat."

Richie, in the bow, said, "Where? I don't see any muskrats."

"They seen you first," Lionel said. "I had a trap I'd stick it in there. That's where they crawl up."

"You eat 'em?"

"If you want," Lionel said. "You can barbecue muskrat, the way I like it, or make a stew. See, but they're bottom feeders so a lot of people won't eat them, afraid they gonna get some toxic-waste dressing in their meat."

Richie said, then what good were they? Lionel

told him a nice pelt was worth six-fifty and Richie said, shit, was that all?

"Watch the sky," Lionel said. "You want ducks, we have to see where they land."

"My jaw hurts," Richie said, "and I'm cold."

It made Armand think of summer, being here a long time ago when it was hot. "It looks different—all this water."

"Maybe you never came down this far," Lionel said, "you and your brothers. There aren't no cats or dogs here to shoot."

"Keep talking like that," Armand said, "I'll turn you into a muskrat." He looked over his shoulder at Lionel in the stern. "I learned how to work medicine from my grandmother. She was gonna turn me into an owl one time."

"Too bad she didn't," Lionel said.

Armand had to twist around to look at him again. "What do you mean by that?"

"An owl knows things gonna happen." Lionel smiled then a little and said, "You gonna turn me into one of these rats, wait till spring when they come in heat. I'll have some fun."

"That's what you already are now," Armand said, "live in a place like this." He was cold and wanted this trip to hurry up and be over. Turning around on the seat, so the wind hit his back, didn't help much. All Lionel had on was the sweatshirt, but didn't appear cold. He wore jeans and dirty sneakers—no, they were running shoes. Look at him. He liked it here and there was no way to insult him. Armand watched Lionel's eyes raise to read the clouds or the wind or some goddamn Indian thing he did.

"How much to take us out tomorrow?"

"A hundred each."

"No special price, 'ey? For an old friend?"

Lionel didn't answer that one, but he said, "You need a twelve-gauge I can let you have one. You buy the shells."

Armand said, "How about that ironworker? You take him out? The one yesterday?"

"Not too much. He's a kind of guy, he don't eat it, he won't shoot it. I think it's more he don't like to clean 'em. My wife does it for hunters. She's what you call a duck-plucker." Lionel grinned. "A buck a duck."

"What's the guy's name?"

"What guy?"

"Your friend, the ironworker."

"It's Wayne."

Yeah, it was the name the woman in the real estate office had called. Wayne.

"You go deer hunting with him, 'ey?"

"Yeah, he's got a private woods there, on his property."

"He seem like a nice guy," Armand said. "What's his name, Wayne?"

"Wayne Colson."

"Where's he live? Around here?"

"Over by Algonac."

"He seem like a nice guy."

"Yeah, I go over there," Lionel said. "Sometimes me an my wife, my little girl, Debbie. His wife says, when we go over there, she wishes they had a little girl. She tells Debbie that."

"So he's married, 'ey?"

"Yeah, his wife sells real estate."

Armand said, "You kidding me."

"What's wrong with that?"

"It seems funny, that's all, an ironworker married to a woman sells real estate."

Lionel shrugged. He said, "They have a grown son, in the U.S. Navy," and looked off at his sky again.

After a while Armand heard Richie yell out, "There's some!" and turned to see land and a flock of birds Armand recognized rising out of an old willow on the bank. Blackbirds.

"I see I'm gonna have trouble with him," Lionel said, grinning. "He'll be shooting at coots thinking they're mallards."

Richie was turned around in the bow.

"What's wrong?"

"Ducks don't land in trees," Lionel said. "Birds, yeah, but not any ducks I know of. That's the first thing you have to learn."

Armand saw the way Richie was looking past

him at Lionel. He said, "Let's go over there and stretch our legs."

"If you want to," Lionel said.

He brought them to the bank where the willow stood empty now and cut the motor. Richie grabbed the tall weeds, stepped out of the boat and both feet sank into mud and water. Armand saw what not to do and jumped past the soft edge of the bank, landed okay, but felt the ground mushy beneath him, weeds up to his waist. He looked around at Lionel, still in the boat.

"You coming?"

"I don't need to stretch any."

Armand said to Richie, "Do him," and expected to hear some excuse. Out here? It's too open. Something like that.

No—he reached under his coat behind him, brought out that nickelplate, cocked it, aimed with two hands like in the movies and shot Lionel three times as he was trying to get out of the boat, that third shot punching him out to drop in the water. They were quick shots too, no hesitation. Loud, but flat out here in the open, the sound just now fading.

"Well, you took more than one," Armand said, "but you knocked him down."

Richie was looking at Lionel facedown in the water, one arm hooked over the side of the boat.

"That pissed me off," Richie said, "telling me

ducks don't land in trees. *I* know ducks don't land in trees."

Back at Lionel's, before they got in the Cadillac and drove off, Armand went in the house and came out with two Remington pump-action shotguns and a couple of camouflaged duck-hunting coats and hats. Richie said, "What's all that for?" Armand told him he'd see. Then, when Armand left the island by way of the swing bridge, heading for Wallaceburg, Richie said, "Aren't we going home? Man I have to get cleaned up." Armand told him to put on one of the duck-hunting coats, they were going to Windsor. They'd leave the car at the airport in long-term parking and pick out another one for the time being. "Then come home?" Richie said. Then cross back at Detroit through customs, Armand said, couple of duck hunters on their way to Algonac. And find out where the ironworker lived.

"What's the big hurry?" Richie said. "If he lives there, he's gonna be there."

"You want to do something else?"

"Well, have a few beers, anyway. Watch some TV."

"After we find their house, take a look at it. You hear Lionel? I'm pretty sure that real estate woman's his wife. The one saw us."

"The one was with him?" Richie sounded surprised. "She didn't do nothing. Was the guy hit us."

Armand turned his headlights on the blacktop moving through farmland, getting dark out there. "I forgot you have to be pissed off," Armand said. "All this blowing away you did, you never blew away a woman, 'ey?"

"I never felt a need to."

"Well, you better feel one now."

Richie was silent. Armand wondered if maybe it was the first time in his life the guy had stopped to think before opening his mouth. Armand waited another few moments before saying, "Let me tell you something. You don't ever leave things undone. You don't ever think somebody's not gonna remember you. Me and my brothers went in that hospital in Sarnia—"

"You already told me about it."

There, he was talking again without thinking.

"Listen to me. My younger brother, Jackie, is holding the elevator. My older brother, Gerard, is watching so nobody comes in the room. He's standing inside by the door, has it open a little bit. A nurse comes down the hall. She don't go by, she opens the door and there's my brother right in front of her, face-to-face, close. He takes her quick into the bathroom, turns out the light and tells her don't make a sound."

"I'd have coldcocked her," Richie said.

"I finish with the guy and say to my brother, 'What about her in there?' In the bathroom, the door's closed. He says, 'I don't think she saw me good.' I say to him, 'What are you telling me? You don't *think* she saw you?' He says, 'No, she didn't see me good.' It was seven months later the police come to the Waverley Hotel—"

Richie said, "The Royal Canadian Mounties?"

"The Toronto Police, that's enough. They come to the hotel where we stay there looking for the Degas brothers. This time they find only Gerard, take him in and that nurse points to him in the lineup. Yes, he was in the room when the man was killed. They find my brother Jackie and shoot him down, they say resisting arrest. That could be true. They find me, the nurse takes a look; no, she never saw me. They have to let me go. See, but I lost my two brothers—one dead, one in prison for life, because Gerard says she didn't see him good. That one time . . . Why did he say that? I don't know, maybe he looked at her. Maybe he liked her face, I don't know. I'm never gonna figure that out."

Richie said, "Well, did you ask him?"

"Sure, I asked him. He don't know either. Now he's at Kingston trying to figure it out."

They drove through the dusk in silence.

Until Richie said, "Well, I don't see there'd be much difference anyway, whether it's a man or a woman. . . . Is there?"

"Not if you don't think about it," Armand said.

7

LATE AFTERNOON, cool and clear outside, three days since the excitement at the real estate office, the phone rang. It was on the wall next to the window over the kitchen sink.

Carmen knew it was Lenore because she had her hands in meat loaf, working a raw egg, onions and bread crumbs into the ground beef and pork, and her mom only called when she was in the middle of something or in the bathroom. If Carmen called her mom, Lenore would answer, *"Who is this?"* in case it might be an obscene phone call. She had worked at one time in the telephone company's Annoyance Call Bureau and knew all about dirty-mouth pervert callers. Just last month she had changed her number after twice answering the ring and the caller hung up without saying a word. She told Carmen, "That's how they find out if you're home, so they can come in and rape you." Wayne said to Carmen, "Tell her don't worry, once the guy got a look at her she'd be safe."

Carmen turned to the sink, rinsed her hands and dried them on a dish towel, the phone still ringing. Sometimes she'd pick it up and say, "Hi, Mom."

But not today. Carmen looked out the window as she lifted the receiver from the hook and didn't say a word.

She saw something move in the woods. Not the far deep woods, where Wayne grew his row of corn along the edge and had placed the salt lick, but in the thicket beyond the chickenhouse, where a section of woods came down close to the backyard. She was pretty sure a man was standing in there, in the tangle of dense branches; not at the edge but back in the gloom, his form blending, most of him concealed. Lenore's voice was saying, "Carmen?" Repeating it. "Carmen, what are you doing?"

Whoever it was just stood there, not moving.

Carmen said, "Hi, Mom."

She didn't say anything about it to Wayne, not right away. He came home—it was on her mind as she got dinner ready and Wayne opened beers for them and phoned Lionel. No answer. Two days now, no one home. Carmen said didn't they have relatives in Ohio they went to visit? Wayne said, "In duck season?"

During the week Carmen would turn on the TV

in the kitchen and they'd watch *Jeopardy* while they ate dinner, sitting at the counter. Wayne was good at state capitals, country music, some history, because it was all he read outside of hunting magazines, and wars. His favorite was the Civil War. Carmen was good at popular music and groups, movie stars who had won Academy Awards and biology. Carmen would get more right than Wayne. *Jeopardy* was on now. Some of the categories were Art, Bowling, Four-letter Words and Kings Named Ed. But they weren't paying much attention to it. Carmen listened to Wayne saying he wondered if he should go over to Walpole, check up on Lionel.

Wayne saying he liked the One-Fifty Jefferson project, he knew most of the guys on the raising gang and the walking boss was an old buddy. One of the connectors got a bunch of flowers with a card signed by five women who'd been watching him from an office building. Wayne saying he was bolting up and doing some welding, but that was okay, it was the kind of story job he liked, put it straight up in the air three hundred feet and go on to the next one. Wayne saying the meat loaf was the best he'd ever tasted. Then going on to say he could never understand why Matthew didn't like it. How could you not like meat loaf?

Carmen, waking up, said, "Oh, we got a letter today."

Wayne gave her a funny look, because a rare letter from Matthew would be sitting right here on the counter. Carmen had to find it, over in a drawer where she filed letters and bills.

Wayne began to read the letter from their son. Carmen took a bite of meat loaf—it was okay but she'd made better—played with her peas and carrots, looked up at the window and saw the kitchen reflected on the glass, the portable TV screen a bright spot. One of the *Jeopardy* contestants had picked the Kings Named Ed category. Something about one of them being a saint and the contestant, a woman, said, "Who was Edward the Confessor?"

Just as Wayne said, "Everything's initials with him now. The A-7Es, the AE-6Bs. He isn't on a carrier, he's on a CVN. Here, he says, 'My new job is to make sure the nosegear towbar engages the catapult shuttle and then stand clear. You don't want to get caught between the aircraft and the JBD.' What's the JBD?"

"The jet blast deflector," Carmen said.

"Well, what's FOD? He says, 'We police the flight deck for anything lying around that might cause an aircraft to FOD-out.'"

"Foreign object damage," Carmen said. "I guess something that might get sucked into the jet engine."

It seemed to irritate Wayne.

"How do you know that?"

"It was in the book he sent, *Supercarriers in Action*."

"I haven't read it yet."

The woman contestant on *Jeopardy* was running the Kings Named Ed category, answering one, "Where is the Tower of London?" in the form of a question, as you were supposed to. The woman was the smartest *Jeopardy* contestant Carmen had ever seen.

She said, "Mom called this afternoon."

Wayne looked up from Matthew's letter. "To brighten your day. Asked what you were fixing for dinner, you told her meat loaf and she said leave the Tabasco out, we're ruining our stomachs."

"She said to be sure to add milk."

"I bet she asked about your dad, what's new with him."

"She hinted around."

"Hoping to hear his liver had finally got him. Guy's down in Tampa happier'n a pig in shit. She's up here drinking her vodka and grapefruit juice, thinking of ways to be miserable. How's her back?"

"The same. She bends over, it's like somebody sticks a redhot poker in her."

"I better not say anything," Wayne said and returned to the letter. After a moment he said, "I like this part. Matthew says, 'The steam pressure it takes to catapult a thirty-ton aircraft off the flight deck would send a pickup truck five miles out over the ocean.' Now something like that I can picture. Then he talks about steam building up in the 'below-deck accumulators.' How's a kid like Matthew know that? He's nineteen years old."

"He's grown up," Carmen said. "You were working when you were his age."

"He says, 'Hoping your days are CAVU and all is well.' You think he's overdoing it a little? What's CAVU?"

"Ceiling and visibility unlimited."

"You know what it is? Being on a new job. You use all the words, like you know what you're talking about. Matthew's out there on his CVN with that JBD and the FODs on a CAVU kind of day."

"Somebody was in the woods," Carmen said, "this afternoon. I looked out, it was when I was talking to Mom."

Wayne said, "Well, that could be," and paused. "You didn't see who it was."

Carmen shook her head. "There might even've been two, I'm not sure."

"You say while you were talking to your mom."

"I didn't mention it to her."

"No, I don't imagine you would. But how come you wait till now to tell me?"

"I was going to right away, but then . . . I don't know, it didn't seem that important anymore. They might've been hunters."

"It's the duck season, honey. There aren't any ducks in the woods. Were they just, maybe walking through?"

"It was more like they were trying to stay hidden, watching the house. That was the feeling I had."

"I don't see how it could be those two guys, if that's what you're thinking."

"No, I don't either."

"They might like to run into me sometime, but they're not gonna hang around on the off chance, with the police looking for them. Or so they say."

Carmen said, "How could they know where we live?"

"They couldn't, there's no way they could find out."

She saw Wayne thinking about it as he finished his dinner. On *Jeopardy* the contestants were getting ready for the hardest part, Final Jeopardy.

"Unless," Wayne said, "that one, the Indian, remembers me talking to Lionel and goes to see him. Hey, but Lionel's away someplace. I don't know where, but he sure as hell isn't home."

"It probably wasn't anybody," Carmen said. "Just some guy. I'm not gonna worry about it."

"No, they'd be pretty dumb to hang around."

Carmen didn't say anything. They were showing the Final Jeopardy question now. She looked at it, then at Wayne as he slid off the kitchen stool and went over to the closet where he kept his hunting gear, his shotguns, boxes of ammunition, coats, boots, lures, old copies of hunting magazines. She could see him in there with the light on.

"Hon, what are two adjacent states, one's a Spanish word, the other's Indian and they both mean red, the color?"

She was pretty sure the states were Colorado and Utah.

Wayne came out of the closet holding his Remington 870 fitted with the shorter slug barrel. He said, "Colorado and Oklahoma," crossing to the door. He stood the shotgun next to it, against the wall.

Carmen said, "I think it's Colorado and Utah."

That was what the smartest woman she had ever seen on *Jeopardy* also thought, and they were both wrong. The states were Colorado and Oklahoma.

It surprised Carmen. Still, she felt good about it, smiling as she said, "How'd you know that?"

"I went bird shooting down there one time," Wayne said. "Remember?"

"Knowing my love of corrections," Donna had said to Richie Nix more than once and in different ways, "for them to treat me the way they did, I have lost all respect for our prison system."

He told the Bird she was always going on about it. It convinced Richie they could trust Donna. At least tell her where they got the van. The Bird said no.

"She's confused," Richie said. "We drive off Saturday in a Cadillac, come back that night in a Dodge van wearing hunting outfits." Camouflaged coats and caps, all green and brown with a little black.

The Bird said, "Let her be confused."

"Yeah, but we don't want her pissed off at us."

The Bird said, "You don't tell a woman use to wear a state uniform your business."

He didn't get it.

"That's the whole point of what I'm saying," Richie said, "she *knows* my business. She *knows* I got felony warrants out on me. It don't matter to her, she spent her life with guys like me. Man, she's a fucking convict groupie. We stay friendly with her, we have a nice little place to hide out. But we hurt her feelings, that'll piss her off. Bird? You understand?"

The Bird said, "Don't call me Bird no more."

That stopped Richie, confused him. "You said they call you the Blackbird."

"Not anymore."

"Well, what am I suppose to call you?"

"My name, Armand."

"*Armand?* You serious?"

They had been having their differences the past couple of days. It had taken that long to locate the ironworker's house, the address in the phone book listed as a rural route number. They had to scout the place then. The Bird's idea, leave the van on a back road and cut through the woods like a couple of hunters, sneak up on the house from behind. Okay, they had done that. Stood in wet weeds and bushes in their camie outfits—there was the house, there was a Cutlass and a boat with an outboard on a trailer in the garage, but no pickup truck. Which meant the ironworker wasn't home and the Bird would not go up to the house till he knew both the guy and his wife were in there. Richie liked the idea of walking into the house, take care of the woman and wait for the guy to get home. Surprise him, we're sitting there. The Bird had said, "Take care of the woman, 'ey? You think you can do it?" Still bringing it up. The Bird didn't like the idea of walking in, he said, because somebody they didn't expect could come along while they were in the house. Maybe cops. These people would have talked to the cops, no? What if the cops stopped by to ask them some more questions? Anything Richie wanted to do, the Bird was against it. Now he had a faggy name he wanted to be called, Armand.

They were in Donna's living room under the pictures of guards, cons and prison officials: Richie and Armand sitting with their drinks among the stuffed animals, Armand fooling with Mr. Froggy's button eyes; while Donna prepared her gourmet frozen chow, banging pans out in the kitchen so they'd know she was there.

Richie said, "Armand?" Jesus Christ, he felt weird saying it. "You notice she's not talking to us? When she makes all that fucking noise like that it means she's getting pissed off. I don't want her to do nothing dumb."

The Bird, Armand, said, "Pimpslap a woman, you want to keep her in line."

"Now that would really set her off."

"If she don't know better," Armand said, "she's in trouble."

Man, this guy was from some other fucking world. "Armand," Richie said, "you're not married, are you?"

"No way."

"You ever live with a woman? I mean outside of your family?"

"What's the point?"

"Armand, lemme tell you something. You're always telling me something, now it's my turn. Okay, Armand." If he kept saying the name it would get easier. "You might've shot a woman or two in your line of work. . . . Have you?"

"Go on what you're gonna tell me."

"Let's say you have. But shooting a woman and understanding a woman are two entirely different things, man. I've lived with women in foster homes and women since then." Richie dropped his voice to add, "I might even still be married, I'm not sure, she got scared and took off on me. That's okay, a woman being scared. But don't ever let 'em get pissed off at you if you can help it. First thing, they'll stop talking to you. Like her out there. You give them any more cause, then look out. A woman won't ever come at you, they got other ways. Put ground-up glass in your chow. Pour gasoline on you while you're sleeping and set you afire. I know guys it's happened to. The least thing they can do is tell on you, that's too fucking easy. Donna knows I got a sheet six feet long besides warrants from here to Kentucky. She can make a case anytime she wants. But, see, that don't worry me. What does is the sneaky shit she's liable to pull, say her feelings get hurt. What I'm telling you, Armand, you have to keep a woman thinking you give a shit what *she* thinks."

Armand said, "So you don't trust her."

"Man, I just got done explaining it to you. I don't have to worry do I trust *her*, long as she trusts *me*."

The Indian took time to finish his whiskey before saying, "What do you want to tell her?" Not sounding so goddamn sure of himself now.

Richie felt he had him. He said, "Watch," and called, "Hey, Donna? Fix us up here, will you?"

There she was, looking like a cartoon spider with her skinny legs and arms and that big butt sticking out. She took their glasses out to the kitchen and returned with fresh drinks filled with ice, checking them now to tell which was which, handing the darker one to Richie, the Southern and Seven, their eyes meeting but he didn't say anything to her, not yet. He knew the Indian was watching all this, watching Donna now coming to him on the sofa, giving him his whiskey, but not even a glance, serious in her hairdo and ornamental glasses. Richie waited until she turned to leave.

"Donna?"

She stopped and said, "What?" but didn't turn around.

"I want to tell you something. You know the van?"

Donna said, "Yeah?"

"I swiped it."

Donna came around about halfway.

"Over in Windsor, at the airport," Richie said. "This blonde was sitting in the van waiting on somebody? After while out come this colored guy must've been seven feet tall, from the terminal. The blonde gets out, she has this real short skirt on, runs up and jumps in his arms and they give each other a big kiss, his hands holding her butt. Then this other seven-foot jig appears, she runs up to *him*. They stand talking a minute and the three of them go in the airport, I figured to get the two jigs's bags. Soon as they went inside I hopped in the van and took off." Richie frowned a little, staring at Donna. "I couldn't help it, seeing this cute little girl waiting on those seven-foot jigs."

Donna said, "What happened to your chin?"

"I got in a fight."

"With the colored boys?"

"No, was way before. Guy got smart with me."

"Well, are you okay?"

"I'm fine."

Donna said, "What happened to *his* car?" Meaning the Indian's, but not looking at him.

"It broke down. We had to leave it for repairs."

"So you decided it was all right to take that van?"

"I'm not gonna hurt it," Richie said. "We'll use it, do a little hunting, then I'll leave it someplace."

Donna said, "Did you want the Weight Watchers chicken patty or the regular?"

Richie grinned. "Who, me? Come on."

"What about him?"

"Give the Bird a double Weight Watchers."

He waited till Donna left them and was in the

kitchen before looking over at his partner. "I did see that happen one time, not over in Windsor, it was out at Detroit Metro. Yeah, this cute girl picks up these two giant colored guys. I guess basketball players. You wonder how those people got so tall." Richie noticed the Indian looking toward the kitchen.

"She believe that story?"

"Who, Donna? She knows it's close to the truth if it ain't right on. She'll ask me some more questions later. Like sneak up and try and catch me. Hey, but what you do now, Bird, I mean Armand, go in there and give her a little pat on the ass. Show her we're all friends here."

8

RICHIE HAD STOLEN THE VAN so he was the driver now. It gave Armand the feeling he was along for the ride, that he was losing his hold on this punk who drove too fast and didn't keep his eyes on the road. They were dressed as hunters, on their way to see the ironworker and his wife. Four days had passed since their visit to the real estate office. And there it was, Richie slowing down as they approached the big house on the river road, crept past, Richie hunched over the wheel to look at the upstairs window.

"You think he's in there?"

Armand didn't answer.

"If I knew for sure he was I'd walk in, go right up to his office. That'd be a kick, wouldn't it? See his face?"

Armand still didn't answer. He was thinking that either one of his brothers would look Richie over and say, "What are you doing with this guy? He's a punk." His dead brother would say, "Guy tries to steal your car, you don't do nothing to him?" His brother in prison would say, "You don't leave him out on the road, keep going?" Try to explain it to them. Well, the deal looked pretty good. His brothers, either one, would say, "Yeah? It did, 'ey? With this guy?" It would be the same as if they saw him in the Silver Dollar with his arm around an ugly woman, buying her drinks. It wouldn't matter how drunk he was.

That place, the Silver Dollar, was changing, full of punks; he couldn't go back there. So he was in this business and it was like waking up with the ugly woman and not knowing where he was, only that he had to find his way out.

His brothers would have something to say about Donna.

Last night Richie kept saying, "Go on, go in there and say something to her. Make her feel good. Give her a little pat on the ass." Okay, so he went in there. She seemed nervous with him watching her getting dinner ready and he could see she was trying to act natural. She had perfume on that smelled pretty good. He liked her body, the way it showed in tight pants and sweater. She asked him if he wanted anything and he said, "If you could be any kind of bird there is, what kind would you be?" She looked at him funny. He told her how his grandmother was going to turn him into an owl one time and what she could make seagulls do. He watched Donna relax and become interested, Donna saying, "No way," her glasses shining in the overhead light when he told her about the seagulls. Armand believed there was a certain type of woman who wore glasses you could tell liked sex a lot. He saw Donna as one of them. He didn't pat her on the butt; he asked her again what kind of bird she'd want to be. Donna looked at him and said she would have to give that some thought. He was getting along pretty good with her until Richie came into the kitchen saying, "Hey, what's going on here?"

Richie a problem since becoming the driver. Richie breaking the silence now.

"We're almost there, Bird."

Armand, alert as they passed fields and woods on both sides of the road, said, "Slow down. Watch for where you turn in."

Yesterday they had followed a pair of ruts that tracked from the blacktop to a deserted, falling-down farmhouse, a patch of woods separating it from the Colson property.

Richie drove past it.

Armand straightened on the seat. "Where you going?"

"I want to look at the house."

There it was, a barn-type roof and dormers coming into view, a big comfortable-looking house sitting among shrubs and old trees. The ironworker's truck was in the drive, by the back porch. The door to the house stood open.

"Jesus Christ, Bird, the guy's *home*."

"Tell me where you're going."

"I'm gonna turn around and come back, pull up right in front. Bang in there, man."

"You want to do it a different way now," Armand said. "Give them a chance to see us coming."

"Don't sweat it," Richie said, U-turning, creeping the van back toward the house. "I want the guy, okay? I'm gonna use a shotgun on him. I never did anybody with a shotgun before. You?"

Armand didn't answer. He was looking past Richie at the house, counting eight columns on the high front porch, thinking that was a lot of columns to hold up the roof, thinking that after this was done he was going to have to shoot Richie in the head, though he would rather do it before, right now.

Dump him out on the front lawn. They were parked off the road now by the trees. Richie, close to him, turned to reach behind the seats for one of the loaded shotguns.

"You ready?"

Armand opened the door and stepped out of the van. Yes, he was ready. He closed the door and put his right hand in the pocket of the hunting coat to grip his pistol. No, he had never killed anyone with a shotgun. What would be the purpose of using one? This guy thought he was in the movies. Armand started around the front of the van.

In the same moment, looking up, he saw the pickup truck through the shrubs backing out of the drive, fast, the rear end turning this way, brake lights popping on and now the truck was taking off in the direction they had come. Armand stepped back, opened the door. Richie was hunched over, starting the van. He glanced at Armand saying, "I got him. You get the woman."

Armand was shaking his head no, reaching up to pull himself in, and the van jumped away from him. He heard Richie saying it again, "I *got* him," taking off after the ironworker's pickup.

Carmen told her mom she was getting ready to fix kielbasa and cabbage for dinner, one of Wayne's favorites. Her mom said, "Oh, is he home for a change? Let me say hello to the big guy." Carmen told her they'd run out of beer and she'd forgotten to pick some up at the A & P, so Wayne had run out to get some. Her mom said, "Uh-huh," and told Carmen that kielbasa and cabbage was a good last-minute kind of dinner, wasn't it, you could throw together whenever the man of the house decided to come home. Carmen, looking out the window over the sink, said, "Mom?" Her mom was saying she fried her kielbasa first, then put it in

with the cabbage to steam for about twenty minutes and served it with mustard pickles. Carmen
said, "Mom, I'll call you right back," and hung up.

The heavyset man Wayne thought was an Indian
had come up the drive and was standing opposite
the porch. Carmen knew him, even in that hunting
outfit, the man facing the door to the kitchen, now
gazing up at the house.

Wayne had come home and run out again, leaving the door open. The shotgun he'd loaded and
placed next to the door last night was still there,
leaning against the wall. But the door was on the
other side of the counter from where Carmen
stood at the sink.

She was thinking that if she had remembered
to pick up the beer, or if Wayne had come home
earlier—but he wasn't home and that's why he'd
placed the gun by the door, for a time like this,
just in case, the Remington she'd fired at least a
dozen times in the past five years, though never
at anything living. Wayne had said she was pretty
good with it. He'd throw cans in the air . . .

The heavyset man was approaching the steps,
his hands in the side pockets of his hunting coat. It
was too small for him. So was the cap, sitting on
his forehead, the peak down close to his eyes.

She didn't want him to come up on the porch. If
he did—she didn't think closing the door and lock-
ing it would keep him out of the house.

So Carmen walked around the counter and watched his head raise, the man seeing her now in the doorway. She picked up the Remington, pushed the safety off and let him see the shotgun too, held in her right hand pointed down, as she stepped out on the porch.

He touched the brim of his cap and seemed to smile. "You going hunting, Miss?"

Carmen didn't answer.

"I was looking for your husband, have a talk with him."

"He's not home."

"I know that. But see, I can come in and wait for him." He shrugged, looking toward the road, then at Carmen again, his face raised with the peaked cap in his eyes. He said, "Okay?" and started to mount the steps.

Carmen half-turned, raising the shotgun in both hands, the stock under her arm.

It stopped him. He frowned and seemed surprised. "Why you pointing that at me?"

"What do you want?"

"I told you, I want to talk to your husband. Why don't you and I go in the house, wait for him?"

"You'd better leave," Carmen said. "I mean it. Right now."

"Or what? You gonna shoot me? That what you do, you shoot people?"

It made her mad, the way he said it, and she didn't answer.

She was holding a shotgun loaded with Magnum slugs, finger curled around the trigger. But the gun was only a threat if she was willing to use it. The man seemed at ease, not believing she would, and that made her mad. She was scared to death of him. She didn't want him to move, come up the steps. But if he did she would have to shoot. He looked out at the road again and up at the house and then at her, in no hurry. It was as though he was saying, This is nothing, I'll come up the steps if I want, do anything I want . . .

He moved to come up the steps and Carmen pulled the trigger and saw his face change, his eyes pop open, in that shattering sound of the gun firing, the shot going past his head. She pumped the gun and held it on him, the man bringing both hands up as he backed away saying, "Okay, take it easy, 'ey? You want me to leave? Okay, Miss, I'm going."

He kept looking back as he moved off, not out to the road but across the drive and the side yard toward the chickenhouse, taking his time and looking back as if to see what she thought of it. Carmen didn't like it at all. She wanted him to *leave*, not lurk around out there. That's what he was doing now, leaning against the front corner of the chickenhouse, watching her from about fifty yards away.

Carmen raised the stock to her shoulder and put the slug-barrel sights on the slat boards of the low structure, close to the man's head. He didn't move, telling her again he didn't believe she would shoot him, and for a moment she felt an awful urge to slide the barrel over, center it on him. Carmen let the moment pass. She fired, pumped the gun in that sound splitting the air, raised it to fire again and he was gone.

What Richie had in mind was to come up on the guy's truck all of a sudden, pull out like he was going to pass, holding the shotgun with the tip of the barrel resting on the passenger-side windowsill, the window open, and as he came even with the guy squeeze one off, blow him right out of his truck. Except once he thought of it they were getting near Algonac and cars were coming the other way, so he couldn't pull out. By the time there was a chance to, the guy put his left blinker on and turned into a 7-Eleven.

Comes home and the little woman sends him to the store.

Richie liked the idea, the guy thinking he was mean but actually was pussy-whipped. Yes, dear. Whatever you say, dear. Donna asked him to go to the store one time. He'd said to her, "Hey, you start on me with that kinda shit, I'm gone." They didn't respect you if you did too much for them. He'd have to remember to tell Bird that, the Bird not knowing shit about women. Which was weird, a man his age. But then the Bird was Indian and they were a weird bunch anyway, believing you could get turned into a fucking owl. Donna didn't know what kind of bird she'd be. Richie believed he'd be an eagle. Shit, be the best.

He had turned into the empty parking area in front of the store, pulled up right next to the guy's truck facing the plateglass windows covered with bargain signs and watched him go in, the guy wearing a jacket that said IRONWORKERS on the back. Like he was proud of it. Look at me, I'm a fucking ironworker, man. Richie's idea was to give the ironworker something to look at when he came out, the muzzle of a pump gun. Then began to think if he needed anything. Yeah, sunglasses; he'd misplaced his shades somewhere. He wondered if he'd have time to run in and get a pair, come back out . . .

Or do the job in there, Richie thought. What's the difference? It even gave him another idea. Do more than the job. Make it a double feature.

He walked into the store carrying the shotgun down at his side. He didn't see the ironworker. The two checkout counters were right in front of him, a girl in there between them, chewing gum as she looked up at him and then down again, not seeming too interested. She was reading a magazine. Richie noticed her hair looked oily. He didn't see the ironworker anywhere.

Then did see him, way down at the end of an aisle, two six-packs under his arm, picking up a bag of potato chips.

The trick now was to do both almost at once. Richie raised the shotgun high enough to aim it at the girl and saw her drop the magazine as he said, "This's your big day, honey. Empty out that cash drawer for me in a paper bag and set it on the counter. And some gum. Gimme a few packs of that bubble gum, too." The girl was about eighteen, not too good-looking, dark, maybe an Indian. When she didn't move he said, "Do it," and she jumped and got busy. He swung the shotgun at the aisle then, yelled out, "Hey!" and saw the ironworker look this way at him, which was the idea, get him looking. But shit, as he fired and pumped and fired, the buckshot blowing hell out of the potato-chip rack and the soda pop on the far wall, the ironworker disappeared. Richie stepped to the next aisle, saw him moving and fired and pumped and fired again; man, raking the shelves, cans flying, bottles busting, but no ironworker lying there. Shit, missed again. Saw him going for a door, the six-packs still under his arm, the ironworker in the doorway as Richie fired his last round and shot out the glass part of the door as it swung closed. Shit.

The guy could be out the back by now. Richie was pretty sure the ironworker had seen enough of him to know who he was. That was better than nothing. Keep the guy jumpy, looking over his shoulder, and get him some other time. There was too much to stand here and think about right now. Richie turned to the girl. He laid the shotgun on the counter and picked up the paper bag sitting there.

"This everything?"

She nodded, holding her hands in front of her, sort of hunched in with her head bent, looking down at the floor.

"Are you Indian?"

The girl shook her head.

"You look Indian. You ought to use something on your hair. You know what I mean? A shampoo with a conditioner in it. Give it some body."

Man, she sure looked Indian. Thinking it made him think of the Bird. Which got him thinking along another line, staring at this girl. He said to her, "Look at me."

She raised her head but couldn't seem to fix her eyes on him, they kept jumping around.

"You sure you're not Indian?"

She was biting on her lip as she shook her head, not chewing her gum now.

Richie said, "Well, it don't matter." He reached behind him, brought out his nickel-plate .38 and shot the girl square in the forehead.

* * *

Now, that was exciting, when it happened spur of the moment. The way the Bird worked it, that's what it seemed like, work, like a job. And thought, Jesus Christ, the Bird. Richie turned the van around in Algonac and headed back out into the country. All the excitement, he forgot he had to pick up the Indian.

What it did was settle his mind, made him realize he'd get another crack at the ironworker. If the Bird was at the guy's house and the guy's truck was still at the 7-Eleven . . . Tell the Bird it was a kick, man, using a shotgun. The Bird would say yeah, but you missed. And he'd tell the Bird not to sweat it, the guy would be coming home soon. Tell the Bird no, there aren't any witnesses, I done what you told me. Hand him the take from the holdup. Oh, here, I almost forgot. You proud of me? See, I went in there to get some sunglasses, account of I misplaced the ones I had. I been trying to remember . . .

It was quiet out here, starting to get dark. Richie slowed down, aware that he was coming up on the ironworker's house, but still in his mind thinking about those goddamn sunglasses, the last time he'd worn them—and was startled, Jesus Christ, to see the Bird appear at the side of the road, coming out of the brush with his arm raised. Richie was past him by the time he braked to a hard stop. The Bird came up to the van in a hurry. He got in saying, "Let's go. Get out of here."

Richie didn't say anything quite yet. He waited till they were up the road, in sight of the highway they'd take to Marine City. All the things he was going to tell the Bird were forgotten. What he finally said was, "Shit, I remember where I lost my fucking sunglasses."

The Bird sat there in his own mind for a while. Finally, all he said was, "This ought to be good."

9

A STATE POLICE INVESTIGATOR told the Colsons they would be hearing from the FBI. With suspicion of criminal activity across a border it had become a federal case.

Wayne said, "You mean you suspect these two guys are criminals? We're moving right along, aren't we?"

After two more days of police from various jurisdictions marching in and out, police cars in the drive, in the yard, police cars creeping by at night flashing high-beam spots on the house, lighting up their bedroom, Wayne stood on the side porch to deliver a speech. He said:

"I got a speeding ticket out at Detroit Metro one time, forty in a twenty-five zone, over there to pick up my wife coming back from visiting her dad, in Florida. It made me think, if you can get stopped for driving too fast at an airport, if the traffic is that light, it doesn't say much for our economy, does it? But that's not the point I want to make.

The point is, it's the only time I've ever been stopped in Michigan for a moving violation. Ohio's a different story. That drive down I–Seventy-five is so goddamn boring you can't get through it fast enough. But soon as you try, they nail you, there's Smokey with his goddamn hat on, every bit as serious as you guys. What I'm leading up to, I want you to understand I've never been arrested or had any trouble with police. I've never swung at a cop, I've never talked back to one, even in Ohio, till the other day, over at the real estate office. I said why don't you go over to Walpole and find out who's driving an '86 Cadillac. If you did, you'd have caught the two guys and Lionel Adam would be alive. But what you guys'd rather do is sit around and drink our coffee and ask the same goddamn questions over and over. How many times you gonna ask me if I saw both guys at the Seven-Eleven? How could I if one of them was here? How many times you gonna ask me what the guy was driving after I told you I didn't see his car? Or did I actually see him shoot the girl? Why is there any question who did it? Who else could have? How many times you gonna go look at that bullet-hole in the chickenhouse? My wife told you she fired the shot and has a sore shoulder to prove it. She told you she wasn't trying to hit him and you act like you don't believe it. Not one of you has said nice going or it was a brave thing my wife did.

Had she shot the son of a bitch would you arrest her for it? I don't see where you guys are doing a goddamn thing besides drink coffee and bump into each other. You sure as hell don't communicate among your different groups or we wouldn't be getting the same goddamn questions over and over."

The State Police investigator told Wayne to take it easy, to look at facts. There was no apparent connection between the Cadillac and Lionel Adam's murder. Investigating one did not lead to the other. Lionel's body hadn't been found in the marsh till three days later.

Wayne had been told that much. Duck hunters had come across the body, shot three times in the chest. "But what day was he killed? Haven't you found that out yet?"

"When we do we'll let you know," the investigator said. "How's that?"

"Yeah, that's fine," Wayne said. "You might also let me know, when you get around to it, why they want to kill us. My wife didn't do nothing to them. Is it they want to shoot her on account of me? Who are these guys? They've been around here a week almost and you can't find them? Where the hell are you looking?"

Local police and county deputies walked off as Wayne spoke, got in their cars. The State Police investigator waited till he was through, then went out to the woods where evidence technicians were still looking around.

Carmen said, "That was some speech," and took Wayne in the house. "But what good is yelling at them? It just gets them mad at you."

"That's the whole point of what I'm saying. They act like it's our fault. Did I antagonize the two guys? Did you aim at the one when you shot at him? I would've, I know that, and if I hit him I'd be in jail up in Port Huron awaiting trial."

"They've been nice to me," Carmen said, "but you rub them the wrong way. Why did you go into all that about getting the speeding ticket and driving through Ohio?"

"Because those are times I got pissed off at cops and didn't say anything, when maybe if I had I would've felt better."

"You feel better now?"

"Not much. Let's have a beer."

Carmen said, "That sounds like a good idea." She said, "You know how when you cross your *t* you put the bar above the stem?"

"You said it meant I was witty."

"It does, but sometimes—I've never told you— there's sort of a downward slant to your *t* bar and that shows a quick temper."

"I'll work on crossing it straighter," Wayne said, "see if I can improve my personality."

"You might just try to lighten up," Carmen said.

Later on, when the FBI special agent called and asked if it would be convenient for them to stop by, Carmen said yes, of course. When she told Wayne they were coming he didn't say a word and Carmen wasn't sure if that was good or bad. She had never seen her husband in a fight or a situation where he ever hit anyone, but believed it could happen almost anytime now.

Two of them, both wearing dark suits, got out of the Ford sedan. The one on the other side of the car walked off toward the woods. Carmen saw the State Police detective out by the tree line looking this way. The one that got out from behind the wheel had thick dark hair, beginning to show gray, and was nice-looking. He nodded to them on the porch saying, "Mr. and Mrs. Colson, I'm Paul Scallen, I called you earlier. May I come up?"

Carmen said, "Please." Wayne didn't say a word.

The man was taller than she'd thought, growing as he came up the steps, taller than Wayne and older, probably in his late forties, showing them his credentials now in a case with a gold shield pinned to it. Carmen saw *FBI* in big light-blue letters and his name printed over it in black, much smaller. *Paul Scallen*. It said he was a *Special Agent* with the *Federal Bureau of Investigation, United States Department of Justice*. On the bottom part was his picture and more writing too small to read. Carmen wondered if there was a difference between a special agent and just a plain agent. She liked his rust-colored tie with the blue shirt and dark-gray suit. No hanky in the pocket. He looked like a businessman.

Wayne was staring at the credentials. Carmen wondered if he was reading the small print until he said, "That's the same color as the guy's car"—meaning the light-blue *FBI* letters—"a big goddamn Cadillac nobody can seem to find."

Swell, Carmen thought. Here we go.

She was surprised when the FBI man said, "You noticed that too," sounding a little surprised himself. "It was the first thing I thought of when I saw the car. The Windsor Police found it at the airport, the one over there."

"So they're gone," Wayne said.

Carmen thought he sounded disappointed. It seemed to perk up the FBI man, who said, "Well, not necessarily. They found it the same day Mrs. Colson chased one of them off, I understand with a shotgun." Giving Carmen a nod as he said it. "And the other one killed the girl in the store. So they didn't fly out and they haven't come back for the car. The Windsor Police have it under surveillance, but we think the two guys dumped it."

Wayne said, "But you don't know if they're still around."

"We think they are."

"You're not sure though."

"Let me say we have reason to believe they are."

"You check the car registration?"

"It belongs to a company in Toronto. We contacted the police there, they followed up and were told the car was stolen. But we don't believe it. We think they gave the car to one of the guys to use. For another matter first, something that happened in Detroit the day before they came to the real estate office." The FBI man looked at Carmen. "I understand you work for Nelson Davies."

"I did; not anymore."

"Well, I can understand, after what happened."

"That wasn't why I quit."

"Wait a minute," Wayne said. "What kind of company loans a car to a guy that kills people?"

"A company that hires him to do it," the FBI man said. "A company that's operated by the organized crime people in Toronto. Mafioso, just like the ones we have here."

"You say they gave the car to one of the guys," Wayne said. "Which one, the Indian?"

"Part Indian, Ojibway, part French-Canadian. His name's Armand Degas, at least that's who we think we have here. We know he was seen on Walpole Island last week and we assume, if it's the same guy, both you and Mrs. Colson got a good look at him." The FBI man paused, staring at

Wayne. "You had to have been pretty close to hit him with that iron-working tool. What do you call it, a sleever bar?"

Wayne nodded and seemed to think about it a moment, Carmen wondering what he was going to say next.

"What I should've done was broke a few bones, put those guys in the hospital, in traction."

Now the FBI man was nodding. "That's not a bad place to question suspects, when they're in pain and can't move."

Carmen watched. Neither one of them smiled but it didn't matter. She could sense that all at once they had tuned in to each other's attitude and were going to get along fine from here on. Now Wayne was asking Scallen if he wanted a beer. Another good sign. Or he could have instant coffee; they were temporarily out of the real stuff. Scallen said no thanks, he didn't care for anything, but went into the kitchen with them and took a place at the counter. Carmen turned on the overhead light. She watched Scallen take a white envelope from his inside coat pocket. Wayne asked her if she wanted a beer and she hesitated because a federal special agent was sitting there and then said, okay, why not? Wayne said, "We're not working, he is." Scallen smiled. He said to Carmen, "That slug barrel gives a kick, doesn't it?" Carmen touched her shoulder and rolled her eyes just enough. He said,

"It took an awful lot of nerve, what you did, to stand up to a man like that." Carmen said she hoped she'd never have to do it again. She saw Scallen taking two black-and-white photos out of the envelope, laying them on the counter. Wayne popped open the cans of beer and handed one to her saying, "My wife's a winner, that's why I married her." She saw Scallen half-turned on the stool, waiting.

He said, "Are these the two men?"

She felt Wayne's arm slip around her shoulders, his hand creeping down her arm, moving with her to the counter. They looked down at the photos, posed, front-view mug shots: the photo of the Indian, Armand Degas, dark; the photo of the other one much lighter, pale skin, a drugged expression.

"There's no doubt in my mind," Wayne said. "They look different there, but those are the guys."

After a few moments Carmen nodded and looked up at Scallen. "If you get them, you want us to identify them in court, is that it?"

"There's nothing we'd like more," Scallen said. "But I should tell you something about them first, before you agree to do it. These guys are both pretty bad."

Carmen pointed to the one with long hair. "What's this one's name?"

Scallen glanced at the photo. "Richie Nix. He's

a convicted felon with a number of federal and state detainers out on him. That means he's a wanted criminal."

Carmen said, "Richie?"

"That's the name on his birth certificate."

She was looking at the photos again. "Both of them have killed people?"

Scallen nodded. "That's right."

Wayne said, "You know they're the ones killed Lionel?"

Scallen nodded again. "Bullets taken from his body match the three that were found in Nelson Davies's office, they dug out of the wall. And, the same gun was used to kill the girl in the Seven-Eleven, when Richie Nix was trying for you."

Carmen looked up. "Is that what you want to tell us?"

"There's more," Scallen said.

Six P.M., nine miles north in Marine City, Armand found a gas station where it looked like only one man was on duty, a run-down place that offered discount prices. Armand drove Donna's red Honda up to the row of pumps, got out and told the man to fill it up and check the oil and the tires. The gas-station man looked at Armand but didn't say yes sir or okay or you bet or anything, just looked at him and walked over to the car. He wore a hunting cap cocked to one side and was older and bigger around in his dark-brown uniform than Armand, but seemed worn out, not much life in him.

Armand went inside the station, picked up the phone on the desk and dialed a number in Toronto. Standing away from the plate-glass window he watched the gas-station man take the hose from a pump and stick the nozzle into the Honda's filler opening. A voice came on the phone saying this was L and M Distributing and Armand said, "This is the Chief. Let me talk to him." He waited, watching the gas-station man move to the front of the Honda and raise the hood while gasoline continued to pump into the tank.

The son-in-law's voice came on saying, "The fuck're you doing? Where are you?"

Armand said, "You don't want to hear about the old man, 'ey?"

There was a pause before the son-in-law said, his voice lower, "It was in the papers, pictures of both of them."

Armand said, "Both?" And said, "Oh. Yeah, I forgot. Listen—what he said, don't tell me it was in the papers. I'm the only one heard it."

"Where're you at?"

"He told me you're a punk, you not gonna last six months. He told me to tell you that. Listen—but the main thing, I need a car, a clean one with papers. I want you to arrange it."

"You call me up," the son-in-law said, "you give me some shit—I don't give a fuck what you need."

"Yes, you do," Armand said. "You don't want me to get picked up for some reason and they start asking me who I work for, who sent me, was I in Detroit last Friday with your car, things like that. Pretty soon they mention, well, if I give them something maybe they let me go home. That's not what you want. What you want to do is call that guy in Detroit, you know who I mean, guy with the cars, and arrange for me to get one tonight."

Armand watched the gas-station man close the hood of Donna's car as the son-in-law was saying he wanted to know what was going on. He wanted to know what happened to the Cadillac, why it was left in Windsor. Armand said, "What difference does it make? It's a blue car, that's all. There's nothing in it can hurt you." Through the window he watched the gas-station man return the hose to the pump and hook the nozzle in the slot. Armand said, "Hold it a minute. Don't go away." He placed the receiver on the desk and stepped to the open doorway.

"You forgot to check the tires."

The gas-station man, coming toward the station now, stopped in the drive. "What?"

"I want the tires checked."

"You do that yourself." Glancing off he said, "Over there," and started toward Armand again. "That's nine-forty for the gas."

Armand moved to the desk, picked up the phone and said, "Listen to me. Tell the guy ten o'clock somebody will pick up the car." The son-in-law started to speak and Armand said, "*Listen* to me. Ten or maybe later. This is for your good as much as for mine."

The gas-station man entered as Armand was hanging up the receiver.

"You just use the phone?"

"It was a local call," Armand said. "How much you want?"

"Local to where, across the river? You people, I swear. You come over here, you expect we're suppose to give you everything. Well, I'm not one of them sees you as poor souls. Gimme nine-forty and go on get out of here."

Listen to him. Armand had to take a moment to stare at this fat, worn-out guy talking to him like that. He said, "What you trying to tell me, I shouldn't come here, 'ey? Is that it?"

"You start anything," the gas-station man said, "I can have the police here in one minute. They're just up the street."

Maybe it was funny. Look at it that way. Armand shook his head. "Whatever you say." He took a ten-dollar bill from his wallet and placed it on the desk. "How about if you keep the change for the phone call? Okay?"

The gas-station guy didn't answer. That was all right. Armand edged past him through the doorway, smelling grease and tobacco, and was crossing the drive almost to the Honda, when he heard the guy call out to him. Something about was he trying to cheat him.

Armand turned.

The guy was coming out, holding up the ten. "This here's Canadian. You owe me another two bucks."

When Armand got back to Donna's house he told Richie about it, in the kitchen while he poured himself a drink. Donna was in the bathroom, taking a shower. Richie said, "Yeah? So what'd you do?"

"I gave him the two bucks. What would you do?"

Richie said, "Jesus Christ," shaking his head. "You didn't teach him a lesson?"

"I want to know what you'd do," Armand said.

"If I had my piece on me? Shit. If I didn't, I'd get it and go back there. No, I'd use the shotgun, blow the place to hell."

"What about the guy?"

"Him too. I know that gas station you're talking

about. You go in there the guy doesn't say a fuck-ing word to you."

"He did to me."

"That's what I mean," Richie said. "He ever talked to me like that and I was a Indian? I'd scalp the son of a bitch." Richie paused and thought about it a moment. "I don't know, that shotgun's a lot of fun. Maybe what I'd do, shoot the place up and then scalp him." Richie paused again and frowned, squinting at Armand, then opened a drawer and took out a paring knife, still frowning. "How do you scalp somebody . . . ?"

"You do all that with the police up the street or maybe driving by, 'ey? Or somebody else that sees you?" Armand said. "You know why I told you about it? To see what you'd do. Now I'm gonna tell you not to think like that, not anymore till we get this business done."

"You want me to think like you, huh?"

"I want you to take it easy, how you think."

"I know you're a cool fucker, Bird, but if that guy didn't get you pissed there's something wrong with you."

"Sure he did," Armand said. "The same as every time it ever happened in my life. But wait a minute, what do we have to think about right now? This guy at a gas station or two people can send us to prison?"

"I'd have still done something."

"Listen to me. That guy at the gas station," Armand said, tapping the side of his head with a finger, "I have him in here, I can go see him sometime if I want. Pay myself to do it. You understand? But we got this other thing to do first." Armand touched his forehead now, tapping it with the tip of his finger. "We have to keep it here, in the front of our heads."

Richie was stabbing the knife at the kitchen counter, trying to hit a crack in the vinyl surface. Like a kid, Armand thought. Don't want to be told anything.

"Donna mentioned it was on the radio," Richie said, stabbing away. "She listens to WSMA, this program called *Tradio* where you phone in and trade shit you don't want no more. It's where she got that pink robe. I go, 'I thought you got it off the Salvation Army.' She gets pissed you kid with her like that."

"You through?" Armand said.

Richie looked up, the knife poised. "Am I through what?"

"Donna mention something was on the radio."

"Oh, yeah, about the Seven-Eleven was robbed, suppose to be they said a couple hundred was taken. Bullshit, it was forty-two bucks, worst score I ever made. No, shit, I take that back. I only got twenty-eight bucks once, place down in Mississippi."

"You told Donna it was you?"

"No, she kept talking about the girl being shot, did I hear about it, hinting around." Richie was stabbing at the counter again. I just go, 'Oh, uh-huh, an armed robbery, imagine that.' See, Donna, she might suspect it was me, but it's talking about it I think turns her on. The idea of a hardcase going in there with a gun. In her life, I bet she's known more guys that packed one time or another than didn't."

"Guys in prison," Armand said.

"Yeah, in the joint."

"Dumb guys that got caught."

"Hey, it can happen to anybody."

"Not to me," Armand said. "Listen, you gonna pick up a car tonight."

"We got a car."

"This is a clean one, with papers. You take the van, leave it someplace in Detroit to get stolen, like you said, and pick up this one we don't have to worry about cops looking for." Armand could tell from Richie's stupid grin he liked the idea, showing some respect for a change.

"You're a slick guy, Bird, you know it? How'd you work that?"

"How do I do something like this, I make a phone call," Armand said. "It's what I don't do is the difference, what you have to learn. I don't leave my sunglasses someplace, I don't leave my fingerprints, I don't do nothing 'less I work it out first and I'm sure." He saw Donna in the hall, a glimpse of her in the pink robe going from the bathroom to the bedroom. "Then all you have to do," Armand said, "is walk in, walk out."

It was half-past nine. Carmen and Wayne were sitting in the living room with lamps turned on talking about a thirty-four-year-old wanted criminal named Richie Nix, referring to a "detainer list" the FBI man had shown them: the detainers indicating crimes he was wanted for in several different states, armed robbery and capital murder.

"What I can't figure out," Wayne said, "he's been doing this for, what, about twenty years. He was in the Wayne County Youth Home when he was fifteen, a few years later he robs a package store in Florida, does something else in Georgia, goes to prison . . ."

Wayne stopped as a spotlight hit both windows from outside and flashed again in the foyer, on the oval glass panel in the front door. There was a silence. Wayne got up from the sofa, walked to a window and looked out.

"They're about five minutes late."

Carmen sat in a rocking chair they'd bought unfinished in Kentucky one winter, coming back from Florida. She had stained the chair with a clear varnish and made an olive green pad for it.

"Why get worked up? They're doing their job."

"What? Shining spots on the windows?"

She watched him walk back to the sofa, fall into it and stick out his blue-jean legs, the heels of his work shoes resting in the rag carpeting. They had furnished the place without much thought, farmhouse traditional; Carmen was tired of it.

"You realize we're actually sitting here talking without the TV on? We haven't done this since you watched me strip the woodwork."

It reminded her again, she wanted to do something with the living room, liven it up. Keep the rocker, paint it a bright color, but get rid of that old green plaid sofa, and the duck prints her mom had given them as a combined present, housewarming and Wayne's birthday, a month late. Her gaze moved to Wayne. She liked to look at him and wait for him to become aware of it. Their eyes would meet and they'd see how long they could stare at each other without smiling—until Carmen would do something like running the tip of her tongue over her lips or she might stick a finger in her nose.

"You want to go to bed?"

He looked over. "It's early."

They stared for a moment. He said, "We haven't done much making out lately, have we?"

"It's been days. Not even hugs and kisses," Car-

men said. The way he shook his head she could tell
he was thinking of something else. "What is it you
can't figure out? You started to say something
about Richie Nix, his record, he went to
prison . . ."

"That's right—three times and they let him
out," Wayne said, getting back into it. "He's in a
federal prison, he sees a guy stabbed to death, he
testifies at the guy's trial that did it and they put
him in the Witness Protection Program."

"It was his cellmate," Carmen said, "the one
that was murdered. I meant to ask Scallen about
that—you notice he called it the Witness *Security*
Program." She saw Wayne anxious for her to finish. "But that's beside the point."

"I don't know," Wayne said. "The thing I don't
understand, here he's supposed to be in prison for
something like twenty years, am I right?"

"He was already there a few years when it happened."

"Yeah, a few. Now they say they have to protect
him, in case the guy's buddies he testified against
tried to get him. So they put him in the witness
program and let him out. How can they do that?"

Carmen paused, seeing the FBI man in the
kitchen talking quietly to them about a man who
robbed and killed and another who was paid to
kill. "I don't think he said Richie got out, not right
away. No, that's when he was transferred to

Huron Valley. He was in the witness program *while* he was in prison, I think three more years, and then for a little while after, till he committed a crime." She had to add, "And that disqualified him. So all these detainers Scallen showed us, the crimes Richie Nix is wanted for now, are things he did in the last couple of years."

"That's what I'm talking about," Wayne said. "They let him out and he starts killing people. He gets a job through a friend, what does he do? He shoots the guy and takes off."

"There was one before his friend," Carmen said, "another one he shot, in Detroit."

"Yeah, he gets out—he's pulling robberies and all of a sudden he's killing people, too. You go down the detainer list, robbed a package store in Dayton, Ohio, shot and killed the store employee. All those others, in Ohio, Indiana, Kentucky, shot and killed store employee, every one of them. He finds out from Lionel where we live—that must've been what happened—and shoots him three times. He didn't have to kill him. The girl in the store, she didn't have a gun or anything, she's a seventeen-year-old girl. He takes the money and shoots her in the head. Why does a guy like that all of a sudden start killing people?"

"Why is he after *us*?" Carmen said. "If we knew that . . . I mean what does he stand to gain?"

"I think getting thrown out a second-story window has something to do with it," Wayne said, "though he doesn't seem to need a reason to shoot people. I guess it's just the way he is. Or right now he's working for the Indian and does whatever he's told. From what Scallen said, the Indian's the one to look out for. I've thought that all along. When I was sitting at Nelson's desk watching him, I think about it now, he didn't touch a thing. They found Richie Nix's fingerprints all over the place, but not the Indian's. We think Richie's bad but, Jesus, what about Armand, the things he's done?"

"There sure isn't much privacy around here," Donna said, "having two men in the house." She was sitting on the side of her bed in her pink chenille robe, rolling up a pair of sheer black panty hose to stick her toes in, the nails painted an orange-red.

Armand stood in the bedroom doorway watching her.

There were furry stuffed animals on Donna's bed, on the purple-red-and-yellow chenille spread done in a big peacock design, and a picture on the wall, over the head of the bed, a color portrait painted on black velvet that Armand believed was supposed to be Elvis Presley. He was pretty sure that's who it was because Donna had a rack of

Elvis Presley records, that Elvis Presley doll dressed in the white jumpsuit and Elvis Presley plates out in the kitchen. Eat down through Donna's TV Salisbury steak and there was Elvis Presley looking at you.

"You want privacy," Armand said to her, "you close the door. But I don't think it's what you want." He could see her thighs where the pink robe was open, pure white thighs. "You know what else I think? You don't have nothing on under your robe."

"That's why I happen to be getting dressed," Donna said, "if you don't mind. What're you, still hungry?"

"Not now. Maybe I will be later."

"I like to see a man enjoy his food. Richie hardly picks at his."

She raised her foot to the edge of the bed, ready to slip her toes into the panty hose she held rolled up. Now he could see the underneath part of her thigh and a dark place that could be only darkness or a dark place that was part of her. He said, "You've been getting dressed for two hours, parading around here. I think you been waiting for Richie to leave."

Donna worked her foot into the panty hose before looking up at him. "Dick comes back, like he might've forgot something? You're in big trouble."

Calling him Dick. Armand almost smiled.

"What do you think he'd do, shoot me?" Armand moved into the room toward the bed and Donna raised her face, stretching her skinny white neck, her eyes unfocused and naked-looking without the glasses, eyebrows darker than her hair, that pile of deep gold, all of it sprayed hard as a rock, shining in the light.

Armand said, "I think you like guys that shoot people, guys that pack a gun. I got one. You like to see my gun?"

"What choice do I have," Donna said. Next thing, Armand heard her sigh and saw her shoulders go slack for a moment as she said, "Well, there's nothing I can do, you're way bigger than I am." Next thing, she was taking off the robe, pulling the panty hose from her foot and letting them fall on the floor. Lying back on the peacock spread, looking up at him with those cockeyed naked eyes, Donna said, "I guess you're gonna do whatever you want and there's no way on earth I can stop you." She paused a moment, still looking at him, and said, "You want to turn the light out or leave it on?"

Earlier in the day Carmen had said, "I've probably done things that made you mad. Maybe once or twice in the past twenty years? But you never once have raised your voice to me, ever. I think about it, I say to myself, well, if he can walk a ten-inch beam way up on a structure, he has control of his feelings, he's not the type to get emotional. But then out on the porch yelling at the police you're a completely different person."

Wayne said, "On the *porch*? The porch is only five feet off the ground. I'll tap-dance on the porch if I feel like it. I'll do any goddamn thing I want on the *porch*."

Carmen tried to picture that, Wayne taking out his anger on those old gray-painted boards, stomping on them, yelling—that's what it was, his anger and frustration coming out, but it still surprised her. Now every few minutes he'd get up from the sofa and go to the window, keeping track of the police surveillance.

"That was the township cops. They're the ones light up the whole goddamn house." He stood with his back to Carmen, looking out at the night.

She wished he'd sit down.

"You going to work tomorrow?"

"Not till they get those guys."

"We could go away."

"Where?"

"Stay with Mom, she's got plenty of room."

That turned him around.

"I'm kidding," Carmen said, "relax." She

watched him, for a moment there on the edge of panic, move to the sofa and slump into it. "Don't you know when I'm kidding?"

"I'd become alcoholic in about two days," Wayne said, "living with her. Maybe one day."

"She loves you too." Carmen rocked back and forth in the Kentucky rocking chair. "You want to turn on the news?"

Wayne glanced at his watch. "It's not on yet."

"You want to know what I don't understand?"

"When you kid," Wayne said, "it's supposed to be funny. That's the whole idea."

Carmen rocked some more, thinking about what she wanted to say. After about a minute she said, "There's a lot I don't understand. But you know what bothers me?"

This time Wayne said, "What?"

"The FBI thinks the Mafia's behind the extortion. Or might be, 'cause it's the kind of thing they do. Or they'd like to believe the Mafia's behind it. I said to the FBI man, 'But Armand's from Toronto. Are we talking about their Mafia or ours?' "

"He thought you were being funny," Wayne said, "calling them *ours*."

Carmen paused, looking at him, but let it go.

"Anyway, he said it could be either one. What they have for sure is a suspect known to work for the Toronto Mafia driving a car that's registered to a company they know is a front for organized crime. Armand was here last Friday, the same day a man, also known to be a member of the Toronto Mafia, was shot and killed in a Detroit hotel, with a young girl. They don't know who she is but they think Armand did it because . . . I guess because he was here and it's what he does. Or they want to believe he did it. And they want us to realize that if it's the Mafia, then we have more to worry about than just the two guys finding us. Is that the way you see it?"

Wayne nodded. "I guess."

Carmen rocked some more, thinking, then stopped.

"Okay, I asked if it seemed likely the Mafia would come to Algonac to pick on a real estate company. Scallen said it wasn't *un*likely. They could come here duck hunting, see a company that's making a lot of money, not much police protection in the area . . . Okay, *then* he said it was possible Armand worked it out on his own, since he no doubt has the experience. I said, 'But he didn't arrive till last Friday. Someone called Nelson Davies before that, to demand the money.' Scallen says yes, and it was probably Richie Nix. But extortion isn't his kind of crime, so they think he was hired to do it, by Armand. Just as they think Richie was told by Armand to kill Lionel. They found Richie's fingerprints on Lionel's boat, but not Armand's. But killing the girl in the store, they think Richie must've done on his own. Scallen said something about his pattern, he robs, he kills. But Armand—he said the fact that Armand wasn't seen before last Friday doesn't mean he wasn't here."

Carmen paused and Wayne said, "Yeah . . . ?"

"That's the part that bothers me."

"What part?"

"They talked to people on Walpole Island who said Armand came to visit his grandmother. That seems pretty weird, a man who kills for a living comes all the way from Toronto to visit his *grand*mother?"

"It's not that far."

"That's not what I mean"—Carmen shaking her head—"I'm thinking if he was in Detroit anyway, last Friday . . . He didn't even know the grandmother had died, he stopped by." Carmen made a face, frowning. "I just have a feeling he wasn't around here before Friday, or someone would've seen him, his car. But Richie Nix was here, he's the one who called Nelson. Ten thousand dollars or I'll kill you—and that's who I think started the whole thing. Richie. Why not?"

Wayne shrugged, not appearing to give it much thought. "What difference does it make who started it? We're deep in it either way."

"Well, you think Armand's the one to look out for," Carmen said. "I think Richie's a lot scarier than Armand." After a moment she said, "I can just see his handwriting. I'll bet it's a mess, full of things that show poor mental health."

Richie had crept up on the gas station, let the van coast into the drive with the passenger-side window down, shotgun ready, and found the place closed for the night. Dark except for a low-watt light in the front part. Shit. He was going to do this one for the Bird. Hack off some of the gas-station guy's hair, if he had any under that hunting cap, and bring it back. See, Bird? This's how you do it. He could still mess the place up, blow out the plate-glass window. Or do it on the way back, with the new car. He could see the Bird shaking his head as he told him, recalled the Bird tapping the side of his head with a finger and then his forehead and Richie thought, Hey, shit. All of a sudden having a better idea than shooting up a gas station.

It took him ten minutes to run down the river road almost to Algonac before cutting inland through a residential part, slowed down coming to the 7-Eleven, open and doing business, braked—it was an idea—and took off again grinning. The Bird'd have a shit fit. "You went *back* there?" The Bird not appreciating spur-of-the-moment moves. No sense of humor, never smiled or nothing.

The road the Colsons lived on was becoming familiar, even in the dark of night with only a half-assed moon, he'd run it enough times. Headlights were coming at him and he slowed to fifty; getting close anyway. It was a cop car. Richie didn't see what kind, either county or township; it wasn't state, all dark blue. And there coming up was the house. There was the ironworker's pickup in the drive, no other cars around, least that he could see. Lights on in a couple of downstairs front windows, probably the living room. Richie drove past, followed a bend in the road, went up about a hundred yards and took his time U-turning, thinking it didn't *look* like any cops were around. Thinking yeah, but they could be hiding. Thinking, Hey, are you pussy or what? Went back around the bend and stopped in the road in front of the house.

Richie aimed the shotgun out his side of the van, fired at one of the lit-up windows and heard glass shatter as he pumped, aimed, fired at the other one, blew it out, threw the shotgun behind him inside the van and took off, tires screaming. He might not've hit anybody, but at least they'd know the truth of that old saying, shit happens. When you least expect, too.

10

THE WALKING BOSS on the One-Fifty Jefferson project was reading blueprints in the front part of the steel-company trailer. He didn't move or look up when the raising-gang foreman came in and said, "We got a man froze-up."

The walking boss, still bent over the print board, said, "Shit. Who is it?"

"Colson."

Now the walking boss straightened in a hurry, turned to the raising-gang foreman standing there in his tan coveralls and hard hat on backward, said, "You're kidding me," and went over to the big window facing the job.

"Where is he?"

"Up on top. That far section toward the river. See?"

They both gazed up at the structure, at the network of columns and beams and girders, a tower crane rising out of the center, the building skeleton exposed, no outside curtain walls up yet, but dark in there with every other level floored to ten, open iron above that.

"I see him," the walking boss said.

A figure on the crossbar of a goalpost, that's what it looked like. Way up on the highest section, standing on a girder between two columns that stuck up against the sky.

"He's not moving."

"That's what I'm telling you," the raising-gang foreman said. "He's froze-up."

"Wayne never froze in his life."

"Well, he's been sitting there, I don't know how long."

"He's standing now."

"He was sitting before, like he was paralyzed."

"You yell at him?"

"Sure, I yelled at him. He heard me."

"He look down?"

"Yeah, he looked down. Maybe he's trying to move is why he stood up."

"Shit," the walking boss said. "There's something wrong with him. He was off a few days, he come back—Wayne ordinarily connects, you know that."

"I know it."

"He come back I had to put him on bolting up."

"I know it, but he didn't seem to mind. He didn't say nothing."

"No, that's what I mean, there's something wrong with him."

"Maybe it's that girl was shot he's having some trouble with."

"I heard guys talking about it," the walking boss said. "I didn't see it in the paper."

"Yeah, it was in, but way in the back. It didn't mention Wayne. I guess it was in the paper up where he lives one of the guys saw, had more about it."

"You think he's eating his lunch?"

"You can see he isn't doing nothing but standing there," the raising-gang foreman said. "He's froze-up. He wouldn't stand there like that if he wasn't froze-up. Would he?"

"I don't know, it never happened to me."

"It never happened to me either, but I've seen it enough. We got to talk him down."

"Who was he working with?"

"I think Kenny. Yeah, Wayne had the yo-yo, so Kenny was holding the roll for him. I saw Kenny come down. I think he went someplace to eat."

The raising-gang foreman followed the walking boss through a doorway to the back half of the trailer where some of the crew were eating their lunch at a wooden table. The walking boss was a young guy about thirty-five. His hard hat was cleaner than most, but he wore it backward like everybody else. He said to the guys at the table, "Anybody talk to Kenny?" They were all looking up at him, but didn't know what he meant.

"Wayne hasn't come down. He's up there like he might've froze." The walking boss raised both hands. "Wait a minute now, sit still. Did Kenny mention to anybody Wayne was acting strange?"

"He didn't say nothing 'cause he wouldn't, not to anybody else," one of the ironworkers said, "but he almost got pitched off. Kenny did."

"You saw it?"

"I was below. I saw him and Wayne moving positions. I think Wayne had just put another fifty feet of hose on his yo-yo. What must've happened, he throws it out to get some slack, not looking what he's doing, and the rubber trips Kenny coming along behind him. I heard Kenny yell—that's when I looked up, I see him grab hold of the beam, he's okay, but he lets go of the beater he's carrying. I'm looking up, shit, I see this ten-pound sledge coming at me. It hits the deck plate, *bang*, missed me by only about a foot. I see Kenny, he's down flat on the beam now, the rubber hanging over it right there—you could see it must've tripped him. And here's Wayne looking at him like, the hell are you doing hugging that beam? He doesn't even know he almost killed his partner. I wasn't gonna say nothing," the ironworker said to the walking boss, "but you asked."

* * *

Last summer when they came downtown to one of the P'Jazz concerts at the Pontchartrain Hotel, it was to see Lonnie Liston Smith, this whole block was a parking lot. They drove past a month ago, it was excavated and the piers laid, the foundation. A big sign said it would become One-Fifty Jefferson West.

Now here he was sitting a hundred and something feet above it on a ten-inch girder. Sitting again, straddling it, feet resting on the girder's lower flange. Get tired of sitting he'd stand up, still looking out at the Detroit River, feeling the sun and a breeze that would become wind as the job rose higher. If he looked at the city skyline he'd think of work. The same if he looked down, he'd see the iron they'd shaken out, ready to hook on to the crane, and he'd be distracted by the job, all the equipment down there, the stacks of floor deck, the compressors, kegs of bolts on pallets, the steel-company trailer, knowing the guys were in there eating their lunch . . .

This was what he needed, to be by himself high up on the iron, after two days of cops everywhere he looked, different police groups coming and going, their presence bringing people out from Algonac to creep their cars past the house. He'd watched cops digging buckshot out of the living-room wall, cops poking around in the bushes along the road and in the woods. Their neighbor across the street, the sod farmer, called to ask if there was some kind of problem. Wayne said, "If I find out what they're looking for I'll let you know." He hung up and Carmen said, *"Evidence,"* gritting her teeth, irritated because he made remarks loud enough to be overheard.

Like when he said, "A glass eye in a duck's ass can see they don't know what they're doing," and a couple of cops gave him their deadpan don't-fuck-with-me cop look.

One thing led to another. Carmen mentioned the framed duck prints that had been shot off the living-room wall and wrecked, saying that was one way to get rid of them.

"If you didn't like the duck prints," Wayne asked her, "what'd you put them up for?"

"If I didn't, who would? Think about it. What do you do around here?"

"I brush-hog the field."

"So you can watch for deer. That's like saying you clean your shotgun."

"I thought you liked those duck prints. They been hanging there for five years."

"Don't tell *me.*"

"You should've said something."

"Who swept up the broken glass?"

Getting picky. He should've told her he didn't give a shit about the duck prints. The only reason they were up, her mom had given them as a present. He was more irritated than ever by then, though not at Carmen. This had nothing to do with the goddamn duck prints. Carmen knew it too.

She said, "This is dumb."

So he eased back saying, "Okay, I won't make any more observations or remarks."

She said, "How much you want to bet?"

He tried, he kept quiet, made coffee for the cops and referred to them as Deputy or Officer when they came up on the side porch for a cup. He even tried to be cordial to the tight-assed county deputy who had asked him in the real estate office if he had an attitude problem. Wayne said to him on the porch, "Well, at least we know those two guys are still around."

"How do we know that?" the deputy said.

"They shot our windows out, didn't they?"

"We don't know it was the same guys," the deputy said.

"If you don't, then I was right," Wayne said, "you don't know shit."

Carmen got him upstairs, faced him with her arms folded and said, "You having fun? Why do you like to antagonize them?"

He shook his head and frowned, wanting her to

believe he couldn't help it. "I don't know what it is. There's just something about those guys that irritates me. Cops and insurance salesmen."

Now he saw Carmen join him in a frown, sympathetic, he was pretty sure. If she didn't understand him it would be the first time in their married life. She said, "Why don't you get away from here for a while? Go somewhere. Go back to work tomorrow."

He said, "I don't know if I should leave you alone."

Carmen said, "If you call four different police departments hanging around here being alone."

Having your windows shot out by gunfire was a hair-raising experience. Carmen yelled his name as it happened, but she didn't scream or lose control. After, when he said, "They're just trying to scare us," she said, well, they were doing a pretty good job, in that dry tone of hers. She said if they were that dumb, to drive by and shoot at the house, the police shouldn't have any trouble finding them. Wayne didn't comment on that.

The State Police investigator arrived as he was leaving this morning in the pickup. Wayne had to wait while the guy thought about it, saying he wasn't sure he liked the idea; he'd have to send a man along. Wayne said, "Up on the iron with me?"

*   *   *

He stared out at the river and Canada from the top of the structure thinking:

Okay, after a while nothing happens, the cops get tired and clear out. Now it's between him and them. He knows they're coming, but doesn't let on to Carmen. Except he'd have to stay home and she'd ask him what was wrong.

"Nothing."

"Then how come you aren't going to work?"

She would know, yeah, but that was all right, it wouldn't change anything, except she'd be scared and want to call the cops again. Anyway . . .

Okay, it's early morning, first light, Carmen reaches over and touches him. "Wayne . . . ?"

And he says, "I heard it, honey. Lie still, okay? Stay right here."

"They're in the house."

"I know they are."

He picks up the Remington from the side of the bed and slips into Matthew's room so that when they come up out of the stairwell he's behind them. The stairs squeak, here they come. Their head and shoulders appear. They're careful, not making a sound as they reach the top, and then stop dead as they hear him rack a slug into the breach. "Morning, fellas." *Wham . . . wham.* Fires and pumps fast as they're turning with their guns.

The cops accuse him of shooting them in the

back. No, that would get too complicated. He'd think of another situation. Okay . . .

The two guys are still outside when he hears them. That's it—he slips downstairs to the kitchen door, opens it a little. Pretty soon two shapes appear out of the woods. As they get behind the chickenhouse he walks out on the porch . . .

Wayne stopped it there. He liked the idea of getting behind them and saying something, taking them by surprise.

Okay, he sees them in the woods and runs out to the chickenhouse, yeah, and is waiting for them inside as they come past it, heading for the house. All the first part would be the same, telling Carmen to stay in bed. Or now he tells her to stay in the house. They go by, he lets them get about ten yards and then steps out of the chickenhouse behind them, that's it, and goes, "You boys looking for somebody?"

"You boys looking for me?"

"You guys looking for me?"

"Can I help you?"

Something like that. They come around with their guns and he's got the Remington on them hip high, *wham*, hits one, the Indian, pumps and fires, *wham*, knocks the other one on his ass, those mag slugs blowing them right off their feet. Or he waits till they get the ten yards, steps out, all he says is . . .

"Looking for somebody?"

He's inside having bacon and eggs as the squad cars arrive flashing their lights. They come because Carmen calls 911 while he's in the chickenhouse. That would work. He steps out on the porch . . .

"You're a little late, fellas."

The cops are looking around. "Where are they?"

"Right over there, where I shot them."

The star asshole sheriff's deputy is standing there. Say to him, "You gonna take me in?"

Or maybe something about doing their work for them, without sounding too much like a smartass.

From his perch Wayne looked east along the riverfront to the glass towers of the Renaissance Center, a job that took them seven hundred feet up when he was an apprentice. Get through that one you could work anywhere. The worst winter of his life, scraping ice off the iron before you dared walk upright. He began to think:

Okay, it's winter, time has passed, the cops are long gone, but you're still hanging around the house, making excuses there's work you want to do, well, or you don't feel good, something. Anyway time passes, Carmen wants to know what's going on. Nothing. Oh, yeah? You're up to something. No, I'm not. Yes, you are, what is it?

And you say, "I'm gonna find them."

She can't believe it. "But they're gone."

"No, they aren't."

The idea is it's dead of winter, the ship channels are frozen over, the coast guard's breaking ice for the Harsens Island ferry and the one to Walpole and he's been going over there on a hunch they're hiding out on one of the islands, in a boarded-up summer cottage or a trapper's cabin, he can feel it, the people on Walpole are acting strange, they know something but won't talk and he senses the two guys have scared the shit out of everybody and are making them bring food, maybe holding a kid hostage. Lionel's wife finally tells him they're hiding out in an old trailer on Squirrel Island where Lionel used to keep muskrat traps, on the edge of a cornfield right across the South Channel from Sans Souci, the bar where the Indians go. For weeks he watched the trailer from a duck blind near the bar until finally one day he sees two figures coming across the channel, shoving muskrat poles in the snow, poking their way along so as not to go through the ice. He raises his binoculars. It's them. They're a mess, filthy dirty fugitives, a couple of human muskrats that have been hiding out on the edge of the marsh, wild looks in their eyes. They don't see him till they're almost to the bank. He's out of the blind, standing with the Remington across his arm, patient, relaxed, wearing his heavy black wool parka with the hood. And he's got a beard now. They stop dead in their tracks. They don't know him from Sergeant Preston of the fucking Mounties till he says, very calmly:

"I've been waiting for you, gentlemen."

Wayne listened to it in his mind. He thought calling them gentlemen because of the way they looked, being sarcastic, would sound good but it didn't, it was dumb. No, leave it off, just say . . . And said out loud:

"I've been waiting for you."

Behind him, the walking boss said, "We're right here, Wayne. What's the trouble?"

The raising-gang foreman was behind the walking boss, both of them standing on the open-iron girder. They watched Wayne look up over his shoulder, welding goggles on his hard hat turned backward, maybe a little surprised to see them, that was all. They watched him get to his feet.

"No trouble," Wayne said. "I'll move out of your way."

The walking boss and the raising-gang foreman watched him walk the girder to the column at the south end of the structure, on the corner, swing out around it, gripping the outer flange with his gloves and the instep of his work shoes, and slide down two levels to the decked-in tenth floor. They watched him pause. From where he was now he could take ladders down to each floored level.

Maybe he was going to and changed his mind, favoring the express route. They watched him slide down the column the entire hundred feet or more, all the way to the ground where the guys were standing around watching, and head for the steel-company trailer.

The walking boss looked at the raising-gang foreman. Neither of them said anything.

11

CARMEN HAD TO WAIT to tell Wayne about the FBI man calling.

Wayne came home talkative, now with another reason to be on the muscle. The squad car parked in the yard wasn't enough. Now they didn't want him at work because they said he almost caused an accident that could have killed a man. "*Almost*," Wayne said. "The whole goddamn job, anything you do on a structure can *almost* kill you, it's the way it is." Having their beers he told her this guy Kenny never looked where he was going was the trouble, it wasn't the first time he dropped a beater, everybody knew Kenny worked in the morning hungover, it was why he went out at noon. Didn't matter. "The walking boss, guy I went to apprentice school with, says take some time off till I get my head on straight. Says nobody'll work with me. You believe it?" Wayne turned to the range, asked what they were having for supper.

Carmen told him Oriental stir-fried chicken and

said, "Wayne? Scallen called." There, she had his attention and could take her time now and watch his reactions to what she was going to tell him.

"He wants us to come down to the Federal Court Building tomorrow."

"Detroit?"

Carmen nodded. "And see a man named John McAllen, with the U.S. Marshals Service."

"What for?"

"I thought maybe they had the two guys. Scallen said no, this was something else."

"What?"

"I asked him, he said it would be better to wait and let John McAllen tell us."

She watched Wayne take a drink of beer. He didn't seem worried. He said, "Tomorrow, huh?" He didn't seem the least concerned, or even curious.

"They're gonna pick us up."

"That's all right, long as it isn't a squad car."

Carmen hesitated. "What do you think it's about?"

"I don't know—what do marshals do? Guard prisoners, take them to court . . . I don't know. What do you think it's about?"

She said she couldn't imagine and after that was quiet, because she couldn't tell him what she was thinking, the awful feeling that the "something else" was about Matthew. Wayne would act amazed and say, "*Matthew?* Why would you think it's about him?" Because she *was* thinking it, that's why. Because she couldn't help it. Because if it wasn't about the two guys but had something to do with the government, someone in the government wanting to talk to them . . . She could see them walking into an office with a flag on a stand where the government official is waiting to tell them, is sorry to inform them, there was an accident on the flight deck of the *Carl Vinson,* CVN 70, their son got between an aircraft and the JBD, or their son had been swept overboard and was missing, not drowned, they'd never say that, they'd say he was out somewhere in the middle of the Pacific Ocean *missing,* as if to say, well, he could turn up, you never know.

Or Wayne might give her his bored but patient look and ask was this her instinct as a mother coming out or the other one, what was known as women's intuition? And she'd get mad and say, "Well, you don't understand," and he wouldn't. So she didn't say anything at all.

Not until the next day, riding downtown in the security of the gray interior of a gray sedan, two men in front wearing gray suits, Carmen and Wayne in back dressed for business, an official occasion, she made sure of her tone and finally said to Wayne in a low voice but an offhand manner, "You don't suppose it's about Matthew."

He looked at her right next to him and said, "So that's it. I've been wondering." He put his hand on hers, holding her purse in her lap. "No, they come to your house. They send an officer, a serious young guy in his dress uniform, to tell you. U.S. marshals don't do that. I've been thinking about it, a marshal's like what Matt Dillon was in *Gunsmoke*. They wear a big cowboy hat. Remember Matt and Miss Kitty?"

The marshal on the passenger side of the front seat turned his head toward the one that was driving.

Carmen nudged Wayne with her elbow. He gave her hand a squeeze.

This U.S. marshal, John McAllen, seemed as big as the one in *Gunsmoke* and was about the same age, around fifty, Carmen judged, and looked familiar in that he fit the role of law officer, appeared to have rough edges and kept his personality to himself, or tried to. She had seen enough law officers recently to recognize the type. McAllen, in his dark suit, was not as neat and polished as Scallen, the FBI special agent, who looked more like a lawyer or business executive and sat off to one side. Carmen and Wayne had chairs facing the marshal at his desk, a big one. On the wall behind him were pictures of three past presidents of the United States and a fourth who was about to leave office.

Greeting them, McAllen had said it was a pleasure and that he appreciated the courage it took for them to come forward, willing to testify at the appropriate time. He said now, with a little smile, "I imagine what you'd appreciate is somebody taking better care of you. Well, that's why you're here."

Carmen thought he even sounded like the one in *Gunsmoke* only more authentically western. She said they would appreciate it a lot, and glanced at Wayne. He was sitting forward, his elbows on the chair arms, not yet moved by the marshal's concern.

"This situation, from our standpoint, is an unusual one," McAllen said. "However since your lives are apparently in danger we feel you qualify for federal protection under the Witness Security Program of the United States Marshals Service."

Wayne said, "You mean our lives appear to be in danger but maybe they aren't?"

As McAllen looked up from a notebook he was opening Carmen said, "I thought it was only for criminals. Wasn't Richie Nix in the program?"

"He was for a time," McAllen said, maybe surprised by the way both of them had come at him, glancing over at Scallen now.

"Everything I've read about it," Wayne said, "it's for people who testify in court to stay out of prison."

McAllen, trying to smile, said, "Whoa now, you people have a misconception about the program we better clear up."

Carmen turned to Scallen as he got into it saying, yes, the program was originally created by the attorney general for the protection of witnesses under Title V—or he might've said Title B, Carmen was still having trouble with McAllen referring to them as "you people." Scallen's tone helped, giving her the feeling he was actually concerned for their safety. He said the program must work, there were about fifteen thousand people in it counting witnesses and their families. He said, "Let's let John McAllen go through some of the boilerplate, basic things about the program. How's that sound? Then we'll see how a modified version might work for you."

It sounded okay to Carmen. She said, fine. Wayne didn't say anything.

So then McAllen recited from his notebook, beginning with the conditions required for eligibility. There had to be evidence in possession that the life of the witness and/or a member of his or her family was in immediate jeopardy. There also had to be evidence in possession that it would be advantageous to the federal interest for the Department of

Justice to protect the witness and/or family or household members.

Carmen began to wonder when Wayne would jump in.

With this evidence in possession the attorney general could, by regulation, provide suitable documents to enable the person to establish a new identity . . .

Right there.

"What you're saying," Wayne said, "you want us to change our names 'cause you can't find these assholes? Is that it?"

McAllen said, "Whoa now," and Scallen got into it again saying, "Wayne, you have to let John finish. The regulation states it's to establish a new identity *or* 'otherwise protect the person,' so we're flexible in that area."

McAllen said he would appreciate their waiting till he was finished before expressing their views. Staring at Wayne.

Good luck, Carmen thought.

The program would provide housing, McAllen said. It would provide for the transportation of household furniture and other personal property to a new residence of the person. It would provide a payment to meet basic living expenses and assist the person in obtaining employment . . .

Wayne said, "Can I ask a question?"

"I imagine," McAllen said, looking up from the

notebook, "you want to know what comes under 'basic living expenses.'"

"I want to know, first, if you're saying we have to sell our house."

Carmen was wondering that too, among other things. But most of all she was wondering, if they did move, what she'd tell her mother. While Scallen was saying, yes, it would involve relocation, for their safety, but he didn't think it would be necessary to sell the house. Carmen thinking that if she told her mother they were going on a vacation her mom would get sick, as she usually did, sometimes putting herself in the hospital. Scallen saying he believed he could make a deal with Nelson Davies, have his company appear to be offering the house for sale and take care of the maintenance.

Wayne said, "Relocate where?"

Scallen looked at John McAllen who said, "Where we have marshals that supervise the program, experienced Witness Security inspectors. Right now we can offer you Lima, Findlay, Ohio . . ."

Wayne said, "Jesus Christ, those're both on I–Seventy-five."

McAllen paused, frowning. "What's wrong with that?"

Carmen said, "Wayne?" with a look that meant, Don't give your speech about driving through

Ohio. She said to McAllen, "What else do you have?"

He was still frowning, maybe confused. "Well, a couple places in Missouri, one especially we recommend. But what I'd like is to finish with the regulations first, if that's agreeable with you."

He didn't say "you people" and his tone seemed okay. Otherwise, Carmen was fairly sure Wayne would have jumped on him. At the moment he was holding on to the chair arms.

Before providing the aforementioned assistance, McAllen said, the attorney general would enter into what was called a Memorandum of Understanding with the person, which sets forth the responsibilities of that person and would include:

The agreement of the person to testify and provide information to all appropriate law-enforcement officials concerning all appropriate proceedings.

The agreement of the person to avoid detection by others of the facts concerning the protection provided.

Carmen was going to say, *What?* But didn't.

The agreement to comply with legal obligations and any judgments against that person.

Carmen felt Wayne looking at her. She glanced over. He was giving her a look, mouth open, that meant, You believe it?

The agreement to cooperate with all reasonable

requests of officers and employees of the government.

The agreement of the person not to commit any crime.

Carmen thought that one should cut Wayne loose, bring him up out of his chair. But he surprised her.

"Now, that's a tough one," Wayne said. "You understand, we could possibly go along with all that other bullshit, but to promise we won't commit any crimes . . ." Wayne shook his head. "I'm sorry."

"Mr. Colson," McAllen said, "these regulations applied originally to federal offenders. I thought we explained that and I'm sorry if we didn't make it clear. They still apply to ninety-seven percent of the people we take into the program, not counting their dependents and so on. The other three percent are honest citizens, such as you and the wife, who're willing to avail yourselves of the program and its resources . . ."

The wife, Carmen thought.

". . . which I must tell you is truly inspiring to us in law enforcement and the administration of criminal justice." McAllen turned to the FBI special agent. "Paul, am I right about that or not?"

Scallen straightened, all of a sudden brought into it. He nodded saying, "That's a fact, yes."

Carmen saw him agreeing but with not much

conviction now, shifting around in his chair as though he might have doubts and wanted to say something. But then McAllen was speaking again, reciting words Carmen believed were from a text.

Something about "in the judgment of the United States government that by reciprocating, protecting you to the fullest extent once you have agreed to testify, we can effect a major action against these elements of organized crime."

After that for a few minutes there was silence, Carmen watching the U.S. marshal line up papers on his desk, getting ready for the next part, while those three ex-presidents and the one about to be looked down from the wall behind him.

"I have a question," Wayne said to the FBI special agent.

Carmen looked over at Scallen, who seemed relieved now, even smiling a little as he said, "I imagine you're gonna have all kinds of questions."

"Just one," Wayne said. "Do we get a ride home?"

A uniformed sheriff's deputy sat in the living room watching television and another one was outside somewhere. State Police would drive by every once in a while.

Wayne and Carmen were in the kitchen having a beer, trying to decide whether to cook or go out.

Wayne said if they went out the cops would come along and he'd rather not be seen in public with them.

They would talk about the witness program, make comments and then not say anything, Wayne with his thoughts and Carmen with hers, taking their time getting into it. Carmen said she had a feeling the FBI agent didn't think too highly of the program, or had some doubts about it. McAllen, she believed, was sincere but used to dealing with criminals. Wayne said he was getting used to being treated as one so what was the difference?

He said, "Can you see leaving here to live in Findlay, Ohio? Jesus. What was the other place, Lima?"

"Lima," Carmen said, "like the beans."

"Yeah, I imagine there's all kinds of structural work down in Lima, Ohio. Can you see moving out and not telling anybody? Not even your mom? . . . Wait a minute, maybe it isn't such a bad idea."

Carmen didn't say anything.

Wayne sipped his beer, watching her. "What're you thinking about?"

"If we did have to change our names," Carmen said, "I was thinking it might be fun, huh? Pick whatever name you want."

"The only one I'd ever think of using," Wayne said, "you know what it is? Mats."

"After your great-grandfather."

"My dad's."

Carmen had seen pictures of him: Wayne with a bushy mustache, Mats the lumberjack, who'd come from Sweden to northern Michigan. Wayne's mother and dad were still up there, near Alpena, growing Christmas trees on three hundred and twenty acres.

"My dad wanted to name me Mats."

"But your mom won," Carmen said, "and named you after a movie star. Moms get away with murder. Mine, you probably think, named me after the girl in the opera."

"Tell you the truth," Wayne said, "I never thought about it."

"She didn't. She named me after Guy Lombardo's brother, Carmen Lombardo, he sang with the band. His big number was 'Sweethearts on Parade.' Mom said it was her and Dad's song when they were going together."

"You're putting me on," Wayne said. "Aren't you?"

"I could change my name to Bambi," Carmen said, "except I'd be afraid you might shoot me. How about Kim? Barbie, Betsy, Becky . . . You have to be little and cute to have one of those."

"You're cute."

"No, I was cute in high school, I outgrew it. When you're really cute that's all you have to be, you make a career out of it. Someone asks you what you do, you say, 'Nothing, I'm cute.' " She looked out at the police car parked in the yard.

Wayne watched her for a moment. "We don't seem too shook up over this."

"If we did move away for a while," Carmen said, turning to him, "we don't see your folks that often, we could be back before they knew we were gone."

"Or go up there to the farm," Wayne said, "if we have to hide, which irks the shit out of me. Or go down to Florida, visit your dad. That wouldn't be hard to take. I think what they said is bullshit, we stay with relatives there's a chance they could find us. I'm leaning more toward what you said, it doesn't have anything to do with the Mafia."

"But they want to believe it does," Carmen said, "and if they're right . . . well, we'd be better off in Cape Girardeau than here."

"I never heard of it."

"It's on the Mississippi . . ."

"I still never heard of it," Wayne said. "You can't tell much from the literature." He took a sip of beer. "What do you think it's like?"

"I don't know," Carmen said. "You want to find out?"

Wayne didn't answer, looking out the window now at the police car. "We'd have to tell Matthew. Make up a story for your mom. Tell her I've become a boomer, gone down to Missouri to work on permit, they got this two-story structure they're putting up."

"It'd be a change," Carmen said.

Wayne turned to look at his wife. "You wouldn't mind doing it, would you?"

"Well, if it's a choice of going to Cape Girardeau or getting shot at." She took a sip of beer and said, "Every once in a while I wonder what it would be like to be someone else. See the way they look at things and what their life is really like."

"You're telling me," Wayne said, "you'd rather be somebody else than who you are?"

"No, I don't mean be*come* someone else, permanently."

"You're just nosy then."

"There was a movie we saw a long time ago," Carmen said, "where Jack Nicholson takes on another man's identity who died and then finds out people are after him thinking he's the guy?"

"Yeah . . . ?"

"I don't remember the name of it or what reminded me. It isn't anything like what we're into at all."

"Jack Nicholson's in it and they're in Spain? He's driving around in a red convertible with this broad he picked up?"

"That's the one."

He watched her nod, calm as always, that clear

look in her eyes. Sometimes she knew things before he could figure them out and she'd tell him you had to feel as well as think. Feel what? She'd say, just *feel*, that's all.

"Why can't we go anywhere we want?"

She didn't answer him.

"We can. Who's gonna stop us?" Arguing with himself.

She touched her hair and seemed to shrug. "They have a house for us, two bedrooms . . ."

"I can just see it."

"It sounded nice, on the edge of a woods."

"We have a woods," Wayne said, "right out there."

The sheriff's deputy from the living room came in carrying a cup and saucer. He didn't look at Wayne. He said to Carmen, "I wonder if you could spare a refill?"

"You having trouble," Wayne said, "staying awake?"

The deputy glanced at him with his blank look, but didn't answer. Carmen poured him a cup of coffee. She got a milk carton from the refrigerator and brought it to the counter where the deputy was helping himself to sugar.

Carmen said, "Would you like some cookies? Or I can make you a sandwich."

Stirring his coffee, the deputy said, "Like what kind?"

Carmen paused. Wayne watched her reconsider and tell him, "Why don't you take the cookies, all right?"

He did, a plateful of chocolate chip with his coffee, back to the living room where the television was going, television laughter letting the deputy know what was funny.

Wayne said, "We have to get out of here."

Carmen nodded. "I think so."

"We'll give them three weeks to find those guys and that's it," Wayne said. "Deer season opens we're coming home."

12

ARMAND HAD TOLD RICHIE, "All right, from now on you don't leave my sight. You go off and do crazy things."

"All I did was blow out a couple of their windows. I didn't get caught, did I? I brought us the car." A nice one, an all-black Dodge Daytona with smoked-glass windows as dark as the body. Stuck in Donna's garage all week. If it was clean why hide it? The Bird had only one thing on his mind:

"You don't leave my sight."

"Okay then," Richie had said, "how about when I go to the bathroom? You want to watch? How about when I give Donna a jump and you're in there looking at *The Price Is Right?* Or you're eating again. Or when I don't hear no snoring in the house and I know you're taking your turn. You want me to come along? She could take us both at once; she's old meat but wiry as hell. Be something to do. How about it, Bird, want me to ask her? Or do we keep pretending you're not fucking her? You think I'd be jealous or what? How long we gonna sit here, Bird? You think I act crazy, shit, this is what makes me. Like being in the hole only there's TV and little stuffed animals with you, a half-breed Indian hit man and a female corrections officer, queen of the cons. Shit, I may as well be in stir. How long, Bird?"

"Okay," Armand had said finally, "we stick our heads out, see what's going on."

Now they were riding along in the black car past open fields in the night, the radio and heater on, the blower going, Richie driving with the seat pushed way back, stiff-arming the wheel, raising his voice over the rock music coming out of the speakers, saying to his Indian buddy in the dark, "The first time? The first time was a guy name Kevin, suppose to be a friend of mine."

Armand hunched over to turn the radio down a notch. "He snitch on you or what?"

"No, I was clean, right out of the joint with this new identity they gave me . . . Wait a minute. Shit, this is weird. You ask me what was my first time and right away I think of this guy Kevin I knew from before. But there was the guy at Terre Haute, my cellmate. Some guys wanted him taken out, so they slip me a knife and say if I don't kill him they're gonna kill *me*. So I did. But then when I

was brought up I laid it on those guys, testified in
court I saw the one guy cut my cellmate's throat.
He got like ninety-nine years added on to the
ninety-nine he was doing and I got transferred out.
Maybe by testifying I talked myself into believing
it wasn't me that cut the guy. You know what I'm
saying? So I don't remember it as my first one. Or
it was 'cause I used a knife, I don't know. Then
when I got my release it was this guy Kevin I knew
hired me to repossess cars and shit. This one
time—listen to this—I had to go in a nursing home
and repossess a wheelchair, this battery-run tri-
cart, they cost just under twenty-five hundred. I
have to lift this cripple woman out of it, put her in
bed, she's going 'Oh, please, I have multiple scaro-
sis, I can't get around without my wheelchair.'
Man, I hated to do it, but she was three months
behind. What was I suppose to do? I had car pay-
ments, rent—see, I was back with Laurie, that's my
wife, I'd hardly seen her in four years. She said it
broke her heart to visit me in the joint, so she
didn't come too much."

Armand turned the radio off, getting rid of that
irritating noise. Richie looked at him and Armand
said, "What about this guy Kevin?"

"I was just getting to him. See, here's Kevin, he
finds out I'm being sent up he tells me he'll look after Laurie, if she got sick or anything, as a friend."

"I can see it coming," Armand said.

"Yeah, well, I didn't think nothing about it till one night me and Kevin are in this bar after work and right out of nowhere he goes, 'I want you to know something. I never fucked Laurie while you were in prison, not once.' I start to think, well, shit, what'd he tell me that for if he didn't? It must mean he did."

"Sure he did," Armand said. "How you gonna stop him, you're doing time."

"I go home ask Laurie, 'You ever go to bed with Kevin?' Her eyes get big, she goes, no, she swears she never did. I hit her a few times, she still claims she never did, swears to it on her Bible. Okay, I'm thinking, maybe they didn't. Couple of days later I come home, she's gone, cleared out with all her stuff. What does that tell you?"

"We're coming to the road where you turn, before you get to that little airport," Armand said. "Sure, she's scared you're gonna find out the truth. She was betraying you."

"And Kevin was fucking her, he musta been. I decide I'd get me a gun and settle the score with him."

"So he was your first one," Armand said, "as you like to see it."

Richie didn't say anything making the left turn onto a hard-packed gravel road, got the Daytona straightened out to head through country, past empty fields, and started to grin as he looked at

Armand. "You aren't gonna believe this. There was another one before Kevin. See, I quit my job, I didn't want to have nothing to do with him till I got myself a gun and stuck it in his face. Man, it tore me up. Here I was working, I had a new name, I was James Dudley, I was clean. I think of it now, the only job I ever had in my life was in the repo business and what's that but legal stealing. I said, shit, go on back to your trade, what's the difference, you can't trust nobody anyway. So I picked up a thirty-eight, not the one I got now, a cheap one—Detroit, you can get any kind of piece you want, buy it off a schoolkid. Okay, I'm ready to go see Kevin. I *think* I'm ready, but you know what? I never shot anybody before. I was gonna shoot that migrant, the one I picked up in Georgia, but I never got a chance to. I'm thinking, I want to be cool when I shoot Kevin, I want to know what's gonna happen. See, I needed cash too, so what I did, I practiced on the guy in the grocery store I held up, little greaseball-looking guy, you seen 'em. Anyway I put three in him and I think, Hey, nothing to it. Aim and squeeze, right? I forgot what I scored, not a whole lot. So by the time I got to Kevin—I caught him in the office late, 'Hi, Kev, how you doing?' and put five in him to make sure—he was actually my third. Though I still think of him, I don't know why, as my first. Weird, huh?"

Armand didn't say anything.

This guy was crazy. Armand remembered his first one like it was yesterday, the Italian coming into the barbershop, offering them a job saying, "The Degas brothers, stick-up guys, 'ey? Think you're tough . . ."

They came to an intersection, a stop sign showing in the Daytona's headlights, the crossroad dark both ways. Richie went through it without slowing down.

Armand didn't say anything.

He was watching now for the road ahead of them to begin curving to the left, remembering the last time they drove to the ironworker's house and Richie wouldn't do what he was told, drove past the house to take a look and when they made the U-turn and approached from this direction, Armand remembered, he'd had the same thoughts then as he did now. That he was going to end up shooting Richie before this was over or right after. Something would come up between them . . .

"The house is just around this curve."

"I know it."

He knew everything in that tone he thought was cool.

"Then slow down," Armand said.

The headlights swept over a sod field and they were close now, the ironworker's place coming up on the left, beyond that mass of trees. Armand looked for cars as Richie braked and let the Dodge coast toward the house, Richie saying it didn't look like anybody was home, or else they were in the sack already. Armand sat hunched close to the smoked-glass windshield. There was something in the yard he didn't remember from the other time. He hit Richie's arm, telling him, "Pull over."

"Where?"

"By the house. Aim the lights at it."

Richie cut the wheel and came to a stop, head-lights shining on dark windows, and there, in the front yard, a Nelson Davies FOR SALE sign.

Armand sat back in the seat trying to think—telling himself it didn't mean they were gone, you don't move till you sell your house—but it was hard to think with Richie talking about the god-damn real estate man, saying there he was again, saying it was like starting all over, it was like this was where he came in, seeing that sign. Finally he shut up. It was quiet for a while in the car.

Till Richie said, "Well, shit, what do we do now, Bird?"

"Don't worry about it."

"Yeah, but they're gone."

"Listen to me," Armand said. "You listening to me? Don't worry about it."

13

IN THE CAPE GIRARDEAU LITERATURE the Marshals Service gave them it said that "You can walk down a busy street with a smile on your face and people will speak to you, not necessarily because they know you; but, because you look like somebody they would like to know. And, if you give them the opportunity, they will take the time to know you."

Carmen read that part and imagined a person stopping her on the street saying, "Hi, you look like a person I'd like to know. You're new in town, aren't you? Where are you from?" She answers, "I'm sorry, I can't tell you. We're in the Federal Witness Security Program, hiding from some people who want to kill us." And the person says, "Oh, uh-huh. Yeah, well, have a nice day." She read the part to Wayne the night before they left home and he said, "Jesus Christ, you sure you want to go?"

Seven hundred miles later they had their first look at Cape Girardeau separately, Carmen in the

Cutlass following Wayne's pickup across the bridge from the Illinois side. It looked nice from this view, a picture-postcard town with church steeples, a courthouse on the hill, lots of trees. But what was that wall for, along the river? A concrete wall about twenty feet high. The wall fascinated Carmen, adding a touch of drama to the postcard look.

They came off the bridge and into the business district, Wayne looking for a street, Carmen following, getting a feel of the place. It seemed kept up, there were new buildings and blocks of old ones that had been gentrified. The chamber of commerce literature said it was a friendly town of sixty thousand with a university campus and a big new shopping center called West Park Mall. Procter & Gamble was here, Florsheim Shoes, Lone Star Industries with a cement plant, Cape Barge Line & Drydock . . . The tallest building was the KFVS-TV Tower—there, Carmen saw it rising about twelve stories above the downtown area, a sight that might give Wayne hope. They drove past a long climb of steps leading to the courthouse and down the hill to the concrete wall that ran along Water Street.

Carmen parked at the curb behind Wayne's pickup, the bed loaded with household stuff and covered with a tarp. She got out of the car stiff and tired. They had left Algonac at four in the morning, still dark, sneaked out with U.S. marshals escorting them to the interstate and maybe beyond, Carmen wasn't sure. Now they were to contact a Deputy Marshal J.D. Mayer, who would show them to their new home and help them get settled. Carmen walked over to Wayne, standing with his hands shoved into the back pockets of his jeans.

"What're we doing now?"

"Did you happen to notice Broadway?"

"I think we passed it, one block over."

"I must've been looking up at all the two-story high-rises and missed it," Wayne said. "I'll call him, but he's probably gone home, it's after five."

Carmen took off her sweater. It was at least twenty degrees warmer here than in Michigan. Wayne hadn't moved. He was looking up at the wall, just on the other side of railroad tracks and a line of young trees, the wall's tan surface shaded by the storefronts across Water Street.

"You know what it's for?"

Carmen said, "I guess to keep the river out."

"Or keep people in. It looks like a prison."

"Well, it's different."

"You get a good look at the river, coming over?"

"How could you miss it?"

"Did you notice a cape?"

"I'm not sure what one looks like."

"I don't see why they call it the mighty Mississippi. It's muddy, yeah, but I wouldn't call it mighty. The St. Clair River's wider, and it's blue. It's a lot better-looking. I'm glad I didn't bring the boat."

"Are you gonna call the marshal?"

"Right now. There's probably nothing but catfish in that river. You like catfish?"

"I've never had it."

"It's like carp. You ever had carp?"

"Go call him, will you?"

Carmen watched him cross the street toward a restaurant decked out with a green awning. It looked nice. So far she had a good feeling about being here, in a new place. Maybe they'd love it and want to stay. Three weeks didn't seem like enough time, not to make a major decision that could change your life. Carmen walked to the corner, to an opening in the concrete wall that was almost as wide as the street that came into it from down the hill. It could be a town in a foreign country.

She stepped into the opening. A giant metal door was hinged to the outside of the wall, where pavement sloped gradually to beds of broken rock along the banks of the river. No, the river didn't appear especially mighty, it looked old to Carmen, about a half mile across to cottonwoods on the Illinois side. A boat pushing flat barges was coming this way from the bridge, out there in the middle not making a sound: a stubby kind of boat that resembled a tug but was much taller. Carmen had never seen one like it before. Moving all those barges, about fifteen of them, tied together three abreast and extending way out in front of the boat.

Carmen turned, looking at the wall from the riverside now, at the massive door they would swing closed when that quiet river rose over its banks, thinking, They didn't build a wall like this for show.

She said to Wayne, coming across the street from the restaurant, "You know what this is? A floodgate. It's my first one. You want to see how high the river rises? They have marks up there by the opening, and dates, almost to the top. I'd call that a fairly mighty river."

Wayne looked up, but didn't appear interested.

"The girl says Deputy Marshal J. D. Mayer isn't in the office. I ask her where I can get in touch with him. We go back and forth, it takes about ten minutes to find out Deputy Marshal J. D. Mayer isn't in 'cause he's on leave of absence and the man in charge now is Deputy Marshal F. R. Britton. I said, well, then tell F. R. Britton that W. M. Colson has just come seven hundred miles to have a word with him, if he isn't too busy. She says, after all this, he isn't there, he's out to the house. I ask her, you mean *his* house? No, he's out to *our* house and we can catch him if we hurry. You believe it? Instead of telling me right away. Nine-fifty Hillglade Drive. I ask her, just where is that, please, and she says,

'Out toward Cape Rock off Riverview,' like, where else could it be? Off Riverview, asshole, don't you know nothing?"

Carmen said, "Are you gonna be a grouch? If you are, let's go home."

She thought 950 Hillglade Drive sounded nice.

On the way there Carmen caught glimpses of the river from high up through the trees, seeing it flat gray, desolate. That's the Mississippi? Wayne had a point, it didn't look important enough. Still nothing on the Illinois side but trees. Maybe Missouri looked the same from over there, except it was hilly.

Street names, Carmen knew, could be deceiving. When Hillglade turned out to be a humped narrow road with ditches on both sides she said, "Oh, well," and followed Wayne's pickup along the road past a lonesome row of two-bedroom subdivision homes with car ports, lights on in some of the houses, bikes in the driveways, suppertime, a development that for some reason hadn't developed, no sidewalks, not much of the land cleared, signs of a builder who'd run out of money. They came to 950 near the end of the street, off by itself in the dusk, windows dark, a red-brick ranch with white trim badly in need of paint. Carmen followed the pickup into a gravel drive sprouting weeds, turned off the engine and sat there. In the Algonac–Port Huron area the house would list for sixty-nine-nine, fixed up, and go for about sixty-seven. Landscaping would help, a new lawn and a front walk. A narrow worn path led from the slab front stoop to where a paneled door, its knob in place, lay across the ditch. Carmen told herself to stay cool.

Wayne came along the side of the pickup as she made herself move, get out of the car.

"What're we doing, starting over? Jesus, twenty years ago at least we had a front walk, and shrubs."

Carmen didn't say anything.

"You want to go to a motel?"

She said, "We're here now," and started across the scrubby yard, Wayne saying after her, yeah, they were here, that was the goddamn problem. Where was the woods? That wasn't a woods, it was a thicket. Carmen looked back at him as she reached the front step.

"There's a note on the door."

A three-by-five card held in place by the metal cover over the mail slot. She pulled it free, began to read the handwritten note, looked up and glanced at Wayne coming across the yard.

"It says, 'Hi, welcome to Cape—' He seems friendly."

"Who does?"

"F. R. Britton, Deputy Marshal. 'I have gone to have supper. Will be back by six forty-five.'" Carmen glanced at Wayne again. "He seems to have an organized mind. Energetic but even-tempered. The way he connects his *t* and his *h*, with most of the words sort of printed, shows originality and intuition."

Wayne said, "Then how come he didn't know we'd be here? We suppose to stand around and wait?"

"It says, 'The side door is open. Make yourselves at home. Signed F. R. Britton.'"

With big loops, Carmen noticed, showing a certain amount of ego.

Wayne walked back to the drive and into the carport at the side of the house. Carmen followed, looking at the note, half written, half printed in a strong right-hand slant. She stopped in the yard, not sure about that circle dotting the *i* in *Hi*. It could indicate he was creative, but not necessarily. Her mom drew circles for *i* dots. The deputy marshal's slant, on second thought, might be a little too much. She'd have to measure it on her Emotional Expression Chart. Carmen looked up, aware of Wayne coming around from the side of the house, Wayne with his grim look.

"What's wrong?"

"You mean outside of there's no electricity?"

Carmen made a face. "Don't tell me that, please."

"That's the good part," Wayne said. "No lights, you can't see the bad part. The place's a goddamn mess."

The young guy wearing a sport coat and tie came out of a cream-colored Plymouth four-door holding up a handful of candles. He jumped the ditch and crossed the yard toward them saying, "Hey, sorry about that. You go see Union Electric tomorrow, they'll fix you up. Or I can take you if I don't have to be in court. Hi, I'm Deputy Marshal F. R. Britton?"

Making it sound like a question. Was it his accent, Carmen wondered, that buttery drawl, or wasn't he sure who he was?

Saying now, "I'd prefer it if you call me Ferris. I don't want you to think of me as your parole officer or anything like that."

And now that stopped Carmen, already surprised by his boyish good looks, her idea of a U.S. marshal being a middle-aged man in a business suit. This one had a full head of wavy brown hair and a muscular build, thick neck and shoulders that made his tan sport coat seem too small, something he'd outgrown.

Carmen said, "Ferris? Is that right?"

"Yes, ma'am, like the wheel, and this must be Wayne Colson," offering his hand now, "and Ms. Colson? How you folks doing, all right?" Holding Carmen's hand he said, "I had to deliver a prisoner up to Marion, Illinois, I come back—did you see my note?"

"Have it right here."

He said, "Good," giving her hand a squeeze before letting go, his eyes smiling at her. "I didn't want you to think I'd forgot you. See, I missed working out this morning on account of going to Marion—I do push-ups and sit-ups, lift some weights, so when I come back I had to get that done—"

"And have your supper," Carmen said.

"Yeah, I had to eat. I imagine you folks stopped on the way?"

"Not since lunch."

"Well, you want to get something first? There's a Shoney's on Route K out toward the mall, not too far."

"We're trying to decide," Carmen said, "whether we want to stay here or go to a motel."

"Or turn around and go home," Wayne said. "Have you been inside that house lately?"

Wayne stood with his arms folded. Next to him, Carmen noticed, F. R. Ferris Britton was about the same height but wider through the shoulders in that tight sport coat. At the moment he seemed confused, frowning as he looked at the house.

"I know the 'lectricity's off, that's why I brought these candles. But it's only temporary, just tonight till you get it turned back on. No, that's a nice little house, I got one just like it not too far from here."

"We did too," Wayne said. "Our first house was this same idea, two-bedroom ranch."

"Up in *De*-troit?"

"That's right, Ferris, near *De*-troit."

Carmen thinking, Here we go . . .

As Wayne said, "The only difference is, Ferris, we didn't keep goats in our house, or pigs or whatever they had living in this one, 'cause it's a goddamn mess, inside and out."

"Gee, I didn't think it was that bad. I know it might need a little work," the young marshal still frowning, showing concern. "Come on, let's us take a look."

It was dusk outside, dark in the house. They went in through the side door, Carmen and Wayne following the deputy marshal, each holding a lighted candle. In the kitchen he turned to them saying, "We could use cups as holders, so we don't drip wax all over."

Carmen, already looking in a cupboard, heard Wayne say, "You think it matters? You can feel the dirt and grit on the floor." There were dishes on the shelves, but not many. Most of them were piled in the sink, soiled, some crusted with bits of food. Carmen opened the refrigerator and closed it quick against the awful rancid odor. There were dirty pans on the range.

"The couple lived here before," Ferris said, "I suspect she wasn't much of a housekeeper. All the woman did was complain. She ran out on him, oh, a few months ago. Then he left, was only last week, right before we found out you all were being relocated here and J.D. Mayer told me I'd be acting-inspector in charge, see to your needs."

"Come here, Ferris, I want to show you something," Wayne said. "I want you to look at the carpeting in the living room. I can't even tell what color it is."

Following Wayne, the deputy marshal said, "I think it's kind of a green."

Carmen watched their candles moving away in the dark. She stepped into the hall to look at the bedrooms, both tiny, twin beds crowded into what would be the front bedroom, the other one empty, cardboard boxes stacked against a wall. Wayne would have a few words to say about the twin beds. She could hear him in the living room telling the marshal to look at the stains and here, look at the drapes, like some animal had been chewing on them, the front of the sofa, the same thing.

The bathroom didn't seem too bad, for a bathroom. Scrub it with a disinfectant, get rid of the shower curtain full of mildew stains. Do something with the window. The windows in the bedrooms, too, all the windows, clean the whole place good . . . if they were going to stay here. Right now it was someone else's house. Carmen followed her candle into the living room. The upholstered furniture, modern-looking, appeared white, the carpeting more gray than green. The walls seemed to be white or off-white.

Ferris was telling Wayne the couple that'd lived here had had a little puppy must not have been housebroken, left its little messes wherever it wanted, little black-and-white shorthaired pup. Looking at Carmen he said, "I know it would try to chew on my shoelace if I wasn't wearing my boots, which I generally do. These here are Tony Lamas I sent away for. I'd give the puppy a little kick, not to hurt it none, you understand, but the woman'd have a fit. She took the pup when she left. Her name was Roseanne—I mean the woman, I forgot the puppy's name." Ferris paused. "It'll come to me. Roseanne, the woman, had real blond hair but was older than you folks. Both of 'em were, her and the guy, her husband."

"These people," Wayne said, "were in the witness program?"

"We call it WitSec," Ferris said, "short for Witness Security. Yeah, they were here when I got assigned last winter, after I finished my thirteen weeks training at the academy. See, I was a police officer in West Memphis, Arkansas, that's my home, before I joined the Marshals Service and was sent to this district."

"You like it?" Carmen said. "I mean Cape Girardeau."

"Yeah, I like it, it's nice. See, I'll work security in the federal court when it's in session, or I'll get a call from the local Bureau office, there two resident agents here, back them up when they make an arrest and then take charge of the prisoner or seize his assets if he's got any, like his car, and arrange for its disposition, you know, sell it at auction or we might use it in surveillance work. Like this house was seized, it was owned by a guy was running dope on the interstate, St. Louis to Memphis, and was using this house as a place to stash it if he wanted, or sell some of it. You know the See-Mo campus is here, Southeast Missouri State? I'm thinking of taking some business courses, maybe computer programming, something like that. I can get home when I want, it's not too far to West Memphis, and there's good deer hunting right over here in Bollinger County."

Carmen watched Wayne. He said, "Is that right?" trying to sound only mildly interested. "Whitetail or mule deer?"

"Whitetail and plenty of him. But getting back to your question," Ferris said, "the one here before

you was a guy name Ernie Molina, little guy, had
this little mustache. He was a loan shark from over
in New Jersey. Ernie and his wife I mentioned,
Roseanne."

Carmen was about to speak, but Wayne beat her
to it. "That's the guy's real name, Ernie Molina, or
the one he made up?"

"His real one. What he changed it to—this's
funny—was Edward Mallon, see, E.M., using the
same initials on account of he had, what do you
call it, his monogram on all his shirts, on the
pocket here. Guy had more shirts'n I ever saw in
my life, like he musta had a good twenty shirts or
more hanging in his closet, I'm not kidding you.
The thing was, it was funny, he's going by this
name Edward Mallon, but you could tell by looking at him he was a greaser. Excuse me, I mean a
Latin. I have to watch that. I come here, Ernie's not
doing nothing, living offa Uncle Sam, I took him
over to Procter and Gamble's and got him a job,
but he didn't care for it, so he quit and got himself
one tending bar. Ernie was a nervous type, I think
drank a lot."

"We were told," Carmen said, glancing at
Wayne in the candle glow, "you aren't supposed to
talk about people in the program, reveal their identity. Isn't that right?"

Ferris seemed surprised. "Well, you're not
gonna tell anybody, are you?" He started to grin.

"Being in the same club, so to speak, as him. No, I take that back. Ernie's gone, so he's not in WitSec no more. Now my responsibility, as far as the program goes, is to protect you folks, keep you out of harm. I know there a couple guys looking for you, they have detainers out on them and you're gonna testify at their trial if and when, but that's about all. See, Marshal J.D. Mayer was given the information and told me you were coming and would be in my care. He's on sick leave, his pump acting up on him, and I doubt will be back. He's funny, I ask him things and he says, 'Look, Ferris, I tell you what you need to know and what you don't won't hurt you.' So all I got is a file with not much in it. I don't know if you're actually married or common-law or even what your real names are."

Carmen said, amazed, "Are you serious?"

"Well, nobody's told me."

"We're Mr. and Mrs. Colson. We're actually married, in church, and that's our name."

"What I have in the report, then—that's your Christian name, Carmen?"

She said, "I don't believe this. Yes, it is."

"That's a nice name," Ferris said. "I like it." He looked at Wayne. "And you're Wayne Morris Colson? That's the name on your original birth certificate?"

Wayne took a moment, staring back at him in the candle glow. "What's your problem?"

"Hey, there's no problem. It was my under-standing that to be in WitSec you have to take on a new identity. Anybody I've ever heard of in it, that's what they did. I'll study out that file again, satisfy my curiosity. It's possible I could've missed something."

"But you sound like you don't believe us," Carmen said.

"No, I believe you, you tell me your real name's Carmen, that's fine with me. I just want to get it straight in my own mind what you have to do and what you don't. As I told you, I wasn't given much information."

"And you haven't been a marshal very long," Wayne said.

"Be a year come January. I might not be up on all the procedures, or you might say the fine print as to what you agreed to. But let me tell you, I know what *I* have to do. I'm armed at all times, got a three-fifty-seven Smith and Wesson on me, and I'm sworn to protect your lives to the death."

Wayne said, "You do some deer hunting, uh?"

"Yeah, I go over to Bollinger County along the Castor River track, it's only about fifty miles, full of whitetail in there."

Carmen went outside. She got her sweater from the car and put it on. It was quiet. She held her arms to her body and rubbed them for warmth.

Trees against the night sky could be trees anywhere, but she could feel a difference knowing she was in a strange place. There were people a block or so down the street in the homes where lights showed, but she didn't know them and couldn't see the town now, out here, with its postcard look from the bridge, the church steeple, the court-house, the friendly town where people might stop you on the street wanting to know you. . . . She thought, How did we get here? How did it happen so fast?

Wayne and Ferris came out of the house and across the yard, Ferris saying, "If you haven't seen one then you wouldn't believe a swamp rabbit. I mean the size of him. He's different'n a cottontail and two or three times bigger. I got me one, was on Coon Island in Butler County, weighed eighteen pounds."

Wayne asked if they were good eating.

"Good," Ferris said, "swamp rabbit's so good to eat people have just about killed him out."

He shook their hands, ready to leave, then spoke for several minutes about motels and places to eat out on the highway, recommending the ones he said wouldn't cost them an arm and a leg, then telling Carmen about West Park Mall, knowing, he said, how women loved to shop whether they needed anything or not. "Hey, Wayne? Isn't that the truth?" He told them he'd be by tomorrow and drove off with a couple of toots from his car horn.

Wayne turned to Carmen. "The guy's a moron."

"But a deer hunter," Carmen said. "Doesn't that make a difference?"

"Ferris does push-ups and lifts weights. I'll bet he likes to arm-wrestle, too."

"Why did he say he doesn't want us to think of him as a parole officer? Did you hear him? Why should we?"

"I don't know. He probably meant as far as we don't have to report to him."

Carmen was silent looking at the sky, picking out faint stars. After a moment she said, "I think he meant something else."

After another moment Wayne said, "The white-tail season here's only seven days, the week before Thanksgiving."

14

"ALL I COULD THINK OF," Lenore said, "you were in a terrible accident. I've been worried sick."

"Mom, you know we got here okay. I called you from the motel, soon as we walked in the door."

"I mean since then I've been worried."

"And I called the other night. Didn't I?"

"Once, since you got there. Don't your neighbors have phones you could use?"

"We don't have neighbors. We're sort of off by ourselves. I haven't met anyone yet. Anyway, Mom . . ."

"You've been gone six days, almost a week counting today. I have it marked on the calendar. You didn't even come see me before you left."

"I told you, it happened all of a sudden," Carmen said. "Anyway, we have our phone now. Southwestern Bell came this morning—I had them put it in the kitchen, well, actually in the breakfast nook. It's like a little booth, you know, with benches built in? You can look out the window . . .

The washer and dryer are in the utility room, right off the kitchen, having the phone here it'll be handy." Carmen letting her mom know she could be seven hundred miles away but was still the happy homemaker, out here baking pies, washing Wayne's coveralls, fixing dinner off recipe cards. "There's a woods behind the house, not like the one we have at home, Wayne says it isn't a woods it's a thicket, but it's nice, you hear birds out there." That might sound as though she was having a good time, so Carmen said, "We've been working since we got here. We had to shampoo the carpeting, the sofa and two chairs in the living room, rent one of those machines, scrub the kitchen floor, do the cupboards, the refrigerator and my least favorite of all jobs, clean the oven. Wayne helped a lot, he didn't report to his job till this morning so, you know, we could get settled. We may do some painting, we're trying to decide, depending on how long we'll be here." Carmen paused to think of what else she wanted to say. . . . Yeah, remind her not to tell anyone where they were. She said, "Mom . . ."

Too late.

"You said a few weeks."

"That's what Wayne thinks."

"I don't see why he has to go all the way to Missouri to get work. Like there isn't any around here."

"It's a change," Carmen said. "He'll know more in a few days. It's not a real big job." He did go see about one this morning, that much was true, though it wasn't structural work. Wayne said he didn't care, he had to be doing something; threw his coveralls in the pickup and took off to meet Ferris Britton at Cape Barge Line & Drydock.

"What's your weather like?"

Her mom would ask that daily, when they were living only thirty miles apart. "It's around seventy," Carmen said, "sort of cloudy, but it's been nice all week."

"It's raining here, and cold. It's suppose to go down to forty tonight. I hate this weather."

"You could move to Florida, nothing's stopping you."

"I don't know anybody in Florida. What if something happened to me? Like one of my back seizures and I can't move, I have to lie perfectly still. There is nothing like that pain when you try to move. I felt one coming on the other day, I called the doctor . . ." Lenore stopped. "I may have to change my number again. Either that or have the Annoyance Call Bureau put a trap on my line, find out where he's calling from and get him."

"You had an obscene phone call?"

"I had two hang-ups the same day. The kind where you know the party is on the line but they don't say anything."

"Didn't even breathe hard?"

"It happens to you, you won't think it's so funny. I thought it was the doctor, I was waiting for him to call me back. You can wait all day, they don't care."

"When was this, Mom?"

"Soon as I started to feel the pain. When do you think? You know they call to find out if you're home, that's how they work it. Call and hang up."

"Or it's someone who got the wrong number," Carmen said. "Have any of our friends called?"

"Why would they call here?"

"I doubt if they will, but if you do get a call . . . See, we didn't tell anyone we were going. Wayne doesn't want the guys in the local to know he's working out of state. I don't understand it myself, but if anyone calls just say we're driving down to Florida and you haven't heard from us yet. Okay? So Wayne won't have to worry about it."

"You don't know when you're coming home?"

Getting an old-lady quiver in her voice. Lenore was sixty-seven years old, she could be tough as nails, dance on a table after a few vodkas with grapefruit juice, or she could sound utterly helpless, real whiny, when she wanted something.

"Wayne says he'll know pretty soon. He just started today, but as soon as we find out . . . We're gonna be talking anyway."

Lenore said, "If I get one of my seizures . . ."

"Try not to think about it."

"I don't know what I'd do, being all alone. I don't even have your number. What's that area code, three-one-five?"

"Three-one-four."

"Are you sure?"

"It's right on the phone," Carmen said, looking at it.

"All right, give me the number." After a moment her mom said, "Carmen, where are you? What're you doing?"

She was looking across the kitchen, through the open doorway to the hall. She said, "Just a second, Mom," raised her voice and called out, "Wayne." She waited.

Lenore was saying, "What? I didn't hear what you said. Area code three-one-four, then what?"

"I thought I heard Wayne come in," Carmen said. She paused before giving her mom the number, listened to her repeat it, said, "That's right." And in that moment looked up again. Sure of the sound this time. Someone closing the side door.

"For all the good it will do me," Lenore said, "if I'm flat on my back and you're down in Missouri somewhere."

Ferris Britton appeared in the hall, looking into the kitchen, looking right at Carmen.

"You remember the last time?" Lenore said. "I was in bed two weeks, I couldn't move and you came every day? You took care of me, you took care of the house . . ."

Ferris Britton, wearing that tight sport coat, thumbs hooked in his belt, grinning at her.

"I don't know what I would have done without you. I couldn't even go to the bathroom alone, remember?"

"Mom, I have to go. Somebody's here."

"Who is it?"

"It's work we're having done."

Ferris was grinning and shaking his head now, showing some kind of appreciation, enjoying himself.

"I'll call you tomorrow, okay?"

"Tell me what time, in case I go out."

"The same time, around eleven."

"I could call you. No, if Wayne's making good money down there, at least I hope he is, you call me."

"I will, don't worry."

"What're you fixing for dinner?"

"Mom, I have to go. Bye."

Carmen hung up, Ferris still grinning at her.

He said, "That was your mom, huh? I don't know if it's a good idea giving her your phone number."

Carmen took a moment. "You walk right in someone else's house?"

Ferris was looking at the electric coffeemaker,

over on the counter by the sink. He moved toward it saying, "Excuse me, but this isn't exactly someone else's house. It belongs to the Justice Department through seizure by the U. S. Marshals Service and is in our care. I thought I told you that." He raised his hand as Carmen started to get up from the table. "Stay where you are, I'll help myself." Ferris took a cup from the dish drainer, filled it with coffee and came over to the table. "Smells good and strong. I don't use sugar or cream, nothing that isn't good for me." Still grinning at her.

Maybe always grinning, Carmen remembering his boyish expression in candlelight, wavy brown hair down on his forehead, country-western entertainer or television evangelist. She said, "Are you gonna walk in anytime you want? If you are, I think we'll find another place." She had to look almost straight up at him standing close to the table and it made her mad. "Maybe we will anyway. I didn't come here to be a cleaning woman for the Justice Department."

Ferris stopped grinning. Carmen watched him squint at her now, squeezing lines into his forehead, another one of his expressions. Carmen believed he had three or four: deadpan, mouth open, this one and his gee-whiz grin.

He said, "You mean you aren't a cleaning lady?"

She watched him set his cup on the table, turn

and inspect the kitchen in a studied way, nodding, before looking at her again.

"Well, you sure could do my house anytime."

There was the grin back again and now he was taking off his sport coat, folding it inside out, making himself right at home.

"Hey, I'm kidding with you. Don't you know when I'm kidding?"

She watched him slide into the breakfast-nook booth, bringing the sport coat across his lap. His wavy hair, his weight lifter neck and shoulders in a short-sleeve white shirt, red-print tie hanging in front of him, seemed to fill the space on the other side of the table. He brought his cup to him and hunched over to rest his arms on the table edge.

"I knocked. You must not've heard me."

"You didn't knock or ring the bell," Carmen said, "you walked right in."

"I hear you talking to somebody I want to know who the person is, or if you're in some kind of trouble, need my help. That's what I'm for."

She watched him pick up his cup and hold it in two hands as he took a sip. He held it in front of him, looking over the rim of the cup at her.

"Mmmmm, that's good. I was in court all week was why I haven't come by. I take that back, I mean during the day. I come by two different nights like around eight, but you weren't home either time. The pickup was here—I looked in the window, saw how you'd cleaned the place up. Man, I thought I musta had the wrong house."

Carmen said, "You looked in our windows?"

"Just the living room. No, I went around to the kitchen too. Where were you?"

"If we weren't home then we were out."

"Well, I *know* that. Where'd you go?"

Carmen took her time, wanting to tell him it was none of his business, but wanting to excuse him, too, because he was dumb, because he was overprotective, took his job very seriously and didn't realize he was blundering into their privacy. She wanted that to be the only reason he was here, sitting close across the table with those huge arms and shoulders, staring at her.

"Let's see," Carmen said, "we shopped, bought a new shower curtain, some dish towels. I called my mother. . . . Oh, Wayne bought a pair of work gloves." She paused, staring at the marshal's innocent irritating expression, and said, "We thought about going to a show, but didn't know if we were allowed to."

Ferris said, "Sure, that's okay, you can go to the show. But call me and let me know which one. See, I have to know where you are, you know, in case something comes up. I think I got your old man a job over to Cape Barge, if he don't mind getting filthy dirty crawling underneath towboats. A dry-dock's the last place I'd ever want to get hired. He told me he was an ironworker before. I didn't ask him, but is Wayne an Indian?"

Carmen said, "An Indian—why would you think that?"

"I heard one time they could only get Indians to go up on those high buildings, either 'cause they're crazy enough to do it, not afraid of heights, or 'cause they're surefooted—I don't know, maybe they wear moccasins and aren't as likely to fall."

"I'm told they fall like anyone else," Carmen said. "I'll bet you also heard you're not supposed to look down when you're up pretty high."

"Yeah, you get the urge to jump."

"If you do, you're not an ironworker. It's looking *up* that can get you in trouble, if you start watching the clouds moving."

"I imagine it takes getting used to," Ferris said. "What'd your old man do before he was an ironworker?"

"He's not my old man, he's my husband."

"I know he's older'n you are, I saw it in the file. He's forty-one and you're thirty-eight, only he looks it and you don't. You look more my age. I turned thirty-one this past July, but I keep in shape. I work with weights I got at home in my exercise room. I can do those one-hand push-ups, I can do nine-hundred and sixty-five sit-ups at one time without stopping. I'll run now and then but I don't care for it too much, I do leg exercises instead. You

ought to see my workout room. It was the den before I got divorced. My ex-wife went back to
Hughes, Arkansas, that's near Horseshoe Lake,
not too far from West Memphis, where I was born
and raised."

"I have a nineteen-year-old son," Carmen said,
"in the navy. Right now he's on a nuclear carrier in
the Pacific Ocean."

"Yeah, I saw in the file you had a boy in the service I expected you'd look like an old woman, but
you sure don't. I can tell you take care of yourself,
like I do. I respect my body. Watch this." Ferris
raised his right arm, cocked his fist and his bicep
jumped out of the short white sleeve. "See? Does a
little dance for you." He looked from his arm to
Carmen. "You like to dance? Get out there on the
floor and shake it?"

"At times," Carmen said. "Why don't you put
your arm down?"

"You want to feel it?"

"That's okay."

Ferris straightened the arm, raised the other one
and stretched, saying, "Oh, man," before laying
them on the edge of the table again, hunching
those huge shoulders at her.

"You have a stereo?"

"We didn't bring it."

"How about a radio?"

Carmen gave him a weary look. She said, "You're too much," and instantly wished she hadn't.

He liked it—grinning at her again.

"My ex used to say that. I'd turn on the stereo and we'd dance right there in the house, the two of us. It's what I miss the most since getting divorced. Well, it and something else. We weren't married but a year. I think we did it more when we were going together'n when we were married, and I'm not talking about dancing now. What I think happens, when it's right there all the time waiting you get so you take it for granted. And I mean just in a year's time. I 'magine after something like twenty years you don't do it near as much, or least not with the same person you're married to. Am I right about that?"

Carmen felt herself boxed in by the table and his big shoulders filling the space in front of her, his shoulders, his wavy hair, his grin . . . She tried staring at him calmly, with no expression—practiced from staring at Wayne, good at it—let this guy know she didn't think he was cute or funny or was afraid of him. She wasn't. She was irritated, but didn't want to show him that either. Irritated by that goddamn grin and now by the thought—all of a sudden popping into her head—that she had missed something in his handwriting, or hadn't paid enough attention to signs of ego. How could a person as dumb as this guy be so confident? That was not only irritating, it was a little scary.

She was wondering if maybe he could grin forever when it began to fade and he said to her, "Oh, well, you think on it and let me know."

He slid out of the booth with his sport coat. When he turned, Carmen saw the revolver holstered on his right hip. She wanted to say something to him, but was more anxious for him to go, get out of here. He started to, he reached the doorway to the hall and Carmen got up to follow, make sure he left. When he turned she stood still, her hand on the edge of the table.

"See, you look to me like a nice person, the kind I'd like to get to know."

"Thanks," Carmen said.

"That's why I know it isn't all rosy between you and your old man, considering what he's into, the kind of people he associates with. I can't say I know what the deal is . . ."

It took Carmen a moment to realize what he was saying. "Wait a minute—Wayne isn't *into* anything."

"I suspect it might be something like labor racketeering, the kind of work he does, and the Bureau's got him up against the wall."

"No—believe me. You've got the wrong idea."

"Am I close?"

"He hasn't *done* anything is what I'm trying to tell you." She watched Ferris put on his frown and pose with his head cocked.

"That's funny, I thought your old man was in the Witness Security Program."

Carmen felt an urge to go over and kick him in the balls, hard. "You don't *have* to be a criminal, do you? Isn't that right?"

"I think it helps," Ferris said, "since I never heard of anybody in the program that wasn't dirty—outside of relatives, wives, like yourself. See, that's why I know you and him have your problems, 'cause as a law-enforcement officer I've dealt with plenty of guys like your old man. I'm sworn to protect his life, but that don't mean I have to show him any respect."

"I don't believe this," Carmen said with nervous energy, too many things in her mind to say at once. She saw Ferris turn to go and then look back at her again.

He said, "I don't have to show you any respect either, if I don't want to."

Carmen took one look at Wayne and said, "Oh, my Lord," not so much at the way he weaved and bumped against the refrigerator, but seeing his coveralls filthy with grease and soot, bunched under his arm.

"I stopped off. I'm not late, am I?"

"For what? We're sure not going anywhere," Carmen said. "Give me those." She took his coveralls and threw them into the dark utility room. "Where're you working, in a coal mine?"

"Close to it. I spent this morning in a coal barge welding in steel plates." Wayne had the refrigerator open now. "The drydock foreman says, 'So you're a welder, huh?' I told him, 'You bet I am, AWS certified.' He says, 'Yeah, but can you weld plates watertight?' I said, 'Hey, I can weld a goddamn building so it won't fall down. Is that good enough?' He liked that, he said, 'We'll try you out.'"

Carmen watched him bump the refrigerator door closed with his hip, a can of beer in each hand, wound up because he was working again and had stopped off with the guys, back into a routine. Carmen was still tense from the deputy marshal's visit, anxious to tell Wayne about it, but saw she would have to wait her turn. He was seated now in the breakfast nook, popping open the beer cans.

"I worked on the coal barge and then this big triple-screw towboat, the *Robert R. Nally,* comes in *side*ways from out in the river—that's called walking the boat, when they do that. The chief engineer, this guy I got to know pretty well, was madder'n hell at the trip pilot. . . . See, there's a pilot they hire for trips, he and the captain take turns navigating, driving the boat. But this one they had caused the *Robert R. Nally* to run aground up here at a place they call the Backbone, Mile Ninety-four. It was pushing sixteen barges and the chief engineer said they splattered, broke the tow all apart. He said what happened, the dummy trip pilot was trying to steer the Backbone when he should've flanked it." Wayne was grinning.

Carmen saw him wrapped up in his riverboat story, into a new trade and sounding like Matthew in his letters full of new words and references. At another time she might be interested. Right now it was beginning to irritate her.

"The trip pilot doesn't work for the company, he's like an independent contractor. He gets two-fifty a day and good ones are in demand. Even taking time off, you know what you could make a year, steering a boat down the river?"

Wayne paused, raising his eyebrows and his can of beer, and Carmen said, "Ferris was here."

"When, today?"

"This morning. He thinks you're a crook, involved in some kind of racketeering."

"Guy's an idiot. He introduces me to the dry-dock foreman and *tells* him I'm in the Witness Security Program. The foreman goes, 'Oh, is that right?' I had to tell him after Ferris left, 'You want to check on me? Call Detroit, call my local.' He says, 'Well, if you can do the job . . . ' "

"I did call Detroit," Carmen said. "I called the Marshals Service and spoke to John McAllen. I told him what happened . . ."

"We finally got a phone. Right there and I didn't even notice it."

"McAllen said he'll look into it."

"Good, straighten the guy out."

"Wayne, I was on the phone talking to Mom—he walked right in the house."

"Who did, Ferris?"

"He didn't knock or ring the bell, he just walked in."

"Was the door locked?"

"I don't know, you went out. Did you lock it? He probably has a key anyway."

"I was with a guy after that mentioned him. We stopped off, the chief engineer and the captain of the boat we're working on—both of these guys've been on the river over forty years. The captain, he wears a regular suit and tie, took me up to the pilothouse, showed me all the controls. But the way I got chummy with him was through the chief engineer. I was underneath the stern of the boat, in the drydock now, they got the old wheel off that was bent . . . The wheel's the propeller, only it's a great big goddamn thing, taller'n I am, they cost ten to fifteen thousand each. I'm welding a plate over the piece that holds the wheel to the shaft, the chief engineer says, 'I got a job you might want to look at.' "

Carmen turned and opened the oven. With hot pads she brought out a casserole of pork chops and escalloped potatoes, placed it on top of the stove and didn't move, standing with her back to Wayne.

"He takes me aboard and down to the engine room, three diesels in there, twelve-hundred horse-power each, and shows me this busted exhaust flex joint."

Carmen got a head of lettuce from the refrigerator, brought it to the counter next to the sink, still with her back to Wayne, and began tearing it apart to make a salad.

"It's a waffle-type joint made of stainless steel, the kind of job ordinarily they'd take out the whole section and send it to the shop. Anyway, I put a weld in there, the chief engineer looks at it, he says, 'We go ashore after work I'm gonna buy you a drink.' I don't care that much about welding, but you know what's the most interesting thing about that operation, seeing how the drydock works. You ever see it?"

Carmen had a chunk of lettuce in her hand. She threw it down on the counter, came over to the table and picked up the can of beer Wayne had opened for her.

"What they do, they fill it with water and the entire dock sinks down in the river. They work the towboat in there between the two sides, pump the water out and the whole thing raises back up with the boat. They took a barge out and put a big goddamn towboat in there in less than an hour."

Carmen slammed the beer can down on the table.

"The guy walked into our house!"

Wayne looked up at her, startled.

Carmen said, "Am I getting through to you?"

Wayne touched her arm. "Why don't you sit down, okay?"

"I don't want to sit down. The guy walked into our house, uninvited. Without knocking or ringing the bell. Do you understand that?"

"Yeah, I understand."

"I could have been undressed, I could have been taking a shower. Did you ask anything about that? What I was doing, what I felt, was I afraid? No, you tell me about this wonderful welding job you did and how the fucking drydock works."

"I was gonna discuss it with you."

"When?"

"Right now. I was about to tell you about this guy that joined us after."

"In the bar?"

"Yeah, a place they go."

"Great. Tell me about the guy you met in a bar."

"Why don't you sit down, okay? Take it easy."

"You want to know something else? The guy who came to our house, Armand Degas?"

"Yeah, the Indian."

"Not once have you asked me what it was like, what I felt, what was going through my mind. You put your gun by the door, just in case—there, you've done your part. Did you think—I'm talking about before now—did you think I might actually have to use it?"

"You did," Wayne said. "You handled it, you ran the guy off."

"How do you know? Did you ask me about it?"

"You *told* me what happened."

"You know what I mean. Did you think about how scared I must've been? You didn't hold me or say anything. . . . I couldn't sleep after—do you remember that? The FBI man, Scallen, he understood. I told him I hope I never have to do that again and you said—do you know what you said?"

"You mean when Scallen was there?"

"You said, 'My wife's a winner. That's why I married her.'"

"Yeah? What's wrong with that?"

"It's like you're taking credit, because you picked me."

"I was complimenting you, for Christ sake."

"No, you weren't. It's always what you're doing

that's important, your job, working on a project—
what am I doing, the ironing, I wash your dirty
coveralls."

"You want me to do it," Wayne said, "when I
come home? Tell me what you want. You don't tell
me, how'm I suppose to know? You start crying, I
don't even know most of the time if you're happy
or somebody died or you got a pain, it doesn't
seem to make any fucking difference. What I need
is something like your Emotional Expression
Chart, a big one I can lay over you and find out
what's going on."

Carmen picked up her can of beer and started
out of the kitchen.

"Wait a minute . . . okay?"

She stopped in the hall doorway.

"You want me to talk to this moron, this asshole
marshal? I will, I plan to, don't worry. He ever
walks in this house again I'll wrap a sleever bar
around his head. How's that?"

Carmen stood there long enough to say, "That's
what you'll do for him. What will you do for me?"

Every once in a while—like getting ice water
thrown in your face—she'd get mad when he
didn't know what she was thinking or how she felt.
Then he'd get mad because he didn't see why he
was expected to be able to read her goddamn

mind. He had wondered if maybe it had to do with her period, mentioned it one time only and got a can of beer thrown at him. He wiped it up from the kitchen floor after she walked out of the house and across the field all the way to the far edge of woods and stood there till it was dark. They made love that night, saying they would love each other forever and everything was fine after. This evening, Wayne had another beer before going to look for his wife and get things back to normal.

She was in the bedroom. The twin beds had been pushed together and Carmen was sitting on the edge of hers, bent over close to the lamp and her can of beer on the night table. She was leafing through the chamber of commerce booklet on her lap. Or going through the motions. Wayne stood in the doorway. He asked her what she was doing.

"I'm reading."

He kept quiet, giving her time.

"I'm finding out," Carmen said, "what a wonderful place this is to live. The Centerre Bank is serving us with three convenient locations. Or we can see Colonial Federal for all our financial needs."

"Are we gonna have supper?"

"If you want."

"Carmen, I'll talk to the guy, okay?"

She didn't say anything. Wayne took a step into the room. "Listen, I mentioned—I started to tell you about meeting a guy when I was with the captain and the chief engineer?" He paused. If she nodded or said almost anything at all it would mean they were friends again.

She didn't.

"Anyway, this guy, his name's Bob Brown, he's a detective with the Cape Girardeau Police. We're talking, I tell him why we're here, he says, 'Oh, so you know Ferris Britton. What do you think of him?' I said, 'You want my honest opinion? I think he's a moron.' And Bob Brown, the cop, says, 'You're being polite. You want anything fucked up, Ferris is the guy you call.'"

Wayne stood there waiting.

Carmen didn't say anything.

"They know the guy, what he's like. He ever walks in here again, call Bob Brown. That's an easy name to remember."

She still didn't say anything.

There wasn't a sound in the house. Wayne shook his head, still waiting. He said, "All right, tell me what you want. Will you, please? So I'll know?"

Carmen looked up at him. "How long are we staying here?"

"Till they get the two guys—I don't know."

"You told me three weeks," Carmen said. "No more than that. But now you have a job you're all wrapped up in, you have your whitetail, so you can go hunting. . . . I guess you're all set, huh? But what do *I* have? Outside of somebody else's house to clean."

Wayne said, "What do *you* have?" getting some amazement in his tone. "Honey, you have *me*, don't you?"

The way she got up and grabbed the beer can from the night table, he knew she was going to throw it at him.

15

DONNA STARTED TALKING about Elvis. She said, "If Elvis was Jesus, you know who I think some of his apostles would be? I think Engelbert would be one. I think Tom Jones would be one. And I think, going way back, the Jordanaires and the Blackwood Brothers. Who do you think?"

Armand said he'd never thought about it before.

This was while Donna was clearing the table, setting the dishes in the sink to wash later on, and Armand was waiting the forty-five minutes it took for another chicken pie to heat. They'd had one each for supper and he was still hungry. Richie was in the living room watching TV. Donna moved on from Elvis and his apostles to Elvis's greatest hits to how she had tried one time to get a job in corrections down there to be near Elvis's home. The West Tennessee Reception Center was her first choice because it was right in Memphis. When they turned her down she waited a year and tried again, requesting Brushy Mountain, DeBerry Correctional, Fort Pillow, any one of those, even the Tennessee Prison for Women in Nashville would have been better than nothing. "And you don't think there wasn't some kind of conspiracy to keep me out?"

Armand never said there was. He was waiting for that Swanson's chicken pie to hurry up and get done.

Donna told him the memory of Elvis was like a giant magnet drawing her to Memphis, that if she lived there she'd visit Graceland every day, the way people visit a church and light candles to get their burdens lifted or find a boyfriend. She'd do it knowing peace of mind didn't come cheap. "But you don't think it wouldn't be worth the seven bucks' admission to have some in my life for a change, after what it's been?"

Armand said, "I believe you," because he could see she believed it herself. She had a look in her strange eyes behind those glasses, like she was drugged or had been hit over the head.

Donna served him the chicken pie, left the kitchen and returned with a stack of color photos taken at Graceland Mansion. She had bought the prints off a girlfriend of hers for two bucks each and kept them in that velvety box a fifth of Amaretto comes in. Armand, mopping up chicken gravy with slices of bread he'd fold over, could look at the pictures as Donna held them up but not touch them.

"This is Elvis Presley Boulevard on a rainy day. This is the Heartbreak Hotel Restaurant, it's not too far. I hear him sing that, I get goose bumps head to toe. I mean still. Okay, this is his famous pink Caddy. This is his lavish jetliner, the *Lisa Marie*. This is inside it. . . . No, this is inside his tour bus. Elvis would bring some of his closer friends along on tours. They'd play cards, Yahtzee, listen to music. They'd cook right in there."

"What's the name of it?" Armand said, wanting to show he was interested.

"The tour bus? It don't have a name. This is the front room of Graceland. That couch seats four-teen people."

"How come his airplane has a name but not his tour bus?"

"If people knew he was in that bus, like if there was anything on it to identify him? There'd be a riot every time it stopped."

"He could've called it some other girl's name, like the jetliner."

"Bird, that isn't just some old girl's name. Lisa Marie's his daughter. Her and I have the same birthday."

"Yeah, is that right?"

"I'll tell you something else," Donna said. "My life number is eight."

"What's that mean, your life number?"

"You add up your date of birth, like February is the second month, that's two. I was born on the first, two and one is three, then nineteen, one and nine is ten, so that's like one. You add that to the three you got from February first, then add up the next numbers—I'm not gonna tell you the year— and it comes to eight."

"Is that right?"

"Okay, now add up 3797 Elvis Presley Boulevard, P. O. Box 16508, Memphis, Tennessee, 38186, and you know what it comes to?"

"Eight," Armand said.

"And you wonder why I'm drawn to there?" Donna said. "Think about it. Okay, this is some of his personal jewelry, his gold Rolex watch, his Maltese cross and solid-gold I. D. bracelet. Here's his famous American Eagle jumpsuit . . ."

"His famous queer outfit," Richie said, coming into the kitchen. "Jesus Christ, Bird, you eating again? I'd take the Rolex and the pink Caddy, the guy did have a certain amount of class." Richie was getting a bottle of beer from the refrigerator now. "But that fucking jumpsuit . . . Would you wear it, Bird? You'd have to get the one he wore after he swole up like a pig."

"You're jealous," Donna said. "You can't look at these without making remarks."

"Jealous of what? You know what the difference is between me and him?"

"Yeah, you're ignorant," Donna said.

"I'm alive and he's dead and that's the only thing counts."

You're alive, Armand thought, watching Richie take a swig of beer, his fist wrapped around the neck of the bottle. But you don't have to be. He noticed Richie was chewing gum with his beer.

"I got news for you," Donna was saying. "After you die, you think anybody's gonna visit your grave? Even if you had a mother I doubt she would. But a hundred years from now, even longer'n that, people will still be going to visit Graceland." She looked at Armand and nodded. "It's true."

"Is that right?" Armand said, feeling a little sorry for her.

Richie was grinning, chewing his gum and shaking his head. "Donna, you're so goddamn stupid. . . . Lemme ask you a question. Which would you rather have, Elvis sing to you or fuck you?" He looked at Armand and winked.

Armand stared back at him. He didn't think Richie was funny, now or anytime before. He watched Donna squinting at Richie, showing him she was being serious.

"I know what you think I'm gonna say," Donna said, "and you'd call me a liar. Well, I can't help that, 'cause it's true. I'd rather have him sing to me."

Armand believed her. He was surprised that Richie did too, Richie looking at him saying, "You know why, Bird? 'Cause he wasn't a con. Elvis wouldn't have been rough or smelly enough for Donna."

"I don't think of him that way," Donna said. "He was a kind, generous person who helped people out, gave them cars, whatever they needed. He believed people ought'n to suffer more than they don't have to. He read books—they say he was ever in search of the answers to life's mysteries."

"I heard he was in search of pussy," Richie said. "Had girls brought to him and he'd take his pick."

It might be true, Armand didn't know or care, but decided that was enough. He was tired of Richie. So when Richie looked at him, fun in his eyes, wanting to be appreciated, Armand said, "Leave her alone."

Richie said, "Who, Donna?"

Maybe a little surprised but still having fun, enjoying himself. Armand decided to push him. He said, "See if you can keep your mouth shut for a while," and the fun was over. He watched Richie's eyes become serious and then dull, sleepy, covering what he was feeling, no longer chewing his gum.

Wanting to hit me with that bottle, Armand thought. Smash it across my face. Now he gave Richie a frown, curious, not a bad look, and said, "What's the matter?"

Richie said, "You ever talk to me like that again . . ."

Armand said, "Yeah, what?" because he wanted to hear how this punk would say it.

"It'll be the last time you do."

Nothing original about that, the guy remained a punk.

They stared at each other, Armand wanting to tell him, Okay, now go watch your TV. But there would have to be more staring if he did and he was tired of it. So he didn't say anything and Richie walked out of the kitchen with his bottle of beer. For a few moments there was silence.

Donna cleared her throat.

"This is Elvis's billiard room," Donna said. "There seven hundred and fifty yards of material, all pleated, covering the walls and ceiling."

The next couple of days the Bird got her to make phone calls for them, seeing if they could locate the ironworker and his wife. Donna would say, "What on earth are you boys up to now?" acting innocent and cute for her age. The Bird wouldn't say anything, but Richie got a kick out of Donna's act and would give her a wink.

When she called the real estate company for them and asked about the house for sale, she was told it was no longer on the market. That was when the Bird finally said, "Let's go." But when they drove past the house—wearing their hunting outfits now, the Bird with that stupid cap on— there was the FOR SALE sign still in the front yard.

What was it doing there? Did they sell the house or not? What in the hell was going on here? The ironworker's car and the pickup were gone, but could he and the wife still be in the house?

Richie fired one question after another, but might just as well have been talking to the fucking steering wheel. The Bird either wouldn't answer or would grunt something like, "Unh," and Richie was supposed to know what that meant.

So he had steam building in him by the time they got the car hidden and approached the house roundabout through the woods, the Bird leading, tramping through dead leaves and making all kinds of noise for a guy who was supposed to be an Indian. An idea began to ease Richie's mind, that all he had to do was raise the barrel of his shotgun, squeeze the trigger and have something to tell his kids, if he ever had any, watching a cowboy movie, one of those good ones they used to have

where you'd see redskins blown off their pinto
ponies. "Yeah, I've done that. There was this time I
was out in the woods . . ." And stopped the picture
in his head realizing he'd already shot an Indian,
the duck guide. Weird, losing count—like he'd
thought of Kevin being his first when Kevin was
actually his third. Which would make the last one,
the duck guide, number seven. Right? . . . No,
there was the 7-Eleven girl with the greasy hair. If
she was Indian it would make the Blackbird his
third . . . Except if he was a half-breed . . . Shit, it
got too confusing. He'd be number nine. Let it go
at that. Richie wondered if smoking weed all his
life except for the past month or so had fucked up
his head. Then wondered if it made any difference.

When they stood at the edge of the woods about
a half hour staring at the house, the Indian playing
Indian, Richie was antsy as hell but didn't say a
word. Why argue? This partnership would end the
minute he couldn't take any more of it. Or the
ideal situation, gun down the Bird the same time
they did the ironworker and his wife and make it
look like they shot each other. That'd be neat,
work something like that out. Read about it in the
paper and see old Donna giving him her innocent
look. What on earth happened to Bird. And he'd
wink or else give her an innocent look back, it de-
pended. Then she'd want to fool with his hair, do

some goddamn thing. Take him out and buy him
some new clothes . . .

The Bird said, "You ready?"

Richie said, "I was born ready," feeling pretty
good about everything for a change.

They were a couple of hunters strolling out of
the woods, looking around, nothing important in
mind; went up on the side porch, looked around
again and became burglars. Let's see what we have
here. Richie's idea, punch out a pane of glass in the
door, reach in, nothing to it. But the Bird stopped
him, saying he didn't like that way, saying cops
would come by and see the door. So Richie went
around back and broke in through a bathroom
window, on the first floor but high up in this old
place and he had to climb a tree to reach the window. What was the Bird's game? Outside of making him do all the work as usual, worried about
leaving his fingerprints, the fucking Bird playing it
safe. As soon as Richie was inside he could feel nobody else was in the house. He went through to the
kitchen and opened the door.

"Well, hi there. Nice to see you."

The Bird came in, his face set beneath that dumb
hunting cap.

Richie left him again to make a quick appraisal
tour of the house, see if there was anything of
value lying around. What hit him right away, it

didn't look anything like a house the people had moved out of. All their furniture was here. There wasn't anything packed in boxes ready to go. Richie went upstairs. He found all kinds of men's and ladies' clothes hanging in the hall closets, a silver jacket with IRONWORKERS BUILD AMERICA written on it. He remembered the guy wearing a blue one, the same words on it, when he shot at him in the store. There were clothes in the two big dressers in their bedroom, shirts and things the guy had left, couple of good-looking sport shirts Richie thought he wouldn't mind having, hey, and a T-shirt from Henry's seafood restaurant, IT'S NICE TO BE NICE. Look at that. It seemed like just yesterday or the day before he was sitting there eyeing the Bird eating his pickerel. Was that what started this whole thing, seeing the Bird? It was weird how one thing could lead to another. You didn't have to plan your life, shit, just go with the flow. Richie went downstairs and stuck his head in the living room again before going out to the kitchen.

The Bird stood by a drawer pulled open, reading a letter.

"Shame on you," Richie said, "reading other people's mail." It was funny the way the Bird folded the letter right away and dropped it on the counter.

"They have a boy in the U. S. Navy."

"I know it, the duck guide told us." He saw the

Bird giving him the old Indian stare. "You don't remember it, do you? When we was in the boat. Then me and you got out and I put him away. You remember that part, don't you?"

The Bird didn't answer.

"Lemme ask you a harder one," Richie said. "How come if they moved they left their furniture?"

"They left in a hurry . . ."

"Didn't pack anything."

"Maybe the movers do that."

"The movers," Richie said. "They pack the clothes too? I don't think these people left *all* their clothes, but enough to make you wonder. Upstairs in their bedroom. The bed's made—they could come home and hop right in."

The Bird said, "Clothes, 'ey?"

That seemed to catch his interest.

"There's a TV in the living room we could use. Better'n the one at Donna's."

"You want to steal the TV," the Bird said, "lug it through the woods all the way to the car?"

"I was thinking, save us getting a hernia, we bring the car around and pick it up."

The Bird didn't like that, being shown how dumb he was. He turned to the drawer, pulled out a Detroit telephone directory and laid it on the counter.

"Look up Colson."

"Donna already tried that."

"Her book's old. Look in this one."

Still giving him orders. Yes *sir*. Telling him last night to keep his mouth shut. Richie opened the book and took his time flipping through pages. Donna had called about a dozen different Colsons; not one of them ever heard of a Wayne Colson. She called the ironworkers' local; they said try him at home, they didn't have him down as working anywhere. Richie found the listing of Colsons and counted them.

"Same ones exactly Donna called. If he's got relatives they're someplace else." Richie closed the book.

He watched the Bird going through mail these people had saved. Now he was looking through a note pad that had loose sheets folded and stuck in it. Something in there seemed to interest him and he took it over to the window by the sink to see the writing better.

Richie looked around. "They got the fridge turned off, nothing in it. That must've broke your heart." It didn't get a rise. Richie thought of something else.

"Bird?"

"What?"

"You gonna kill Donna?"

That got him to look up.

"Why?"

"I just wondered."

"You worried about her?"

"I told you, not as long as she trusts me."

"That don't make sense."

"You don't know her like I do. I'm her boy."

The Bird looked at the note pad for a moment, Richie waiting for him. The Bird looked up and said, "What does that make me, her man?"

"I don't know," Richie said. "I get what I want, I don't have to look at her Elvis pictures. I don't even have to listen to her if I don't want to."

Richie felt good, giving the Bird little jabs, playing with him. Then felt himself jump and said, "Jesus Christ!"

The phone was ringing.

Loud and close to them in that little kitchen on the wall behind the Bird, Richie seeing the Bird looking back at him. Richie jumped but the Bird didn't. He didn't move, not even his eyes under that dumb hunting cap, while the phone rang seven times before it stopped.

It seemed quieter than before.

The Bird said, " 'Ey, was that the phone?"

The son of a bitch, giving it back to him now because he had seen him jump. Richie thought fast and said, "Well, why in the hell didn't you answer it? You want to talk to somebody knows them— why didn't you pick up the goddamn phone?"

"Anybody that calls, if they don't know they're

gone," the Bird said, "they don't know where they went. That's why. But how about somebody that moves and they don't have the phone disconnected?"

"What've I been trying to tell you?" Richie said. "All the furniture, for Christ sake, the clothes upstairs."

The Bird wasn't listening to him. "They put that sign up, we suppose to think they moved. They didn't move, they coming back."

"You finally figured that out? Christ, look at all the stuff right here they left."

The Bird still wasn't listening, he was studying that note pad again, looking at some of the loose pages that had been stuck inside.

"There some phone numbers here they wrote down, but no names or anything."

"Then what good are they?"

"Like you look up a number and write it down. Or somebody gives you a number over the phone, it isn't in the book, so you make a note of it."

"Bird, they're coming back. We know that."

"I'm tired waiting."

"It can't be too long, all their stuff here."

"And I'm tired hearing you talk," the Bird said, not sounding mad or with any effort, the same way he had said last night to shut up. He turned to the wall phone with the note pad and began punching numbers. Each time he got an answer the Bird would listen and then push the button to disconnect, not saying a word.

After watching him do this a few times Richie had to ask him, "Who was that?"

"Plumbing and heating company."

After each call then Richie asked him who it was and the Bird told him, That was the Amoco station. That was a Chinese restaurant. That was a number no longer in service. That was a place does hair. Now the Bird was looking at a note, holding it up to the window. "Here's one that says 'New,' underlined three times and the number."

"You aren't doing nothing but wasting our time," Richie said. "We're gonna have to wait, that's all. You don't like it, go back to Canada. I don't give a shit."

The Bird was holding up his hand, listening to a phone ring, then shaking his head, about to hang up the receiver, when a woman's voice came on even Richie could hear, ten feet away.

"Who is this?"

"Yeah, I'm looking for Wayne Colson," the Bird said.

There was a pause.

"He isn't here."

Both Richie and the Bird straightened and didn't move.

"You know where he is?"

"Who gave you my number?"

Richie could hear her voice clearly. She sounded like a mean old broad. The Bird was already stumbling, not knowing how to talk to women of any age, telling her, "I have it written down here." Yeah, where? What did she care it was written down someplace. The Bird telling her, "See, I'm looking for Wayne Colson." Dumb fucking Indian. Richie walked over holding out his hand. The Bird let him take the phone, no problem, relieved.

The woman was saying, "Who *is* this?"

"Ma'am? Excuse me," Richie said, getting a little smile on his face. "That was a fella works here was just on I asked to call you. See, we been trying to get hold of Wayne. . . . He gave us this number before he left—"

"He gave you *my* number?"

"Well, actually he gave it to the boss and the boss gave it to me, only he's not here now. He said you'd know where he was, Wayne."

"I don't understand this at all."

She sounded like an older woman. Richie took a shot and said, "Ma'am, you aren't by any chance Wayne's mom, are you?"

"No, I'm not." The woman hesitated. "I'm Carmen's mother. But I don't know where they are, outside of she said they were driving to Florida."

"Yeah, that's right. Wayne said something about going down there. You don't happen to have a number where I can reach him, do you?"

There was a silence on the line. Richie looked at the Bird's serious face, waiting.

"See, I have this check I want to send him."

"Oh, you're from work?"

"Yes, ma'am. I guess he was in a hurry to take off." Richie paused to see if that would get him anything. It didn't, so he said, "The boss told me, see, if I could get this check to him. I imagine him and your daughter would like to have it, down in Florida on a vacation."

Richie and the Bird waited, staring at each other.

"You don't have an address, huh?"

"No, she hasn't given it to me."

"I was thinking, if you've talked to them . . ."

He waited and there was a silence. He waited a little more and said, "Hey, I got an idea. How about if you give me your address? I can mail you the check or drop it off. See, then when you find out where they're at *you* can send it." Richie paused again, giving her a little time. "I know if it was my check I'd want to have it."

Carmen's mom said, "Well, I guess that would be all right. I live on Gratiot Beach, if you know where that is. You have a pencil?"

16

CARMEN HAD LOCKED the bathroom door. She stood under the shower facing the spray, eyes closed, trying not to think. She had read somewhere that enlightenment through meditation only worked if you could clear your mind of pictures and things swarming around in it and concentrate on nothing. Which seemed impossible to do, things just *came*. So she tried concentrating on the water, feeling it, saying to herself, "Mmmmmmmm," and thought of Jack Nicholson about to take a shower telling the black guy who worked in the hotel there wasn't any soap and the black guy saying yes, or that was true.

It was the Jack Nicholson movie that starts out in North Africa, in the hotel in a desert village, bugs on the wall, where Nicholson switches identities with the man in the next room who dies of a heart attack. Carmen remembered the name of the movie now, it was *The Passenger*. Nicholson, what he's doing in the movie, is running away from his own life. He steps into the dead man's life and lets it take him on a trip to different places, England, Germany, Spain, where he meets the girl in Barcelona and it's fascinating, sort of dreamlike, not knowing what's going to happen next, Carmen thinking that if it's fascinating to watch it would be fascinating to do it, become someone else, at least for a while. But something funny is happening in this movie. Nicholson remembers seeing the girl in London, before, yet doesn't think it's strange when she shows up in Barcelona. He doesn't even mention it till much later. He knows, with his new identity, he's in a dangerous business and there are men after him. But he doesn't seem to care, he's only concerned with escaping his past. So he lets his new life happen. He lets it carry him along as a passenger to the end and the end is fascinating. At least it was fascinating to watch, the way it was filmed, not like any other movie Carmen had ever seen, it was so real in a way that she could *feel* what was happening without actually seeing it. Even now she could feel sorry for Nicholson. Poor guy, a passenger all the way. Not knowing when to get off.

Carmen put on a terry-cloth robe and patiently wrapped ten electric curlers in her hair, head down, eyes raised, staring at herself in the mirror, thinking that if she were Jack Nicholson she would have gotten out of there somehow, run like hell or

explained who she was. The whole thing a big mis-
understanding. Go back to the other life and face
it, work it out. Nicholson's wife seemed okay, she
did look for him. But even if she hadn't and even if
bad guys weren't after you and you were free to go
anywhere you wanted, how long could you hang
out in Barcelona or drive around Spain in that convertible? . . . Or past real estate offices in Cape Girardeau, Missouri, in her Cutlass or walk through
West Park Mall. It was okay, it was a very nice
mall as malls go, nice people, though no one had
stopped her to say she looked like a person they
would like to know. Come home and look out the
windows hoping a cream-colored Plymouth didn't
turn into the drive. Fix supper, wait for Wayne to
walk in full of his new job and listen to him speak
in a new language as he turned from ironworker to
riverman, amazed to hear it. No more spud
wrenches and beaters. Now it was cowtails and
hula hoops, chain slings, ratchets, the jewelry they
used to tie barges up for a tow—three wide and
five long on the Upper Miss on account of they
have to pass through locks. But did she know what
the record was on the Lower Miss? No, what?
Seventy-two barges, a world-record tow the *Miss
Kae-D* hauled from Mile 304 near Baton Rouge to
Hickman, Kentucky, in May of '81. A fleet more
than a quarter of a mile long, with a load capacity
of 113,400 net tons. How did he remember that?

Moved by rail it would've taken 1,152 boxcars, a freight train 13 miles long. By truck, shit, it would've taken 4,300 18-wheelers in a convoy, legally spaced, that would stretch 173 miles on the interstate. He remembered it because he was a man who could look up at a high-rise he'd helped build and tell you how many tons of structural steel were inside its skin. He was reading a book on Mississippi River navigation and the Rules of the Road, showing her maps. Did she know the Mississippi started way up here by Minneapolis–St. Paul? Yeah, she knew that. It was called the Upper Miss down to Cairo, Illinois, where the Ohio came in, and the Lower Miss down to New Orleans. He told her, by the way, the *Miss Kae-D* was a triple-screw tow, same as the *Robert R. Nally* that had run aground on the Backbone, up by Mile 94, that tow he was working on and wouldn't mind going out in sometime, take a little cruise on her. Carmen asked him how come if it was a *her*, it was named the *Robert R. Nally*?

She walked out of the bathroom in her robe and curlers, glanced down the hall and stopped dead.

A man she had never seen before was standing near the doorway to the kitchen. It was his yellow sport coat that stopped her, made her look and held her rigid. She saw the yellow coat—the man in it beefy, with short legs and arms. She saw his arms raise, saw the palms of his hands extended toward her.

He said, "Take it easy, okay? I'm not gonna hurt you." As if to reassure her, keep her from screaming or running out of the house. "I rang the bell— listen, I didn't mean to walk in on you like this, I'm sorry."

"I'm getting used to it," Carmen said, more irritated than afraid, even though she was fairly certain this guy must be the previous tenant, the Mafia witness from somewhere in the East, New Jersey. He was in his upper fifties, about five-seven, with a little gigolo mustache and hair that was too dark and thick, too perfect, to be his own. Carmen was good at spotting rugs.

So this was what a loan shark looked like.

"You're Mr. Molina, aren't you?"

His expression changed just a little.

"Yeah, I used to live here."

"Well, you don't anymore. What do you want?"

It startled him; he seemed more surprised now than when she said his name.

"I stopped by—my wife thinks maybe she left one of her rings here she can't find."

Carmen said, "You want to search my house?"

"No, it's okay. I won't disturb you."

"I'll tell you something, I cleaned this place from top to bottom and didn't find anything but dirt."

She was at ease, confident, standing up to this guy. Then began to lose it—Oh, my God—as she nodded toward the spare bedroom and felt the curlers in her hair and felt Mr. Molina staring at them.

"Unless it might be in there. I didn't touch those boxes."

"No, that's nothing, some junk. Old clothes I was gonna throw away or give to somebody. Listen, I'm sorry the way the place was."

Carmen looked at him again. He did seem sorry.

"My wife was already gone and when I left . . . Well, I left, that's all. I decided and that was it."

"How long did you live here?"

"Almost five years."

"That seems like a long time."

"You kidding? It was five years too long, if you know what I'm talking about, the kind of situation I'm in. I think you do, since you know my name, probably where I'm from, my life history." He came toward her taking cautious steps, as if testing the floor.

Carmen didn't move. She could tell now, absolutely, he was wearing a rug, a good one, a style popular with a number of movie stars, but still a rug. She decided if he didn't feel funny wearing it there was no reason to be self-conscious about her curlers. She was even beginning to feel comfortable with this man.

When he said, "It was that deputy marshal that told you, uh? That kid Britton?"

Carmen said, "We call him Ferris, so we won't think of him as a parole officer," and saw the man's expression change, his eyes open with obvious surprise. Carmen put out her hand. "Mr. Molina, we're both in the same club."

The last time they drove up the river to Port Huron they crossed the Blue Water Bridge to Sarnia and got Richie's chin stitched up at the hospital and Armand had waited in the blue Cadillac to think of what they would do next. When was that, last year? It seemed like it. This time they came to visit the ironworker's mother-in-law, and Armand was still thinking of what they would do next on this trip that didn't look like it would ever end.

They had stopped at Donna's house while she was off driving her school bus to change from the hunting outfits to regular clothes. Now Armand had on his suit and Richie, driving the car because he was the driver now, had on his nice-to-be-nice T-shirt under a silver jacket he had taken from the guy's closet. "Show the woman," Richie said, "look, I'm an ironworker and a really nice guy." The jacket was an old one, too big for him, but that was okay. The idea would be for Richie to do the talking, continue to play the company guy he was on the phone with her. He said, "You may as well wait in the car, Bird. It won't take both of us."

That was the punk talking.

Armand didn't like to hear it. There were things he wanted to tell Richie, to try to keep him under control, but didn't say anything about it driving along the river. If he told him too soon it would be in and out of the punk's head. So he let Richie play the radio and slap the steering wheel in time to the rock music until they had driven through Port Huron and now were catching glimpses of Lake Huron, gray and overcast, between the homes spaced along the shore. Armand turned off the radio and said, "Let's think about what the woman knows and what she doesn't."

It got a mean look from the punk.

"That's what I'm gonna find out. Get her to tell what *we* want to know."

"Yeah, but first of all, I don't think she knows where they are."

"You mean she says she don't."

"No, what I mean—yeah, she could know where they are, like they're in Florida, but not know their address for some reason, like they're not gonna be in one place too long, so she don't need it to write them letters or anything. See, when she wouldn't say nothing to you, that was when she knew something but didn't want to tell you. Like when you asked did she have their phone number. She didn't answer. But when you asked her if she had their address, she said no, she didn't."

"She could be lying, couldn't she?"

"I don't think so. She didn't expect that phone call, anybody asking about them, so the woman didn't have any lies ready. When she didn't want to tell you something, she didn't say nothing, she kept quiet. You understand what I mean?"

"Hey, Bird, I don't give a fuck what she said or didn't. If she knows where they are I'm gonna find it out. That's what we're here for."

This guy continued to be a punk and would never change.

"That's what we want to do," Armand said, "but when you talk to her you got to be cool, 'ey? Like when you talk to her on the phone. See, what I'm thinking, if she'll tell us their phone number, then we can find out from it where they are. Call the operator and say where is this anyway, this number?"

"*If* she'll tell me?" Richie said. "She's gonna be dying to tell me."

"Yeah, but you have to take it easy," Armand said, wanting to punch this guy in the mouth as hard as he could. "You don't want to get rough with her."

Richie said, "I don't?" slowing down and hunching over the wheel. They were getting close now, the road lined with a wall of wooden garages and fences, one after another on deep, narrow lots along here. Richie was looking at the house numbers that were nailed over the garage doors or painted on. Some of the places bore names, "Lazy Daze," "E-Z Rest" . . .

"No, we want to keep her friendly," Armand said. "Maybe she can't tell us something today, but then she finds out tomorrow they gonna be someplace for a few days, yeah, we can send the check there. See, you get rough then we can't use her no more, she calls the cops. What's this? All this time they think we took off, we're gone. Oh, those guys are still around, 'ey? They put up roadblocks and we can't go nowhere, we can't fucking move or we get caught and you go back to prison. You don't want nothing like that, do you? . . . Hey, you hear what I'm saying?"

"There it is," Richie said. The house number was painted on the gate in the board fence. He pulled up close to it and opened his door. "You don't want to come watch? Or you don't want her seeing what you look like? Shit, I know your game."

"Remember that it's nice to be nice," Armand said.

He got a look at the house, a quick one—three stories counting the windows in the attic, narrow, straight up and down, white frame with green trim—as Richie went through the gate and it swung closed again.

Armand sat back thinking, You let him go in there with a gun.

So what difference does it make he has a gun or he doesn't have a gun, a guy like that?

So you don't care, do you?

He thought some more and decided, yeah, but not much. He had come this far, now he was along for the ride.

Carmen and Mr. Molina were in the living room, facing each other from opposite ends of the white sofa: Carmen dressed in a shirt and jeans, curlers gone from her hair, Molina smoking cigarettes, stubbing another one into the ashtray on the coffee table.

"All this stuff I was dealing in," Molina said, "the bonds, the stock certificates, were either stolen or counterfeit. I was the middleman, you might say. I'd go up to Toronto every couple months and lay it off on the family there. They knew what it was, they were only using it as collateral, buying up property downtown. So I got to know those people. What was the guy's name again?"

"Armand Degas," Carmen said.

"No, I never heard that name. He could be connected, but I can tell you he's not family. This's going back, what I'm talking about, eight nine years. He could've come along since then. I still can't see an Indian in any kind of position with those guys."

"He kills people," Carmen said.

"Yeah, well, whatever he was doing in Algonac, Michigan, doesn't sound to me like a family operation. I was in a different position, one phone call I could find out for you, but from what you told me"—Molina shook his head—"they're not gonna go after a real estate company for any ten grand. They'd want a piece of it, steady income off the top. Same way it happened to me. I'm in the printing business, it's slow, my accounts receivable are fulla deadbeats, like I owe a paper house fifteen hundred past due a hundred and twenty days. So I borrow it from a shylock. By the end of the year— listen to this—I've paid them twenty-seven thousand and they're into my business. I can run off phony bonds or end up in the Susquehanna, that's my choice."

He paused to light a cigarette and Carmen stared at his hairpiece, its abrupt line across his forehead, the part, the wave in front, permanently combed.

"Ferris told us you were a loan shark, from New Jersey."

"Ferris doesn't have the right state even," Molina said. "I don't know how he got out of school, if he ever went. Seven years I've been in the government witness program. Started out, went to Washington, D.C., for orientation. I've met I don't know how many U.S. marshals and every one of them was a decent guy except this asshole. There was one other one wasn't too bright I can tell you about. But this guy Ferris, he comes on like he's running for office—am I right? Next thing you know he turns into a fucking Nazi. I'm sorry, but there's no other way to say it. Listen, at the time my wife had enough of this and left, I went back to Scranton for a week, talked to the FBI and the marshal there, the people that got me into this. They took me before a Senate committee and I told them my experiences as a protected witness."

Carmen said, "You've been in it seven years?"

"That's right, but it isn't just the time spent. My first wife I was married to for twenty-six years divorced me. I haven't seen my kids—I got three grandchildren I probably won't ever see."

"So you didn't start out here."

"No, the first place I was relocated . . . Remember them telling you they're gonna, quote, provide suitable documents to enable the person to establish a new identity?"

Carmen nodded. "I remember, but we didn't change our names."

"I had to," Molina said. "And you know how long it took to get suitable documents? Four months for a driver's license. Almost a year for a social security card. I still don't have a birth certificate. Try and get credit when you don't have a history. Try and get any kind of a job on your own. The kid marshal takes me out to Procter and Gamble, they put me on the Pampers line. I'm fifty-nine years old with this white smock on making diapers. You know how long I lasted? I tell all this to the Senate Committee on Governmental Affairs. They're sympathetic, up to a point. The chairman says, 'Well, our survey shows that seventy-three percent of the people in the program want to stay in it.' I said to him, of course, they want to stay in. You leave it, you're dead. I could've done ten at Allenwood instead of this shit and I'd be out by now, good behavior."

"You didn't like the first place they sent you," Carmen said, "so you left? Can you do that?"

"The only thing that was good about it, I met my present wife, Roseanne. If we get along half the time it's better than nothing. But that's when they were bringing me back to Scranton to testify and the marshal—this's the other one that wasn't too bright—puts me on a direct flight." Molina paused. "You understand what I'm saying? You land at Avoca, the airport there, anybody watching for you knows where you came from. That's not bad enough, we're leaving the courtroom after the trial, people all around, the guy, the marshal, tells another marshal where we're going. I mean he says it right out loud, anybody could've heard it. There people still in the courtroom, friends of the guy I just got done testifying against. I said to the marshal, 'You crazy? I'm not going back there.' They had to drag me on the plane. But then I bitched enough after that . . ." Molina paused, his head raised. "You hear a car door slam?"

"It could be Wayne," Carmen said. She watched Molina stub out his cigarette and get up.

Walking over to the window he said, "I've been doing this for nine years. I hear something, I jump."

"Is it a light-tan pickup?"

The man didn't answer and Carmen started to get up.

By the time he said, "I hate to tell you this, it's that fucking Nazi . . ."

Carmen was out of the sofa. "We won't let him in. I'll put the chain on."

"Don't," Molina said. "I did that one time, he busted the door."

Carmen's mother's home had a sun porch across the front with a wide-open view of Lake Huron, gray as the sky, nothing to see. Richie stood there, giving the woman a look at his ironworkers-build-America jacket before turning to the living room again: dark in here, full of old furniture and pictures of birds all over the dark-paneled walls, color prints of birds and some that looked like a little kid had drawn them with crayons. Richie figured there were about thirty bird pictures in here, all different sizes and all framed. It was warm in here, too. He could hear a radiator hissing steam.

Richie said, "You like birds, huh? I notice you have feeders out'n the yard."

"I've always loved birds," Lenore said. "My mother named me from a poem about a bird. I guess I just love nature." She gave a girlish shrug, but then looked at him hard through her glasses and said, "Don't you?"

Like she was testing him. Richie felt he'd better say yes if they were going to get along. He said, "You bet. I even have a friend named Bird," and gave the woman a smile, though loving nature made no sense to him. What was there to love about it? Nature was just *there*, outside, wherever there wasn't something else.

Lenore gestured toward the crayon drawings and said, "Matthew did those when he was little. I've kept them."

Like he was supposed to know who Matthew was. "They're nice," Richie said.

"He's in the United States Navy, aboard an aircraft carrier."

Richie nodded along, wondering about a kid

who liked to draw birds and ended up joining the navy, the kid sounding like a fucking re-tard. So it caught him by surprise when the woman said:

"What job are you working on?"

"Oh, well, we been on different ones."

He'd better be careful, stay alert.

This woman's eyes reminded him of Donna's the way they seemed magnified by her glasses, her eyes hard and dark in silver frames. She was all red and grayish, red lips and rouge on her cheeks and grayish-blond hair to the shoulders of her flowery blouse. Another one trying to look girlish, but in a different way than Donna worked it. This one was a lot older and heavier, more like a foster mom he'd had named Jackie, who worked hard with six of her own kids in the house and was always sweating. Had little beads of perspiration on her upper lip like this one. Jackie could look you in the eye and tell if you were lying.

"I was wondering if you might be working on that Cobo Hall expansion."

This woman seemed to know the business.

"As a matter of fact we were," Richie said, hoping she wasn't setting him up, trying to trip him. She didn't appear suspicious. He'd still better cut the chitchat before he got in trouble. It was funny how he had the feeling of being back in a foster home.

"Anyway, what I started to tell you, I don't see

what difference it makes who mails the check, you or us. But the boss says we have to do it. I guess since it's up to the company. You understand it's not the boss doesn't trust you. I told him you were a nice lady to offer in the first place."

"And I told you," Lenore said, "I don't have their address. She never gave it to me. The only thing I have's their phone number."

Richie felt an urge to slap this old woman across the face and tell her to, goddammit, wake up. Why didn't she say so on the phone and save them a trip? He had to wait till he could act natural and sound surprised before saying to her, "You didn't mention that, did you, you have their number?"

"Not on the phone I didn't," Lenore said. "I wasn't absolutely positive whom I was speaking to. I've had some problems with the wrong kind of people calling me, if you know what I mean."

"I understand," Richie said, forgiving the woman now that it seemed so easy. "You can't be too careful."

"Anything the least bit suspicious I report to the Annoyance Call Bureau. That's what they're for."

"I don't blame you," Richie said, not knowing what she was talking about, but wanting to get this deal moving. "Well, I don't see any problem now. You know we're like family. Ironworkers build America and they look out for each other. Let's call and get that address so we can send Wayne his check."

"Ironworkers drink more than anybody in America, too," Lenore said. "You give him that check, you know where he'll cash it, don't you? The nearest bar."

"You're saying Wayne drinks?"

"You know an ironworker doesn't?"

"I barely touch it myself," Richie said, thinking, Wait a minute. Jesus, is that all . . . And said it, "Is that all you're worried about, he'll spend it on liquor?"

"The way I look at it," Lenore said, "if he doesn't have extra money to spend, he won't be tempted beyond what little willpower he might have. I don't see why I should make my little girl's life any harder than it is, with all she has to put up with."

Man, here was a woman who could ruin your life knowing what was best for you.

Richie felt himself on the verge of causing her pain. Ask her to tell him the number. If she wouldn't, bend her old-woman arm behind her back till she did. Or grab a handful of that skin hanging from her throat and give it a twist. He wouldn't hit her. He had never hit a woman with his fist. Well, maybe once or twice. He'd punched Laurie that time, trying to find out if Kevin had been fucking her; but that was different, they were married. He was thinking of what he might do here, like start tearing her clothes off . . .

When Lenore said, "There's only one way I'd consider making the call."

It stopped Richie, just as he saw himself about to rip open her flowery blouse.

"And that's if I leave it up to Carmen. If she says send the check, she can use it, then all right, it's okay with me. But I won't tell Wayne about it if he answers and I won't let you talk to him, either."

"That's fine with me," Richie said, experiencing a relief and then a tender feeling as they went to the phone sitting on a table and the woman bent over to look in her address book. Richie laid his hand on the warm, moist material covering her back and gave it a few gentle pats.

Lenore said, "Have you ever had back trouble? Mine is just killing me."

Richie moved his hand down her old-woman spine, exploring. "Where? Right there?"

Ferris stood in the doorway to the hall: hands on his hips, no sport coat today, wearing a white shirt with the three top buttons undone, the short sleeves turned up to show more arm and muscle, and a big revolver snubbed high on his right hip.

The pose, Carmen thought. Saying, Look at me, Ferris Britton, Deputy Marshal. Dumb enough to be a TV star, he had the hair, the build, the fake boyish grin. . . . The only trouble was he was real.

"I rang the bell."

Carmen waited.

"You heard it, didn't you? You can't say I just walked in on you."

"What do you call it?" Carmen said. "I didn't notice anybody opened the door for you." She stood between the window and the sofa only half-turned to him, arms folded in her own kind of pose.

"I bet you even saw me drive up. Ernie, you heard me ring the bell, didn't you?"

Molina, seated again, said, "Yeah, I heard it."

"Then why didn't you come to the door?"

"I don't live here no more."

"I guess that's true enough, Ernie, but you could've answered the door, couldn't you?"

Ferris serious was annoying as Ferris grinning. "The reason we didn't open the door," Carmen said, "was because we didn't want you to come in. It's that simple."

"Why not?"

"Jesus, what difference does it make? Just leave, okay? Take your shoulders and your wavy hair and *leave*, will you, please?"

Ferris raised one hand to his head, frowning. "My *hair?* Man, I'd like to know what is going *on* here. I already got a bone to pick with you, lady, calling De-troit on me. I like to got in trouble. I said, well, why didn't somebody tell me the guy wasn't up on charges?" Ferris looked at Molina. "Her old man. You ever hear of a government witness wasn't dirty? I haven't."

The phone rang in the kitchen, the sound coming from behind him. Ferris held up his hand.

"I got it—don't nobody move. It's prob'ly for me." The phone rang again. "If it isn't, I bet it's a wrong number." The phone rang again. "How much you want to bet?" He waited for another ring before turning and crossing the hall to the kitchen.

Carmen started after him and Molina said, "Don't bother." She hesitated and came around slowly.

"It's *my* house."

"Yeah, and he walks in, he answers the phone. He'll look in the icebox, complain if you don't have fresh orange juice . . ."

They heard the phone ring again, once.

Carmen stood still, listening, then needed to move, do something, and looked at Molina, at his perfect hair as he brought out his cigarettes. He seemed at ease lighting one, used to having a U.S. marshal in the house, blowing the smoke out in a slow stream.

"You don't need this," Molina said.

"I *know* that, for God's sake."

"Take it easy. You got to stay cool, but you got to watch him, too. What I mean by you don't need this, you don't need government protection. So you got two guys looking for you—go someplace else, wherever you want, you don't have to stay here. Just don't tell nobody."

Carmen stepped around the coffee table and sat down thinking, Why not? Sell the pickup, get in the car and *go*. She said, "My husband has a job. He likes it here."

"So what? You don't. Tell him you've had enough of this shit, you want to leave. Go where you want, California, someplace out there. You know what the kid marshal wants, don't you? What he's gonna get around to before long," Molina's voice fading as he said, "if he hasn't already."

"Well, I was right," Ferris said, coming in from the hall. "Wrong number. They called twice. The second time—you hear me? I go, 'Hey, I just gone done telling you there's nobody here by that name.'" He came over to the coffee table. "So what're you talking about now?" Looking from Carmen to Molina. "Ernie, you telling stories about me? Man, I thought I was rid of you. Here you turn up again."

"Mr. Molina's wife left something," Carmen said. "He came to get it."

"Oh, that's right, it's Mr. Mo-*leen*-ah," Ferris

said, winking at Carmen. "I keep forgetting how important he is, big Mafia witness, and call him Ernie. Hey, Ernie? What'd Roseanne forget, her diaphragm?"

Carmen watched Molina. He didn't bother to answer.

Ferris moved around the end of the coffee table to get closer and look down at him.

"You and her back together?"

"Everything's fine."

"Gee, I'm surprised," Ferris said. "From the way she acted I thought, well, she either had enough of you or she wasn't getting enough *from* you, one." He looked at Carmen. "Roseanne liked company. Old Ernie'd go to work tending bar, Roseanne'd call me up. 'Hi, watcha doing? Why don't you come over and have a drink? Me and Bitsy are all alone here.' Her and that goddarn dog. You still have Bits, Ernie? Nobody's kicked her little teeth in?"

"We still have her, yeah."

Molina drew on his cigarette, blew the smoke out in a sigh and Ferris began waving his hand at it.

"Ernie, what're you doing?" Sounding disappointed, glancing at Carmen as he said, "I've been trying to get him to quit ever since I got assigned here. Ernie, you *know* what smoking does to you."

Carmen watched him take hold of Molina's

hairpiece, grab a handful and lift it from his head. Molina didn't move.

"It makes your hair fall out. This here," Ferris said, inspecting the rug closely, feeling it now, a small animal in his hand, "is from a lifetime of smoking."

Molina's eyes raised to Ferris for a moment, Carmen watching him. He looked at her then and seemed to shrug. Carmen pushed up from the sofa.

She heard Ferris say, "Where you going?" as she walked out of the living room, crossed the hall to the kitchen and could feel him behind her by the time she reached the table and picked up the phone. "Who you calling?"

"The police."

"Hey, come on. Who you think I am?"

"The biggest asshole I've ever met in my life," Carmen said, dialing the operator.

He reached past her and took hold of the cord. "I'll yank it right out of the wall."

Carmen put the phone down. She stood against the end of the breakfast table, her back to Ferris. She could smell his after-shave, feel his hands slide up on her shoulders.

"That's not nice, talking like that," Ferris said, his voice low, close to her. "You want me to wash your little mouth out with soap? I will, I'll wash

your little ears, too, and your little neck. I'll wash
any parts you want. How's that sound to you?"

"You're sure," Richie said, "you didn't dial it
wrong."

"I was a telephone operator twenty-five years. I
don't dial wrong numbers."

"And you're positive when you wrote it
down—"

"Listen to me, will you? I know numbers. I hear
a seven-digit number it registers in my head till I
jot it down. And there it is, right there."

He looked past her shoulder where she was bent
over the desk, hands flat on the surface, staring at
the number.

She'd said they were in Missouri someplace. St.
Louis? No, that wasn't it. Richie said he'd never
been to Missouri. He'd been to East St. Louis, but
that was over in Illinois. East St. Louis, shit, you
had to stand in line to commit a crime, but didn't
tell her that.

This woman was pretty smart. She knew something was wrong and even said it, though more to
herself than to him. "There's something wrong
somewhere."

"You mentioned you had trouble with your
phone."

"I had trouble with callers, not the instrument. I told you, I referred the matter to the Annoyance Call Bureau and they put a trap on my line."

"They listen in?"

"No, a trap records what number is calling this number. That's how you catch obscene callers."

"You had any?"

"Yes, I did, I'm sorry to say."

"What'd he do, talk dirty to you?"

"I would never ever in my life repeat one word of what that man said."

"You have to wonder about people like that," Richie said, "what gets in their head and makes them become perverts. Here, let me help you." Lenore was groaning as she tried to straighten up from the desk. Richie got under one of her arms and lifted.

"I should never bend over that far from the waist," Lenore said. "It's like somebody stuck a knife in me."

"That's your sacroiliac. I mentioned I could give you a back rub. I learned how from a foster mom I had one time named Jackie. She was some kind of therapist before that, worked with cripples. Let's get you on the couch. . . . No, let's get you down right here on the floor, over here on the carpet. I'll get a pillow for your head, so you'll be comfortable."

Lenore eased down to her hands and knees on

the living-room floor. Now she looked up at Richie taking off his ironworker's jacket.

"You sure you know what you're doing?"

"Yes, ma'am."

"You aren't gonna hurt me, are you?"

17

CARMEN OPENED HER EYES to see the lamp turned on, Wayne kneeling next to the bed looking at her, waiting.

"You awake?"

"I am now. What time is it?"

"Quarter after two."

"You must've closed the bar."

"We barely made last call. I've been working since I left here this morning till just a while ago. Had supper on the towboat, it wasn't bad either."

Carmen could smell the strong soap Wayne used. She stared at his face, for a moment wanting to touch it, the tough weathered skin shiny clean but drawn. He looked worn out.

"Why didn't you call?"

"I tried to. I forgot the number and the operator wouldn't tell me 'cause it's unlisted. I said, it's *my* house. Didn't do any good."

"I called the drydock when you didn't come

home," Carmen said. "Whoever it was said you hadn't been there all day."

"The foreman knew where I was." Wayne smiled. "That's why we sound a little cool, huh? I'll show you my coveralls, you'll see I wasn't out chasing women. You know where I was? On the *Curtis Moore*, the harbor tug. We brought some barges up from Westlake, putting together a tow. They're gonna leave first thing in the morning, like in four hours. That boat I helped repair."

"Your new life," Carmen said.

"Well, I'm looking it over. You get out there, talk to guys who've been on the river a while, they wouldn't think of doing anything else."

"Maybe it's all they know."

"It's more than that. I think the river gets to you."

Carmen rolled her eyes at him.

"Well, it's what you said, it's a life, it's not just the river. It's places, it's . . . like they're talking about running the Lower Memphis bridge south-bound, how you come along Interstate-Forty, stay close to Mud Island and point at the High-Rise Motel. Like you're driving along the highway, only you have a quarter of a mile of barges out in front of you."

Carmen said, "Not like walking on high steel."

"It's different, yeah, but you get the same kind

of feeling that, you know, you're doing something. It's not just a job where you get paid, you go home and put hamburgers on the grill and sit there thinking, Shit, I gotta go to work tomorrow."

"When did you put hamburgers on the grill?"

"You know what I mean."

"It's big stuff," Carmen said.

"That's right. It's not a building you can look at after, but you know you've done something."

"Like today?"

"Yeah, putting that tow together, getting ready . . ." He stopped and said, "What'd you do today?"

Remembering her. He did it sometimes when she least expected and it made her feel comfortable, nothing to worry about. She said, "You first."

"Well, this morning I'm on the drydock, a company boat arrives with a tow. They come down from Burlington, Iowa, with hopper barges loaded with grain they have to get to New Orleans by a certain day, a ship's waiting at the dock, so it's what they call a hot tow. But they also have eight coal barges they're supposed to drop off at Cairo, Illinois, a thousand ton of coal in each one, you talk about big stuff. But if they stop at Cairo they won't get to New Orleans on time . . . You listening?"

"A thousand tons of coal in each one."

"You feel all right? You look tired."

"I *am*. I just got to sleep before you came home."

"What were you doing?"

"Lying here *trying* to sleep . . . thinking."

"You want to leave, don't you?"

"Whenever you're ready."

"You know what I hear is a good place? St. Louis. A hundred and ten miles north of here. Burlington, where they picked up the grain, is another couple hundred miles. Anyway, they have to get to New Orleans, so they leave the eight coal barges here for the *Robert R. Nally*, the boat I worked on. It's repaired now, ready to go. We used the *Curtis Moore* to bring up eight barges of crushed rock from the quarry at Westlake and now we've got a sixteen-barge tow. What they'll do is drop the coal off at Cairo and haul the rock down to Louisiana to use as building revetments. See, the federal government won't let contractors use shell anymore, you know, seashells, to mix their concrete. So they use this crushed rock from up here."

Wayne paused and Carmen waited, knowing he wasn't finished. Finally she said, "Yeah . . . ?"

"They asked me if I want to go."

"Are you?"

"It's okay with the drydock foreman. I could get off just about anywhere I want and catch a northbound tow to come back."

"Is that river talk?"

"What?"

"Catch a tow?"

"I don't know—I'd only be gone a few days."

"Then why don't you go?"

"I'm thinking about it."

"Well, if they're leaving this morning . . ."

"In about four hours."

"You'd better get some sleep."

"I thought maybe I'd get in with you. It's been a while, and if I'm gonna be gone . . ."

"We made love last night," Carmen said. "You don't remember?"

Wayne stared at her thinking about it. He said, "Was that last night? Uh-unh, it was the night before, after you threw the beer can at me." He said, "Well, I can wait if you can." He gave her a kiss good-night, got in his own bed and said to her in the dark, "We could check it off on the calendar each time and keep score. The way your mom used to do it."

He thought that was funny. He'd say, well, it is. You take things too seriously.

Lying awake listening to him snore. Trying not to resent the way he could fall asleep almost at will.

She could say something that was really funny and he wouldn't get it, but she was the one who took things too seriously or was too sensitive. He'd say, if that's the word. Sensitive. He didn't trust it. When she used to have problems at work, someone in the real estate office stealing her leads, she'd be afraid to tell him. He'd say, well, you settle it or forget it, don't piss and moan. Now she had Ferris making the moves, touching her, telling her he'd be back, he'd look for her car in the drive and stop in when she was home, telling her he was a patient man and once she got to know him . . . But if she told Wayne she was afraid he would go after Ferris and get in trouble, threatening or assaulting a federal officer. Or was she afraid he might not and say she was imagining it? Why would the guy make the moves on a woman ten years older than he was? Seven years. All right, seven years. Good-looking guy, he wouldn't have any trouble getting girls. Wayne would say that being a moron had nothing to do with it. But being smarter didn't solve the problem either. Getting straight A's twenty years ago. If she mentioned Ferris tonight, Wayne might decide it was a problem to be settled now, not put off or forgotten, and he'd miss his boat ride. So maybe you're playing the martyr, Carmen thought.

And then thought of her mother. She'd better call her tomorrow.

That business about keeping score, marking a calendar each time you made love, was something her dad had told Wayne. Her mother never said a word about it. The way Wayne had told it to Carmen:

"Your dad says, 'You understand, all those years of marriage we're using the rhythm method of birth control. It gives you about a week a month when it's safe to do it. So it became known as Love Week with us and among some of our friends, all the micks. The problem was, the wife could hold it over your head. Say you're at a party and she wants to go home and you don't, you're having a good time. She whispers in your ear, "We go home right now, buddy, or you don't get any." You have to decide quick. You want to get smashed, have a good time? You do, you're gonna have to wait a month to get laid. This goes on for years of marriage. One night I'm not feeling so good, I'm constipated, sitting in the bathroom trying to get something going. Lenore says to me through the door, "If you want to have sexual intercourse"—that's what she called it, sexual intercourse—"you have to come right this minute." I sat there thinking about it and decided, that's it for Love Week. No more. I left the house the next morning and we got a divorce.' He tells me all this, I say, 'Yeah, but there's one thing you didn't mention. Did you have sexual intercourse that night?' And your dad says, 'Why not?'"

Maybe it was funny.

* * *

Wayne rolled out of bed saying, "Jesus, I'm late. I'll never make it."

"That clock's fast," Carmen said. She stood in her robe watching him. "The coffee's made. What else do you want, a sandwich?"

"Why didn't you wake me up?"

"I did, twice. I thought, well, if he wants to go he'll get up. If he doesn't, he won't. Isn't that the way you'd look at it?"

Less than ten minutes later he was in the kitchen, clean coveralls over his shoulder. Carmen sat at the breakfast table with toast and coffee, looking out at the backyard in a mist of rain.

"I can't find my goddamn keys. I bought new gloves, I can't find them either."

"The gloves are on the refrigerator."

"I know I didn't leave them in the pickup. I used my house key to come in." He stood looking about the kitchen saying, "Shit, I don't know where they are."

"I made you a meat-loaf sandwich," Carmen said. "Sit down, have some coffee."

"No, I gotta run. Listen, I'll have to take the Olds. You mind?"

"Didn't you park behind it, in the drive?"

"I can get around the pickup. I'm not worried about ruining that goddamn lawn."

"What if I have to go somewhere?"

"Well, the keys're here someplace, you'll find them, you're good at finding things." He came over to the table, picked up the sandwich, took a bite and gave Carmen a kiss. "I'll call you when we get to Cairo. It should be early this afternoon."

"I wish I knew what time," Carmen said.

"I think early, by two anyway."

Wayne walked out of the kitchen, was gone only a few moments and came back in.

"You have the keys for the Olds?"

Carmen was positive Ferris would stop by sometime today. She had made up her mind, the moment she saw that cream-colored Plymouth coming up Hillglade she'd call the Cape Girardeau Police, 555–6621, she had the number memorized. Or, she'd run out back and hide in the woods. The only problem was she had to find Wayne's keys and call her mother, and she didn't want to be down on the floor looking under the dresser or in the kitchen talking to her mom and hear Ferris walk in. Not again. It was not ever going to happen again. She could leave here, call her mom from the mall or somewhere once she found the goddamn keys. But it was hard to stop and think where they might be when she had to keep running into the living room to look out the window. She decided, finally, to make the call. Get it over with.

Carmen sat at the breakfast table, dialed the number, cleared her throat and waited. She listened to it ring several times, thinking, Come on, will you? She got up from the table with the phone and brought it across the kitchen as far as the cord would reach, the phone ringing several more times. From here she could look straight into the living room and see the big picture window and its view: the back end of a failed subdivision where cars seldom went by. She saw the road directly in front of the house and trees beyond in this morning's mist of rain. The phone continued to ring, Carmen listening, thinking, One more. But let it ring twice again, staring at the front window, and was startled to hear her mother saying, "Who *is* this?"

"Mom? It's me."

"Well, where are you?"

"The same place. Did I call at the wrong time?"

"I was lying down on the floor with my legs on a chair. It's the only way I can get any relief, if I lie perfectly still and not move."

"What's wrong, your back?"

"I had to *crawl* to the phone. My back has never been this bad in my entire life."

"I'm awfully sorry, really. Did you call yesterday?"

"I called twice. You gave me the wrong number. I've been in terrible pain ever since that man was here and gave me the back rub. Oh, my Lord, when I try to move. I have to crawl to the bathroom to go the toilet. I didn't sleep all night with the pain, I couldn't."

Carmen stared at the front window in the living room.

"What man? Who was it gave you the back rub?"

"From the company Wayne was working for, when you left. They want to send him his check."

"He picked it up," Carmen said. "I'm pretty sure."

Her mother groaned saying, "I've never felt pain like this. I imagine you can tell from my voice. It's just something terrible when I try to move."

"Mom, you let a man give you a back rub you don't even know. What's his name?"

"He seemed nice, he said he learned from a therapist how to do it. Now I can't walk, I can't dress myself or take a bath. I should've known better than to let an ironworker touch me. I'm *not* going to the hospital, the way they treat you. If I lie here on the floor and try not to move . . . It's so cold in the house, I'm gonna have to see if I can reach the thermostat and turn the heat up. But I raise my arms, it just about kills me."

"Mom, if I was home you know I'd come. I'm seven hundred miles away."

A car appeared in the front window. There for a moment creeping past the house. A light-colored car.

"How long would it take you?"

Carmen stared at the window, empty now.

"Not more than a day, would it? . . . Carmen?"

"I can't just drop everything and come. Wayne's off on a job."

"I don't *need* Wayne. You drove your car, didn't you?"

"There must be someone you can call, one of your friends."

"Like who? They work or baby-sit or have husbands they have to take care of. Doctors don't make house calls, they don't do you any good anyway. Sit and wait hours to see them, they give you a prescription . . ."

The car appeared again and Carmen was ready. A cream-colored Plymouth, Ferris's car, no doubt about it, creeping by, going the other way now. She couldn't see the driveway in the window. The car passed from view but might have turned in.

"They give you so-called pain pills that don't come near reaching the pain I have now. If you ever suffered from it you'd know what I mean. Well, I'm gonna *try* to get up those stairs and go to bed. I have that extra-firm mattress with a board under it . . ."

"Mom, I'll have to call you back."

"Not that it did me any good last night, and I can't *stay* up there, but I just don't know what else to do."

"Mom!"

"What?"

"Someone's here. I'll call you back, okay?"

"Who is it?"

Carmen said, "I'll call you as soon as I can," placed the phone on the floor and ran into the living room.

Wayne's pickup stood in the drive. There was no sign of a cream-colored Plymouth.

Carmen stood by the window knowing Ferris would be back, wanting to be ready but thinking about the keys for the pickup too, wanting to get out of here.

She had looked everywhere in the house Wayne might have dropped or left a ring holding a half dozen keys and a St. Christopher medal. She had looked in the pockets of his dirty coveralls, the pants and shirt he'd worn yesterday, on top the refrigerator, where his new work gloves were lying and he'd forgotten them, even inside the refrigerator and behind it. She pictured him entering the house last night, turning the light off in the kitchen, he might've gotten a beer but she didn't think so, coming in the bedroom then. She tried it again, pictured him entering the house and stopped, almost certain where the keys were.

She found them, the house key still in the side door, the rest of the keys hanging from the ring, the door open a few inches, like that since Wayne had run out of the house this morning.

Carmen changed her clothes, from jeans to a pair of good beige slacks. She stood in the bedroom in her cotton bra trying to decide what to wear on top, a blouse, a turtleneck, wanting to hurry, get dressed and get out of here. But couldn't make up her mind and ran into the living room in the bra and slacks and felt the hairs on the back of her neck stand up.

Ferris's Plymouth was coming up Hillglade Drive.

She watched it slow down, coasting, and creep past the house, its windshield wipers sweeping back and forth, side windows streaked with rain, a figure inside that had to be Ferris. The car disappeared up the road, past a stand of trees.

Carmen moved closer to the window and stood watching for several minutes, wondering why Ferris hadn't stopped. The only reason she could think of, he saw the pickup in the drive and thought Wayne was home.

It could be safer to stay than leave. She turned a chair to face the window and sat down. About ten minutes later the phone rang. Carmen remained in the chair.

By noon it had stopped raining.

At twelve-thirty the cream-colored Plymouth came up Hillglade Drive again and crept past the house. The car's side window was down and this time she saw Ferris behind the wheel, his face, sunglasses on, looking at the house.

Fifteen minutes later the phone rang. Carmen didn't answer it.

Ferris drove by again at one-thirty. Carmen was sure he was going to stop this time. The car seemed to pause at the driveway before continuing up the road. She waited for the phone to ring, but no sound came from the kitchen.

At two o'clock she changed back to her jeans, took off her bra, put on a tank top and a clean white Oxford-cloth shirt and returned to the window to watch and think some more, though she was almost certain now what she was going to do, tired of watching, tired of being here.

As dumb as Ferris was he could find out Wayne was off somewhere on a towboat. Or even if he thought Wayne was home he could ring the bell to find out, or he could walk in—why would he be

afraid of Wayne? And if she saw him coming up
Hillglade again, called the Cape Girardeau Police
and told them he was driving past the house . . .
Oh, is that right? They could find him *in* the house,
so what? It was his. They would have to catch him
ripping her clothes off . . .

Carmen went into the kitchen, stood at the
breakfast table, dialed a number and waited.

"Who *is* this?"

"Mom? I'm coming home."

"Well, it's about time. Are you watching Phil
Donahue?"

"No, I'm not." Carmen brought the phone
away from the table to stare through the living
room at the front window, bright sunlight outside.

"He's interviewing couples who live together
and engaged couples who say they aren't going to,
you know, have relations till they get married.
They show one of the girls real close and the word
virgin comes on the screen telling that's what she
is, a virgin, like she's some kind of rare bird. Can
you imagine? It's like they're saying, 'Look at this
virgin, everybody.' You didn't see it?"

"Mom, I'm leaving as soon as I hear from
Wayne."

18

THE CAPTAIN OF the *Robert R. Nally* said to Wayne up in the pilothouse, "Put your hand on your chest halfway between your neck and your belly button. Now look over there at your elbow. That's the kind of bend I'm coming to at Gray's Point and have to get around without stubbing my tow on a sandbar. If I do, this whole shebang will come apart on me and I won't look too good, will I?"

In the rain and mist, fog shutting them down as they approached the Thebes railroad bridge and the captain told Wayne Thebes was where the rivermen sued the railroad for building these obstructions, Abe Lincoln represented the railroad and the scudders won. Wayne said, well, you have to have bridges, don't you? "Nineteen and forty-eight," the captain said, "I was a deckhand on the *Natchez* when she hit the Greenville bridge and went down in ninety feet of water, twelve drowned. Abe Lincoln might've freed the slaves, but he didn't help rivermen none." The captain in his suit and tie stood there working his chrome-plated controls staring straight ahead, his three football fields of barges hidden in the mist. He had radar and two deckhands on the front of the tow with Handie-Talkies, but still couldn't run a bridge in fog, so an eight-hour trip was going to take about ten.

Wayne drank coffee with the captain in the pilothouse, with the chief engineer down in the racket of diesel engines, with the mate and the two off-duty deckhands at the long table in the lounge. Coffee with noon dinner and pie for dessert, the woman cook asking Wayne if he wanted her to a-la-mode that for him. The table reminded him at first of a steel-company trailer at noon hour, except here they talked about Cardinals and Cubs instead of Tigers and Jays and the deckhands were young guys, they were loud and laughed at stupid remarks.

The mate, on the river twenty years, sat hunched over his coffee, holding it on the table with two hands. When he stood up he was still hunched over, one of those skinny guys with high bony shoulders and slicked-back dark hair Wayne saw in cheap downtown bars after he came off the steel. The mate said the work suited him, he liked the thirty days on and thirty off. He was leaving the boat at Cairo to go visit his girlfriend in

Marysville, she was doing a stay at the Ohio Women's Reformatory. Wayne asked him if he wanted to be a pilot. The mate said he knew the river and the Rules of the Road backward, but the chickenshit government people wouldn't let him have a license on account of he only had one eye, this one here was glass. Once of the deckhands said the mate had as much chance of getting up to the pilothouse as growing hair on his tongue. The other deckhand thought that was pretty funny and the mate got up and walked out of the lounge. The deckhands told Wayne the mate had been fired and was being put ashore for getting caught drinking on the boat. It wasn't allowed, unless you went overboard and if you came up they might give you a shot.

They talked about barge lines they'd worked for, about captains and pilots that were pricks, about guys falling overboard, some popping up astern, some not and getting carried downstream to be found on a sandbar or lying cold on the riprap, the crushed rocks you saw along a revetment. It was slippery out on the barges from all the grease and shit, or you could trip on a ratchet, and if you went over at night you better have a flashlight on you. It sounded like they wanted him to understand this was no place for sissies. Wayne could have recited the book to them on falling from all kinds of places, buildings, bridges, factories, but didn't; or tell them his trade or where he was from and the deckhands didn't ask.

He began to think you had to start young in this river business. As in any other.

He was alert the first few hours of the trip, then felt it becoming tiresome. Even if you were working there wasn't that much to do when the boat was under way, and with all those barges it only went about eight or ten miles an hour. They'd be moving south making headway, flank around a bend and be going in the opposite direction for the next hour or so. There was nothing to see but mist and rain most of the trip and you had to wear a life preserver when you went on deck. When he tried to forget it on purpose, the mate caught him, asked Wayne if he thought he had special privileges. Once in a while that morning there'd be a glimpse of shore or an island. There's Counterfeit Rock. There's Burnham. Over there's Commerce, Missouri. The sky cleared by the time they got to Dogtooth Bend, a name to store away and tell Carmen. After that the points of interest were Greenleaf Bend, the I-57 highway bridge, Eliza's Point on the Illinois side, some more bridges and finally Cairo.

To the mate: "Is it a nice town?"

"What, Cairo? No, it ain't."

"I'm thinking of getting off with you."

"Do what you want," the mate said.

With the end of the trip in sight Wayne returned to the pilothouse. He could actually see a line where the two rivers met, the muddy Mississippi running past hard, the beautiful Ohio settling in a pool to keep out of its way. Rounding Cairo Point the captain said, "Now I'm gonna stick my head over into the Ohio, leave my stern in the Mississippi and just kinda flip her around, like the catch on an outhouse door."

"It's been a trip," Wayne said, "but if you don't mind, I'm getting off here."

"We have better days than this, when you can see the countryside. We have worse ones too."

Wayne said, "There's all that engine noise and vibration," and was surprised he thought that; ironworking was way noisier. "Or else I'm too old to learn a new trade."

"Ride down to New Orleans with me," the captain said. "That town will make you feel young again."

By the time they tied up at Waterfront Services, Wayne was out of his coveralls and had on his ironworker's jacket. He picked up his overnight bag and followed the mate carrying his suitcase across barges to get ashore. They walked past the floodwall and through a decaying area where bums hung out, sat in discarded chairs and car seats around a fire that became a cloud of smudge rising in the damp air. Wayne said it looked like more rain was coming. The mate didn't say or care. They walked a long block to the Skipper Lounge—Beer, Wine, Liquors & Pizza—that was maybe one notch above a skid-row bar. No cars in front, full of guys off boats.

They ordered bourbon and shells of beer, the mate looking around at the rivermen in here, nodding to some, Wayne looking at his watch. Ten to five. He'd have one and call his honey, tell her the good news, that he'd be home in the morning if not before. They tossed down the shots and ordered another one each.

"I have to see about a ride back," Wayne said. "I was told it can be arranged. Here or down at Waterfront Services."

The mate stood hunched, leaning on the bar. He looked past his shoulder at Wayne. "You had enough, huh?"

Wayne shrugged, sipped his beer.

"I could've told you."

Wayne watched him straighten to drink his shot.

"You could've told me what?"

"You weren't ever gonna cut it."

The mate looked at the bartender for another shot, pointing a finger at his glass. Wayne looked at his watch. It was still ten to five.

"How'd you know that?"

"What?"

"You don't think I can cut it."

"You remind me of these college boys come along in the summer, looking for a trip on the river. They last about two days. But that's longer'n you did—up there Mr. Big Shot in the pilothouse." The mate tossed off his bourbon and got back down on the bar before he said to Wayne, peeking past his shoulder at him, "What I wondered was if the captain let you suck him off."

Wayne's overnight bag was sitting on the bar. He pushed it aside and leaned on his arms to get down closer. "You don't know who I am, anything about me. Why would you say something like that?"

"Well, you're a queer, aren't you? Isn't that what queers do?"

Wayne studied the man's one-eyed face, his dumb mean expression, one of those nasty drunks Wayne could never understand, why booze turned them bitter, made them want to fight or tear up a place or drive their car into a tree. It had an opposite effect on Wayne, it made him feel warm and witty, able to abide even assholes and mime the tune "My Girl" the way the Temptations did it, with all the moves. But he wasn't drunk now or anywhere near to feeling good. He said to the mate, "Which one'd you tell me was your glass eye?"

It caused the mate to stare, hesitate, but only a moment. "You don't know shit, do you? Can't tell a towboat from a coal hopper, a real eye from one that ain't."

"The clear one," Wayne said, "that isn't all bloodshot. You lose it in a bar?"

"Boy hit me with a bottle."

"I can believe it, the kind of mouth you have. I'm surprised you aren't dead by now."

"We're getting to it," the mate said, "aren't we?"

Wayne said, "No, we're there." He straightened and put his hand on the man's bony shoulder. "And I'll tell you where we're at. You're gonna quit mouthing off, okay? You don't, I'll pound that glass eye into you so hard you'll be using it to peek out your asshole." Wayne got a grip on the man's coat, pulled him straight up and held him there one-handed looking into his good eye. "Is that what you want? Nod or shake your head, but be careful you don't speak."

The poor dumb one-eyed drunk seemed to shake his head. Or was that a nod? It didn't matter—what was the question? The guy's breath was so bad Wayne had to put him down. He saw the bartender coming over with a stern look.

"I'm okay, but give him one. Where's your phone?"

The bartender was a big bald-headed guy in a

plaid wool shirt. He hooked his thumb toward the
back of the room.

Moving along the bar Wayne looked at his
watch. Not yet five. He had hoped to call earlier
and was anxious now, getting a quarter out of his
pocket as he reached the phone booth, stepped inside and closed the door. He'd reverse the charge,
no problem, Carmen would be home. He raised
the quarter to drop it in the slot and an awful
feeling came over him. It caused him to say out
loud in the quiet confinement of the booth,
"SHIT!"

He didn't know the goddamn number.

It was in his mind last night when he was talking
to Carmen, telling her how the operator wouldn't
help him—*Write it down before you go to bed*. He
could remember telling himself that. And forgot to
do it.

Wayne looked in his wallet. He had the number
of Cape Barge Line. But they didn't have his. He
didn't have a phone when he had filled out the job
application. What he did have was the office number of the U.S. Marshals Service. They'd have
his—if that moron Ferris wrote it down. It was almost five. Wayne could see the moron and his sec-
retary leaving for the day, the door swings closed
and the phone starts ringing. He had about five
minutes. But first he'd have to get change at the

bar. He couldn't imagine Ferris accepting a collect call.

Carmen packed all the clothes her big canvas suitcase would hold and put it inside the pickup on the seat. She would have to come back sometime for the rest of her things, but wasn't going to worry about that now. Her plan was to leave at five. If Wayne didn't call by then she'd write a note and tape it to the refrigerator. Ferris could walk in and read it if he wanted, it wouldn't matter, she'd be gone. She felt less edgy with the keys in her hand and her bag in the truck. She had enough money for gas. What else? She got her navy wool coat out of the closet, and a sweater she hadn't packed and took them out to the pickup. Coming back into the house she heard the phone ringing and thought of Ferris.

"How're you doing, honey?"

"Wayne?"

"I'm gone one day and you don't know who I am. We were late getting in on account of fog. You run a bridge you have to see where you're going."

Carmen stood in the middle of the kitchen with the phone, looking into the living room.

"Where are you?"

"Cairo, but I'm coming home soon as I can catch a tow. Probably get back tomorrow morning, early."

It surprised her and she was curious—even as she continued to stare at the front window.

"You said you'd be gone three days."

"Well . . . I'll tell you about it when I get back, but you know what the thing was that turned me off. Don't laugh, but you have to wear a life preserver. I never wore a safety line on the job—you know I'm not gonna work someplace you have to wear a *life* preserver. These guys talk about falling overboard, shit, they don't know what a fall is. It was okay, I had a pretty good time. Now I'm gonna go look for a ride."

"Wayne, I won't be here when you get back." She said it fast. "Mom's sick, I have to go take care of her."

"Your *mom*? Your mom's always sick. Jesus, what's the matter now?"

"Her back, she can't move."

"That woman snaps her finger, you jump. Jesus Christ, don't you know she's using you?"

"Wayne, I'm going."

There was a silence.

"All right, listen, I'll leave right this minute. You can wait till tomorrow morning, can't you?"

"I want to get out of here," Carmen said, staring at that front window. "I waited all afternoon for you to call. I'm packed now, ready to go."

"I forgot to write down the number. I had to call Ferris."

"Oh, shit, you didn't. I'm leaving, right now."

"Wait a minute, will you? Did he come in the house again?"

"He's been driving by all day, sneaking around. If he knows I'm alone—he could be on his way right now."

"His girl said he was out on the job."

"Wayne, I have trouble telling you things you don't want to hear or you don't believe. This guy, this creep, is after me. He walks in the house and thinks he can do anything he wants. Do you understand that? He has *told* me he's coming by when you're not home. Now do you want me to stay and wait for him?"

"I'll call him up."

"Wayne, I'm walking out of the house. I'm leaving right this minute."

There was a silence.

"All right, then I'll see you at home. I mean our real home. Yeah, that's fine with me, I'm ready. I'll see you tomorrow. It'll be later, but I'll see you. . . . You found the keys, huh?"

"Yeah, I found them."

"I knew you would."

"Wayne, I'll most likely be at Mother's."

There was a silence again.

"Well, if you are, I'll see you at your mom's," Wayne said. "That's how much I miss you."

This was a low-life place but comfortable, a workingman's bar; the only thing different about it was the pizza smell. The guys, though, could be in any trade. Wayne looked around, but didn't see the mate anywhere. The bartender brought him a shell of beer and Wayne said, "You know of anybody in here's on a boat going north?"

The bartender said, "I look like a travel agent? Ask around."

He started to move away, the size of him making a slow turn, and Wayne said, "Wait a minute. Where's the bag was sitting here?"

The bartender looked over his shoulder at him. "Your buddy took it."

"That was my bag," Wayne said. "That wasn't his."

The bartender came around to face him. "He's into you for the drinks too. Four dollars and eighty cents."

"I went to make a phone call, I said give him *one*."

The bartender said, "Are you gonna be trouble?"

* * *

Carmen made a sandwich, fast, to take with her. She put the meat loaf back in the refrigerator and stood there with the door open looking in at the milk that would sour, the food that would spoil, grow a furry white mold and smell awful, remembering the odor when she opened the refrigerator that first night in the dark, in candlelight, Ferris saying the woman wasn't much of a house-keeper . . .

She slammed the door closed, amazed at herself, worrying about food spoiling, leaving a mess, when she had to get out of here right now. She'd let Wayne take care of it, but would have to remind him, leave a note. Going to the breakfast table she began composing it in her mind. *Unplug the fridge, throw everything out, leave the door open . . . Be careful with my nice car, I'll try not to wreck the truck. See you late tomorrow. Love . . . No, I love you . . .*

The phone rang.

Carmen jumped and stood rigid, because she knew it was Ferris. It could be Wayne, but it wasn't, it was Ferris. She said, Yeah, it has to be. And began to relax then, wanting it to be Ferris, Ferris somewhere else, not here or on the way. She did, thinking about it as the phone rang, she

wanted it to be Ferris and felt so sure it was, and so
confident about herself at the same time, that she
picked up the receiver and said, "Ferris?"

"Hey, how'd you know?"

"Where are you?"

"You sound different, real calm for a change. I
mean not all, you know, up in the air."

"Are you at your office?" All she wanted to
know was where he was, how near.

"Yeah, I came in, I see a note here says your old
man's out of town. I wish I'd known. Listen, don't
look for me tonight, I have to run down to New
Mad-rid, pick up some confiscated items, like
guns. But I can make it tomorrow, no problem.
How's that sound?"

"I won't be here," Carmen said, still calm, about
to tell him she was taking off and what he could do
with his house, wanting to rip into him; but
stopped, aware that maybe she was overconfident.

"You going out?" Ferris said. "I could come by
early, catch you in your jammies."

Or he could come right now if he thought for a
moment she was leaving. She had to be careful. Say
too much, even if it would make her feel better,
and that cream-colored Plymouth would be cutting
her off at the bridge.

Carmen said, "Do what you want," and hung
up, proud of her restraint. That was cool. *Do what
you want*. Just right.

The phone was ringing again as she left the house, slammed the door. It wasn't until she was driving away that she realized, if Ferris did come tomorrow, he could walk in the house and find Wayne there.

19

DONNA SAID TO ARMAND, the two of them sitting in the living room this evening among the stuffed animals, the TV off so they could talk, "I'm gonna tell you something I never mentioned before."

"Yeah? What is it?"

"There's people that believe it and there's your skeptics who don't. There's people won't believe nothing even if they're looking at it. Take my word."

"That's right." Armand nodded, thinking he wouldn't mind pushing this woman over on the sofa.

"People make up their minds something is true or isn't and there's no way you can get them not to be convinced of it. Well, I'm not one of those persons. You know why?"

Armand shook his head. "Why?"

"Because I think you have to believe what you see, sure, but also things beyond what you see, when something tells you it's true, if you know what I mean."

Jesus Christ, Armand thought.

This woman could put you to sleep. If she wasn't sitting in her pink robe showing him that dark place in there the way she had one leg raised, her foot on the sofa, he might have trouble keeping his eyes open. He was thinking of saying to her, "Why don't you tell me whatever it is in the bedroom, we get comfortable." Take hold of that dark place down there and she'd forget in a second, this one going off like a gun when you touched her hair trigger. He'd do it right now, except Richie would be home pretty soon and make remarks through the door. "What you two doing in there? You want me to get in with you?" That kind of shit. He had gone out to call the woman who had a trap on her phone. Richie, if he was here now, would tell Donna to shut up. "Jesus Christ, you don't know what you're talking about." And she would, she would shut up. Armand wanted to ask her what she thought of Richie, but felt he had to listen to her first. She was still talking, saying something else, and then she said:

"That's why I know Elvis is still alive."

Armand said, "You believe that?"

"I don't believe it, I know it."

"You showed me a picture of his grave."

"I didn't mention it at the time," Donna said, "but did you notice the name on it? Elvis Aaron Presley. Aaron with a double *a*?"

"Yeah."

Donna leaned toward him against her raised knee. "It so happens that Elvis spelled his middle name with one *a*."

"The person in the grave then," Armand said, "is a guy that spelled it with two?"

"I don't think there's necessarily a body in there. What they're saying is, hey, Elvis isn't in here. Don't you think we'd have spelled his name right? Come on." Donna squirmed her butt on the sofa cushion. "Listen, I saw a man, it was on *Kelly and Company*, who has actually seen Elvis since his death. They also had on a girl who recorded a song with him and I *heard* the record."

"Maybe it was somebody imitating him."

"You mean impersonating? There some that try to. But, see, I know Elvis's voice and it was Elvis. There's not a doubt in my mind."

Armand wished she would sit back, she was too close for him to see anything.

"Why would he want to pretend he's dead?"

"That's something we'll have to wait and see. I believe it will be revealed before too long, there too many people love him and miss him. And I believe it will happen at Graceland. Which is the main reason I want to go down there."

"Why don't you get Richie to take you?"

"Richie doesn't even like Elvis. He's jealous of him. I don't suppose you do either."

"What, like Elvis? Sure. I like that 'Hound Dog' song."

" 'Heartbreak Hotel' is the one tears me up."

"That's a nice one too."

Donna hummed some of it, moving her shoulders in the robe, her eyes half closed. She stopped, her eyes in the glasses open now, and said, "Bird, can I tell you something? I don't know if I should but I want to."

"Yeah, but don't call me Bird."

"I'm sorry, I hear Richie . . ."

"You want, you can call me Armand."

She said, "Armand," in a soft voice. "That's a real nice name." Then livened up her tone saying, "Hey, I'm not being very polite. Can I get you something, a snack?"

"No, I don't think so."

"I got a can of cocktail weenies I could fix."

"Maybe later."

"I enjoy watching a man likes to eat." She said, "That Richie eats like a bird," and said, "Oh, I'm sorry, I didn't mean that."

There was something wrong with this woman's brain. Maybe the weight of all that hair on it.

Armand said, "What is it you want to tell me?"

Now she had those magnified eyes staring at

him, wanting to trust him, or wanting to hold him so he'd keep looking at her and believe her.

"I'm scared to death of Richie," Donna said.

"Is that right? You let him stay here . . ."

"What choice do I have?"

Now she twisted her shoulders back and forth a couple of times like she was trapped in that robe and didn't know what to do. She picked up one of the stuffed animals, Mr. Froggy, and held it against her raised knee so that it was looking at Armand.

He said, "It's a nice place. I'm getting to like it." He said, "It wouldn't be too hard to get Richie out of here. Have you thought of that? What you're doing? They could arrest you too, for harboring, 'ey? Unless you turn him in first."

"I'd never do that."

"It's something to think about."

"I got news for you, he'd find out I did."

"Yeah, but if they put him away, so what?"

"They'd have to catch him first, and he's slick. Even if they did, he'd get out. I don't mean escape. He'd do a few years and then come looking for me." Donna shook her head. "I would never snitch on him. I'm not that kind of person."

"They got some pretty heavy stuff on him," Armand said, "what sounds to me would get him life or worse. I don't think you'd ever see him again."

Donna was shaking her head. "I wouldn't do it.

He said to me one time, if I ever even thought of calling the police on him he'd know it."

Armand said, "You believe that?" And thought, Well, if she believes Elvis Presley is alive . . .

Of course she did. Cocking her head to the side as if thinking about it, then nodding with that dreamy look on her face, the one that was supposed to mean she knew things he didn't. Believing in something—how did she say it?—beyond what you can know. He could see the inside curve of one of her breasts hanging there in the robe. It was elderly but not bad. The way she was sitting, he couldn't see the dark place. Maybe if he moved back a little and tried it, getting a stuffed animal out from behind him. He glanced down. Ah, there it was.

She said, "You seem to have doubts."

Armand shrugged. "I don't see how he could know what you're thinking."

"He just would."

"You mean 'cause of how you're acting then, nervous?"

"I guess partly."

"Listen, you don't have to be afraid of him."

Donna was still holding on to him with her eyes in the shining glasses. She said, "You're not afraid of him, are you?"

He pushed against the back of the sofa to sit up,

reached over and very gently lifted off her glasses to see her eyes naked. Donna didn't move. She blinked. Now she was looking at him again, or seemed to be. She looked like a sister of the Donna before. Now she turned her head slightly and touched her pile of hair. Armand believed it was a gesture that meant she wouldn't mind getting laid.

"No, I'm not afraid of him," Armand said. "You know why?"

She was trying to give him a soft look with those cockeyed eyes. He didn't know why seeing Donna without her glasses made him more aware of her being naked beneath the robe, but it did.

She said, "You're bigger than he is," lowered her head just enough and smiled, becoming a little imp now, this fifty-year-old woman and her Mr. Froggy, both looking at him.

He said, "You know who I am?"

"Who you *are*? Sure."

"You know what I mean. Richie told you, didn't he?"

"He said you're from Toronto."

"What else?"

"I don't know."

"Why can't you say it?"

"I don't know what you mean."

"The kind of thing I do for a living."

"It isn't none of my business."

"Yeah, but Richie told you. Don't he tell you everything he's doing?"

"He brags a lot. You know Richie."

"But he did tell you about me."

"It really doesn't matter," Donna said. "I've enjoyed your company, I think you're a nice person and, well, I wish you all the best." She looked off at the room. "I don't know—I hope you didn't mind my cooking too much. It isn't the easiest thing in the world, trying to please two different men."

Armand said, "You think I'm leaving?"

"Well, I guess you will sometime."

"What did he tell you?"

"Nothing, really. I just, you know, have a feeling."

"He told you what we're doing?"

"No, uh-unh, he's never said a word." Donna shook her big hairdo back and forth, brushed Mr. Froggy from her knee and stared at him, those poor eyes of hers saying, Please believe me. She said, "I don't know anything about your business and I don't want to. I made those phone calls. . . . Richie says things, you never know if he's giving you a bunch of bull or what, so I just let it go in one ear and out the other. I would never, *ever*, repeat anything that was said to me, whether I was told not to or I wasn't. It's just none of my business."

"Are you nervous?"

"Not the least."

"You seem nervous."

"Well, I'm not. I have no reason to be."

"So, you think Elvis is still alive."

"I'm pretty sure of it."

"Maybe he is. Who knows, 'ey?"

"Even if he wasn't, I'd still like to go down there."

"What else? Would you like it if I killed Richie?"

"Oh, my Lord," Donna said. "Would I."

"What will you give me?"

They heard the back door open and slam closed.

Richie came in through the kitchen, saw them on the couch with the TV off, Donna's glasses off, what's this? They weren't playing Yahtzee or looking at Elvis pictures. Richie stopped chewing his bubble gum. What's going on here? In some kind of serious conversation that could be about him. Or else the Indian was getting ready to dive into her muff. Either way, Richie didn't like the looks of it. But lightened up his manner saying, "Goddamn it, Bird, I do all the work and you have all the fun. Did I mention that before? I don't like to repeat myself. Donna, go take a leak or something, the Bird and I want to be alone."

Look at that. Now she was staring at the Bird, like it was up to him, or he'd give her permission, those big bald eyes of hers trying like hell to focus.

"Donna, you hear me?"

"He don't like to repeat himself," the Bird said to her and motioned with his head, go on.

She still took her sweet time getting up, straightening her robe, walking out, head of gold held high, retired queen of the cons—never had it so good and never would again. Richie stepped over to give Donna a pat on the behind. He looked at the Bird, who looked back at him, but waited, chewing his gum, till he heard a door close.

"You ready?"

"For what?"

"I call the woman, okay? She starts in bitching at me, her back's killing her and it's my fault."

"Am I ready for what?"

The Bird trying to act cool.

"I ask her," Richie said, "did she ever get hold of her daughter and Wayne. She goes, 'Yeah, and you don't have to send the check now, they're coming home.'"

That hooked the Bird.

"You kidding me. When?"

"They already left. She says her daughter's coming to take care of her, on account of she's in terrible pain and can't move." Richie watched the Indian, waiting for him to catch on. "They're coming 'cause I gave the woman a treatment. You hear what I'm saying? *I* did it, man, rubbing her old bones. I got them to come *home*, you understand? Saved us a trip."

The Bird looked like he was still trying to figure it out. "She's going to her mother's house."

"That's right."

"What about the guy?"

"The guy, he'll go with her, or he'll stay home. Or they'll both stop home first, I bet you anything, 'cause it's on the way. We go to their house right now, tonight, and wait. They don't come by, we go to the mom's house."

"Maybe," the Bird said. "I'll think about it."

Fucking Indian.

Ten feet away. Take one step, hop on the other foot and kick him right in the face. Uh, what did you say, Bird? There's nothing to think about, man. You want to know everything's gonna happen? There's no way in the fucking world you can know everything. You don't even *want* to know everything, not have any surprises in your life?

No more partners, man, that was for sure. He should never have brought the Indian into this deal. That caused his mind to pause and think, Wait a minute. What deal? There wasn't a dime to be made off it, unless he called up that real estate man sometime.

Just then the Bird said, "Okay, we go to their house."

And they were back together again, Richie grinning at him, anxious to tell more, but blew a bubble, popped it and was chewing again before saying, "Bird? Guess what? I even got us provisions. We spend the night there we're gonna be hungry. I got us some pizza you put in the oven, I got us a bunch of different kinds of like frozen dindins, I got us some potato chips, candy bars . . . Hey, I picked up a magazine at the checkout, I'm waiting there? Bird, it shows a picture of a guy weighs twelve hundred pounds. You ever hear of anybody that big in your life?"

"Twelve hundred pounds?" the Bird was squinting at him. "Three horses don't weigh twelve hundred pounds."

"I got the magazine out'n the car."

"What's the guy eat?"

"You won't believe it," Richie said.

Armand, holding a bottle of Canadian whiskey in a paper bag, looked into Donna's bedroom. He said, "We're leaving now. See you tomorrow."

She was over by her dresser, still wearing the robe. It hung open and she left it that way turning to look at him, one hand on her hip, showing him

everything she owned. Donna didn't say anything.
What could she?

So Armand said, "I don't know what time I'll be
back." She was scared but still didn't say anything.
He took another look at her, that white body with
the dark place showing, and closed the door. He
waited in the hall for Richie to come out of the
bathroom.

"You ready?"

Richie looked surprised to see him standing
there. He said, "Yeah, let's go."

They went through the kitchen and out the back
to the Dodge parked in the narrow drive. Armand
had to edge past a tangle of bushes to open the
door and get in his side. Richie was already behind
the wheel starting the car. He got it going and sat
there a moment.

Armand thinking, He forgot something.

Richie looked at him, giving him a glance, no
more than that, and opened the door.

"I forgot something."

"What?"

"I want to bring some booze."

"I got it right here."

"Not what I drink, you don't."

Armand didn't say anything else. He waited as
Richie got out of the car and went back into the
house. Armand turned off the engine and sat listening. He saw Donna the way he had looked in

the bedroom at her naked beneath her robe. He sat listening, thinking that Richie would use his gun if he was going to do it. He sat listening not wanting to hear that sound or have Richie come out and tell him he did it some other way, if that's what he was doing. He sat listening until Richie opened the door and got in, handed him the bottle of Southern Comfort and started the car. They backed out and drove away from the house, lights showing in the living room. Armand didn't say anything and neither did Richie.

20

ELEVEN-THIRTY THAT EVENING Carmen stopped at a Kountry Kitchen south of Gary, Indiana, tired and hungry, halfway home.

The hardest part of the trip was getting out of Cape Girardeau, crossing the river and following county roads east to find I-57. After that there was nothing to it. Turn left and drive straight up through almost the entire state of Illinois. Turn right on I-94 and cut across a corner of Indiana, where she was now. She'd have something to eat, get back on 94 and it would take her all the way across southern Michigan, through Detroit and to within twenty miles or so of home. Mom could wait.

Carmen was anxious to walk into her own house again, that drafty old barn with its cramped kitchen, its foyer bigger than the living room, its creaks and groans, the steam pipes making a racket in the winter. The house would be cold, it didn't matter. She wanted to see it, make sure it was still there after more than eighty years, look out the kitchen window at the woods and the brush field and Wayne's Chickenshit Inn. She'd call him when she got home, which would be about six-thirty in the morning if she could stay awake and drive straight through. Find out what time he was leaving. Check to see if Mom was okay and maybe wait for him. Mom could be all better now, knowing her little girl was coming home. Wayne could have already left by the time she called. But if he was there, she'd tell him not to be surprised if Ferris drops in, and if he does, be nice, okay? Just say good-bye. And Wayne would say, yeah, uh-huh, what else you want me to do? How about if I give him a hug? . . . Or not mention Ferris at all. He was three hundred and fifty miles behind her, back in southeast Missouri with his muscles and wavy hair, Carmen thinking of him now as a clown who used to walk into her house, an annoying jerk rather than a serious threat. She should have spoken up to him more. Got mad and told him to get the hell out, goddamn it. And got mad thinking about it, cleaning up her plate of bacon and eggs, cottage fries, rye-bread toast and coffee, Kountry Kitchen No. 3.

She should've thrown something at him. Something heavy. She threw beer cans at Wayne, but beer cans were for show. Or she should've hit him with something. Keep a sleever bar handy for creeps who walk in the house uninvited.

Carmen finished, got the check and went to the counter to pay. A guy in a John Deere cap reached it at the same time. He touched the bill of the cap funneled over his eyes and said, "After you." Carmen nodded, glanced at the guy, saw his eyes and the sly grin and thought, Oh shit, another one. He said, "I imagine there's all kinds of boys after you," and Carmen got out of there.

The pickup stood close, angle-parked in the lights of the Kountry Kitchen. She unlocked it, climbed in, reached for the door to swing it closed and the guy in the John Deere cap caught it, held it open.

"Excuse me. I just want to ask, if you got time . . ."

Carmen started the engine, revved it.

"Wait a sec now, I thought we might have a drink. There's a spot up here before you get to the Michigan line, the Hoosier Inn off Exit Thirty-nine? You ever been there?"

Carmen took time to look at him, his face raised, hopeful now. She said, "Do you really think I want to go to a place called the Hoosier Inn off Exit Thirty-nine? For a drink or any reason at all? Are you serious?"

Carmen put the pickup in reverse and backed away from the Kountry Kitchen, the open door bringing the guy along against his will, the guy yelling now, "Hey, for Christ sake!" Scrambling to stay on his feet. Carmen braked, shifted, took off in low gear and left him. The door swung closed as she drove away.

Hit them with a truck if you don't have a sleever bar.

Twenty years married to Wayne.

She followed her headlights along the nighttime freeway, not as tired as before, thinking about Wayne now, seeing them together. They're in the kitchen having a beer and she's describing the guy in the John Deere cap, oh, about thirty-five, not bad-looking. She tells what the guy said, word for word, memorized, beginning with "After you," and then what she said, very calmly, after he invites her to have a drink. "You really think I want to go to a place called the *Hoosier* Inn, off Exit Thirty-nine?" Wayne would be grinning by then. "Are you serious?" He'd love it. It was the kind of thing Wayne would say. Or he'd ask the guy if he was out of his fucking mind, but "Are you serious?" still wasn't bad. She wanted to hurry up and get home, call Wayne, and if he was still there tell him to get on his horse.

They told Wayne at Waterfront Services there were northbound tows leaving but none that had to stop at Cape. A guy who worked for the Corps of Engineers, a civilian employee, was in the office. He said Wayne could ride with him as far as Thebes, where he lived, and it was only another nine miles to the Cape bridge, but he first needed to see a man over at the Skipper Lounge. Wayne thought he meant ride in a boat, but it was a Ford pickup they drove to the pizza-smelling saloon and the man the guy from the Corps of Engineers had to see was the bartender. He had to see him keep pouring Jim Beam into a glass until the fifth was used up. By this time it was eleven-thirty at night.

Carmen, Wayne believed, would be somewhere around Chicago, while he was stuck down at the ass end of the state. The bartender kept watching him to see he didn't lift the guy from the Corps of Engineers off the floor and threaten or shake him.

The guy kept telling Wayne to take her easy, have another, he'd still get home quicker than by towboat. Wayne, who only had every other drink with the guy, said, "Okay, if you let me drive." Sure, hell, they'd both go to Cape and have one and the guy, smashed out of his mind by now, would drive himself home from there. Which was okay with Wayne, as long as he wasn't riding with him.

They got to Thebes and Wayne said, "Which way now?" The guy said turn here, turn there, okay stop. They were at the guy's house. Wayne said, "I thought we were going to Cape." The guy from the fucking Corps of Engineers said, "You're going to Cape, I'm going to bed." Wayne almost stole his truck. It took him three hours and forty minutes to hike it half in the bag, from Thebes to the bridge, not seeing one goddamn car on the road. He picked up the Olds at Cape Barge Line, got home feeling like shit and there weren't any aspirin in the medicine cabinet. Carmen had taken them with her. Thanks a lot. There was a note on the refrigerator and his new work gloves he'd forgotten lying on the breakfast table. Wayne set the alarm and went to bed.

He woke up at seven wearing his Jockey shorts and the yellow cowhide work gloves, hung over, feeling mean and craving ice cream. For about fifteen minutes he lay there thinking about a chocolate milk shake. He had downed many of them in a hung-over state while other guys drank cold beer or hard stuff as a pick-me-up. Wayne believed drinking before noon could get you in trouble and ice cream was better than sweating out the clock. Carmen had bought some, he was pretty sure, the other day, a half-gallon of butterscotch ripple. He jumped out of bed to check and there it was, Thank you, Jesus, in the freezer part of the fridge. But hard as a rock. He took it out to soften while he showered and got dressed.

But then in the shower with water streaming over him, hair lathered with shampoo, he thought, Hell, bring the ice cream in here and it would soften enough to drink, just like a thick milk shake.

Wayne left the shower on and closed the curtain so the floor wouldn't get wet. He walked out of the steamy bathroom naked and wet, tiptoed along the hall to the kitchen, on the right, and stopped, catching a glimpse of something to his left. Through the living room and out the window. A cream-colored Plymouth pulling into the drive to park behind the Olds. Deputy Marshal Ferris Britton getting out of the car, coming to the side door.

What would he want this early in the morning?

If the doorbell rings, Wayne was thinking, yell at him to go away. But the doorbell didn't ring. He heard a key turn the lock and knew what Ferris wanted.

Wayne slipped back along the hall to the bedroom, closed the door partway and stood listening. He heard the side door close.

Ferris was in the house.

Wayne got a clean pair of Jockeys from the dresser and put them on. He was still wet, hair creamed and swirled with shampoo. He looked at his new work gloves, never used, lying on the bed.

Ferris was in the hall, looking in the kitchen. He came to the bathroom and for a moment stood in the doorway. He stepped inside.

Wayne came only a few moments later, into the steam and sound of the shower going behind the flowered plastic curtain. He stood looking at Ferris's back, close enough to reach out and touch the big grip of the revolver on his belt, the shirt stretched across those solid shoulders, short sleeves rolled up, the muscles in his arms tightening as he raised his hands to his hips. Wayne was going to tap him on the shoulder and say . . . whatever you said to a guy who thinks he's about to surprise your wife in the shower. He hesitated, watching Ferris's right hand reach up to take hold of the curtain. Maybe you don't say anything.

Ferris did. He said, "Surprise!" Yelled it out as he tore the shower curtain aside, ripping part of it off the rod . . . and stood looking at wet tile, the shower streaming into an empty tub. He stood like that for several moments, as though thinking, well, she must be in there somewhere. Wayne got ready.

He waited for Ferris to turn, saw his face, all eyes, and hit him. Hit him with his right hand in that yellow cowhide work glove, hit him as hard as he had ever swung a ten-pound beater, hit him one time with everything he had and Ferris went into the shower, bounced against the tile and slid down to lie cramped in there, legs sticking up over the edge of the tub. His eyes opened to stare dazed through the stream of water.

Wayne bent over, hands on his bare knees, to look at him. He said, "Oh, it's you. Shit, I thought it was somebody broke in the house."

The phone rang in the kitchen.

It rang five times before Wayne got to it, taking off his gloves, and answered.

Carmen's voice said, "Wayne? I'm home."

21

"I JUST WALKED IN THE DOOR."

"How was it? You have any trouble?"

"It wasn't bad. When did you get there?"

"Four A.M. I got up at seven, had a shower. At the moment I'm having some ice cream. Butterscotch ripple."

"Are we a little hung over?"

"You took the aspirin with you. That was a cruel thing to do, you know it?"

"Wayne, why don't you leave as soon as you can. In case Ferris stops by."

"He already has. He's here right now."

"You mean he's right *there*, in the kitchen?"

"No, in the bathroom. I think his jaw's broken," Wayne said and told her about it.

Carmen listened. She said, "Wayne, you better get out of there, now."

"Soon as I clean out the refrigerator."

As he said it, and told her he didn't see a problem, he'd ask Ferris if he wanted him to call Emer-

gency Medical or the cops, Carmen was aware of
a humming sound, familiar, one she was used to,
and turned from the sink to look at the refrigerator. The door was closed and it was running.
Wayne was telling her now he planned to keep his
foot on the gas all the way and try to make it in
ten and a half hours, set a new Cape to Algonac
speed record.

"We turned off the refrigerator," Carmen said,
"didn't we? I mean the one here."

"We shut everything off but the phone."

"Well, somebody turned it on." She paused, listening. "Wayne, I think the furnace is going."

"Check the thermostat."

"I can feel it. It's warm in here."

"Maybe Nelson had the house open, trying to
sell it. I wouldn't put it past him."

"Maybe," Carmen said, looking across the
kitchen to what had been a pantry and now was
Wayne's closet, where he kept his hunting and fishing gear, stacks of outdoor magazines. She listened
to him speculate, Nelson gets an offer and the next
thing they know he's trying to sell them a two-
bedroom over at Wildwood, your choice of decorator colors. The shotgun must be in there, in
Wayne's closet. It had to be, they didn't take it with
them. The closet would be locked and the key was
on the ring with the rest of his keys, in her purse.

"Call your buddy Nelson and ask him."

She'd get the shotgun out and put it by the door. It startled her, all of a sudden remembering the two guys.

"Carmen?"

"I will. I have to call Mom first."

"You gonna be home when I get there?"

"I'll see how she is."

"Get her permission."

"If I can leave her, I will. Okay? That's the best I can do."

"You get pissed off at Mommy and lay into *me*."

"I'm tired," Carmen said.

"Call the State Police, that detective, whatever his name is. Tell him you're home."

"I will. Hurry, okay?"

"I'll see you about six, six-thirty. We'll probably need a few things, huh, some beer?"

"It's weird," Carmen said, looking around the kitchen. She saw the oven door open a few inches.

"What is?"

"I don't know—the feeling. I walked in, it wasn't like coming back to a house that's been closed up."

"It's only been a week but seems longer, that's all. Call Nelson."

"I will."

"And that cop."

"I'll see you," Carmen said. Hesitated a moment and said, "Wayne? I'll be here." She pushed the button to disconnect, dialed her mother's number, waited and was surprised to hear:

"Hello?" The tone almost pleasant.

"Mom? Did you know it was me?"

"I prayed it was. I've been worried sick."

"I'm home. How are you?"

"Well, I'm walking now. The pain is still something awful, but at least I'm on my feet. When're you coming over?"

"You sound much better."

"Well, I'm not."

"I could stop by later, for a while anyway. Wayne'll be home this evening and I want to have his dinner ready."

"I haven't seen you in so long . . ."

"Do you need anything at the store?"

"I'll have to think, I'm so used to looking out for myself," her mom said. "Well, I could use a bottle of Clairol Loving Care. The light ash blonde, number seventy-one."

"Anything else?"

"Oh—I got the report from Annoyance Call. There was a whole bunch of calls from where you were, three-one-four. There was one from Algonac, your house, and three from public phones. One Marine City and two Port Huron that must've been the hang-ups. That's what they do, call from a pay phone so they don't get traced, they're slick articles."

"I didn't know you were having trouble."

"I told you the day you had your phone put in, and you called? I was gonna see if a trap would catch him."

"You must've had it done before we left."

"It was right after, I know, because I was worried sick I hadn't heard from you."

Carmen said, "And one of the calls was from this house?"

"It's your number on the list."

"But we weren't here, Mom."

Her mother said, "Well, somebody was." She said, "How's your weather down there?"

Thirty miles away. Carmen wanted to hang up and walk out of the house—the weather was all right, it was weather, about 50 out, overcast, quite windy—walk all the way around the outside of the house and look at it good—her mom saying it was 52 degrees in Port Huron—look in the windows and find out for sure, was this her house? It looked like it, everything was in the right place, but it didn't *feel* like her house, someone had been here and touched things. Everything *wasn't* in the right place, the phone book and note pad she kept in a drawer were on the counter. Someone had been here and left a smell, the kitchen smelled, someone had been cooking, used the oven she never left open like that, plugged in the refrigerator humming away, what else? Looking around now—her mom asking what time she was coming—Carmen telling her she didn't know offhand, she had to shop (think of something), she had to get a tire fixed, and heard a sound from somewhere in the house, hard, clear, a metal-hitting-metal sound. Carmen told herself it was a radiator clanging, hot air banging in a pipe, and told her mom she'd be there around noon, bye, I missed you too, Mom, yeah, okay, see you in a little while, bye. And hung up. She moved to the range, stooped to push the oven door open and looked inside. Three wedges of cold pizza and a few crusts lay on a cookie sheet. She could smell them. Carmen straightened, closing the oven, turned to the refrigerator and jumped, sucking in her breath.

Richie said, "How's Mom doing?"

He stood in the doorway to the dining room wearing an ironworker's jacket, Wayne's old one, and sunglasses, holding a shotgun across his arm.

Now the other one appeared, coming into the kitchen past Richie Nix, also with a shotgun but holding it at his side, pointed down. Armand Degas, wearing the same dark suit he'd worn that day at the real estate office. He said to Carmen, "It looks like we gonna be together for a while, 'ey? Till six or six-thirty?"

Richie Nix said, "Bird? Here, hold this," and handed him his shotgun.

He came toward her and Carmen tried to look him in the eye, tried hard, but lowered and turned her head as his hand came up and she thought he was going to slap her across the face. "You got nice hair," Richie said, touching it, stroking it. She was looking down at his cowboy boots toe to toe with her white sneakers. "Has body, you don't have to use a lot of sticky spray on it." He moved against her, his hands going to her shoulders. "Mmmmm, smells nice, too. I can see you believe in personal hygiene, you keep yourself clean. I like your sweater-and-shirt outfit. You look like a little schoolgirl." His hands came down to take hold of her hips. "Scoot over, I want to get something here."

Carmen looked up. She saw the diamond in his earlobe and saw Armand Degas watching them. Richie had the oven door open. He brought out a wedge of cold pizza and took a bite as he moved to the window over the sink.

"How come you had to drive the pickup?"

"It was there," Carmen said. Her voice sounded dry.

"Whatever that means," Richie said, looking at her now. "It don't matter. Where's the keys?" When she hesitated Richie stepped over to her purse lying on the counter. "In here?"

Armand said, "Put the truck in the garage and close the door. Let's get that done."

Carmen watched Richie look up and stare at Armand before he said, "That's what I'm gonna *do*, Bird. Why do you think I want the keys?" He brought them out of the purse and walked around the counter that separated the kitchen work area from the door.

"I thought you might want to keep talking," Armand said, "till somebody drives by, sees the truck."

Richie stopped and took a bite of pizza. He said, "Hey, Bird?" in a mild tone of voice. "Fuck you."

It didn't seem to bother Armand. Carmen watched him. All he did was shrug, reach over and lay Richie's shotgun on the counter against the wall.

She moved to the window over the sink, not wanting to be alone with Armand looking at her. She had to make up her mind how to think about this, how to accept it—her mouth dry, trying to breathe, telling herself to take a deep breath and let it out slowly—how to act, passive, or let herself go, think of Wayne walking in and let the tears come, plead with them, please . . . Or think of a way . . . First get the keys back from Richie, with the key to Wayne's closet, the Remington inside. She thought of it without knowing if it was possible or if she'd have the nerve, it was hard to picture, if she did somehow get to the gun—would it be loaded?—and held it on them . . . then what? Through the window she saw Richie inside the pickup, starting it, both hands free, what was left of the pizza slice sticking out of his mouth. He might leave the keys in the ignition. She watched the pickup creep ahead and turn toward the garage, out of view.

Behind her, Armand said, "You want to fix us some breakfast? We brought food, it's in the icebox."

Carmen turned and they were as close as the day he tried to come up the porch steps, his face raised with the hunting cap hiding his eyes, the day she could have shot him and wished to God, now, she had.

She said, "What do you want?"

"There some waffles if you have any syrup."

"I don't mean to *eat*. What do you *want*?"

"We're waiting for your husband."

Making it sound like a visit.

"And when he gets here . . . ?"

She watched him shrug and then look up. A hammering sound was coming from the garage, Richie—it would have to be Richie—pounding on metal. The sound stopped.

"I know why you're here," Carmen said. "Why can't you say it?"

"Well, if you know that . . ." He gestured with

his hands, let them fall and said, "Don't talk so much, all right?"

"Or what, you'll shoot me?"

"I'll get tired hearing you and put a gag on your mouth, tie you up. You want that? I don't care."

Richie came in holding Wayne's sleever bar. "Look it, Bird. What the guy used on us. I knew he kept it in that tool box. It's just what I been looking for."

Armand didn't say anything.

Richie dropped the keys on the counter going by and Carmen didn't hesitate. She stepped over from the sink, picked up the keys, ready to shove them into her jeans, and stopped. Richie was at Wayne's closet. She watched him wedge the pry end of the bar into the seam between the door and the frame, Richie saying, "I been wondering why you kept this locked." He put his weight behind the bar, pushing on it. "I never even noticed it till this morning." He grunted, pushed hard and the door popped open.

Carmen stared at the closet. She could see Richie inside now with the light on. Armand, close to her, said, "You gonna fix us breakfast?"

"Fishing poles and a bunch of shit for hunting," Richie said, his voice raised. "I thought there'd be a gun. Hey, Bird, didn't you?"

Carmen didn't move, staring at the closet,

Richie inside looking around. Close to her Armand said, "There was a shotgun." She didn't look at him. "That one you had, 'ey? Where's that one?"

"In Cape Girardeau, Missouri," Carmen said.

"That's where you were? It sounds French, no? But I never heard of it. So your husband has the gun, 'ey?"

She was thinking that last week or the week before or whenever it was, she had brought the Remington inside and Wayne had come back from the store where the girl was killed and picked it up. . . . It wasn't next to the door when they left and Wayne didn't bring it with them, she was sure of that. He had put it somewhere . . . she thought in his closet.

"I remember that gun, with the slug barrel on it," Armand said. "I remember I asked you, you shoot people with that thing? Oh, you wanted to shoot me that time. I watched you, I could see it. Didn't you?"

Carmen stared at Richie in the closet, Richie holding something in his hand, looking at it closely.

"But you couldn't do it," Armand said in his quiet voice close to her. "Maybe your husband's different, I don't know. But you don't shoot people, do you?"

Carmen didn't answer, watching Richie coming

out of the closet with a plastic bottle in his hand, holding it up.

"Hey, Bird? What's Hot Doe Buck Lure?"

Armand inspected the entire house again in daylight. Upstairs in the bedroom he pulled the phone cord out of the wall, in case the ironworker's wife sneaked up here. She might do it, but could never jump out of one of these windows without hurting herself. She would have to go through the two panes of glass, the window and the storm sash, once he locked them, using all the strength in his fingers to twist each catch in place. There were storm windows downstairs too. The living room was on the wrong side of the house to watch from, but the dining room was good. Armand liked the dining room, the big oak table, the window in front and the row of windows along the side, where the ironworker would drive in. There was still plenty of time. It was only eleven-thirty. He'd have one drink, a swallow from the bottle, that's all.

He was getting used to the sounds around this place. It had been quiet all night except for Richie, but now the wind was gusting, rattling the windows, and those big cargo planes from the Self-ridge Air National Guard base were flying over low, with a roaring noise like they were coming into the house. It would shut Richie up for a few moments. Armand felt himself coming to the end of Richie, the irritation of this guy, this punk, reaching its peak, and by the end of this day that would be enough of him. Richie hadn't mentioned Donna yet but he would, Armand was pretty sure.

Earlier, they had eaten in the kitchen, the waffles you put in a toaster. The ironworker's wife had syrup. She made coffee and stood by the window while they sat at the counter, Richie talking, trying to impress her, the punk talking with his mouth full. He asked her if she had ever met a bank robber before. She said no. He asked her if she liked Missouri. She shrugged her shoulders. He said did she know Jesse James was from there? He said he was going to Missouri and rob one of the banks Jesse James robbed, that would be cool. He showed her all the flat frozen-food boxes in the icebox, not in the freezer, thawing on a shelf, so you could cook them quicker, and told her he ate chicken every day. You know why? She said no. He said because Wade Boggs ate chicken every day of his life. He said, Bird, you know who Wade Boggs is? Armand had heard the name, they spoke of Wade Boggs in the Silver Dollar in Toronto, cursing him; but that was all he knew, the name, so he didn't answer. Richie asked the ironworker's wife, calling her Carmen, if she knew and she nodded. Maybe she did, maybe she didn't. Richie said, Tell the Bird who he is. Carmen said, He plays third

base for the Boston Red Sox. Richie said, And belts
the shit right out of a baseball. He told Carmen he
had wanted to be a major-league ballplayer, but his
deprived youth as an orphan had fucked up his
chances, so he became a bank robber instead.
Chewing gum by this time, the punk would blow a
bubble and pop it, showing off.

Next thing, Richie told Carmen to take her
clothes off, he had an idea. She said no, shaking
her head at him, determined not to do it. He said,
Okay, not all your clothes. You got on undies,
don't you? You can leave on your brassiere if you
wear one and your panties. You wear a brassiere?
She turned away as he reached for her and Armand
watched Richie rub his hand over her back, feeling
it, and then his whole face smiled and he said, Hey,
she don't wear one, Bird. He told her, Okay, strip
down to your panties if you got any on and you'll
be our little topless bunny, serve us drinks and dinner. How's that sound, Bird? Armand didn't say
anything. The way this punk kept talking had him
at the edge; still, he wouldn't mind seeing the ironworker's wife without her clothes on. She held her
arms tight to her body when Richie tried to pull
the sweater off. When she kneed Richie in the
crotch, hard, and he doubled over with the pain,
Armand thought Richie might pull his gun. He
could hit her if he wanted, but shoot her, no. Her
mother might phone worried sick, wondering

where she was. Or the ironworker might call from the road and think something happened if she didn't answer and then maybe he'd call the police too. But Richie didn't pull his gun. He tried to slap her with one hand, holding his balls with the other, and she got away from him and went to the other side of the counter and picked up a knife. Richie thought that was funny. What he did, he opened the bottle of Hot Doe Buck Lure and threw deer piss on her clothes, doused her with it good and the smell was so bad it could make you sick. Richie made her go into the bathroom at the end of the hall, telling her to take off those clothes and wash herself. He closed the door and they stood in the foyer by the stairs waiting. The door opened. She came out wearing something that looked like an undershirt and white panties very low on her hips. Jesus Christ. Richie said, Hey, I want you topless. But looked at her some more and said it was a cute outfit, he liked it. Armand didn't say it but agreed with Richie, the ironworker's wife looked pretty nice. She stood up straight, not folding her arms or trying to cover herself, and looked right back at them. Though didn't seem too happy about it, no.

They were in the dining room now, at the table Carmen and Wayne had bought at a farm auction.

Richie sat at the end toward the doorway to the

kitchen. He had Wayne's jacket off, hooked to the back of his chair. The nickel-plated revolver she remembered lay on the table next to his low-cal gourmet chicken.

Carmen sat with the windows behind her, hands folded on the table edge in front of her; she felt less exposed here. The tank top smelled and she'd breathe through her mouth whenever she got a strong whiff of doe urine and would remember the night Wayne brought it home. She wasn't shaking the way she did at first, chills running through her. Now she could sit without holding herself rigid, not exactly relaxed, but at least aware. The hardest part was trying not to think of Wayne coming home or Wayne in tender moments or Matthew; she didn't dare think of Matthew, especially as a little boy. If she did an urge to cry would come over her and she was afraid if she started she wouldn't be able to stop.

What she did to hang on and not panic or come apart was think of Wayne in a different way, Wayne here, close to her, so that she wasn't alone. Wayne in her mind but real, because she knew him so well. She asks him if he's scared and he says, for Christ sake of course he's scared, you'd have to have brain damage not to be scared of these assholes. Don't let their chitchat, that casual bullshit, fool you, these guys are fucking maniacs. Stay low, don't make a lot of noise, don't piss them off, and if they give you any more than thirty seconds' lee-way take it, run like hell for a door. Don't try a window, you'll never get the goddamn storm open. She says, Thanks a lot. Wayne shrugs. What else can I tell you? You run if you see the chance. You get your hands on a gun, use it. None of this put-your-hands-up-while-I-call-the-cops, use it. She asked him where he'd put the Remington. He wouldn't tell her. She clenched her jaw. Wayne, goddamn it . . . He still wouldn't tell her.

Armand, wearing his suit coat and the tie with tiny fish on it, sat across from her eating Swedish meatballs and noodles. The opening to the foyer and the stairway was directly behind him. Richie, to Armand's left at the end of the table, would stare at her tank top chewing his food, sucking his teeth. He looked at her the way Ferris did; but Ferris was an actor, Richie was real. Ferris was noth-ing. Armand would glance at her as he looked up from his food to gaze at the row of windows be-hind her, rattling in the wind. She had been right when she told Wayne, a long, long time ago, Richie was scarier than Armand.

They'd had drinks now, Richie a Southern Com-fort and 7-Up, one, Armand four whiskeys with a splash of water, and were talking to each other more than they did earlier.

Carmen listened to them, waiting for the phone to ring, Mom calling, *Where are you? It's almost one o'clock*. They began talking about the shot-gun, Wayne's Remington, as if she wasn't sitting at the table with them. It gave her a strange feeling, till she began to concentrate on the gun that was somewhere in the house.

Richie saying, "He might have it, but he's not gonna walk in here with it."

Armand saying, "Oh, you know that?"

Richie saying, "Why would he? He thinks his little wife's in here fixing supper. Comes runing in, 'Hi, honey, I'm home.' "

Armand saying, "How do you know he won't have the gun?"

Carmen thinking, Because he doesn't. Because it's here.

Armand saying, "What did she say to him on the telephone? Something funny is going on here and he told her to call the cops."

Richie saying, "To tell them she's home, that's all." Looking at her then and saying, "Isn't that right?" Carmen nodded and he said, "I guess you figured out we was listening in upstairs."

Carmen thinking that's where it would have to be. But if it was there, why didn't they see it? If Wayne took it upstairs he wouldn't have hidden it.

She looked at the glasses and plates and food containers on the table—extra ones in the middle Armand would pick from, macaroni and cheese, lasagna, sweet potatoes with sliced apple and brown sugar—looked at the stains on the plastic tablecloth she had put on to protect the wood finish. It reminded her of looking in the refrigerator yesterday at 950 Hillglade, worrying about food spoiling when she was dying to get out of there. Instinctively the good little housewife. Now sitting in her underwear with two guys who were going to shoot her husband when he walked in the door and then shoot her or shoot them both at the same time. . . . She had never thought about dying or even getting old or what she had heard on television called the terrifying middle-age crisis. . . . They might use the shotguns leaning against the table next to where they sat. They might take them down to the cellar. She thought, Well, if we're together. And thought, Bullshit.

Mad. The way she was on the porch the time Armand came and she fired twice. Mad because he was so goddamn sure of himself. Fired when he was close and fired again, when he was out by the chickenhouse. After that she went inside.

Now think.

She had laid the gun on the counter.

Wayne came home from the store where the girl had been shot and killed. Probably by the nickel-plated gun lying on the table to the right of Richie's plate, the stubby barrel pointing at Armand. The police arrived. No, they got here before Wayne, because he was questioned at the store for about an

hour, came home and a different bunch of cops
started on him and they didn't like his attitude.
They never liked it. Wayne saying if they weren't
going to handle it, he would. Wayne furious, in his
way, showing contempt, cold anger. *Wayne reload-
ing the shotgun in front of them.* Carmen remembered it now, yes, and the police didn't like it at all,
Wayne's Charles Bronson gesture. And the next
night—or was it the night after that?—the front
windows were shot out as they sat in the living
room and threw themselves on the floor and the
duck prints were blown off the wall, yes, and that
night Wayne took the shotgun upstairs. He said,
They could walk right in the goddamn house if
they want. He said, We'll clean that up in the
morning. He took the shotgun upstairs with them
saying, We'll hear this step squeak if they try it. She
remembered she didn't say anything. He stood the
gun against his night table but didn't like it there.
He said, I get up to go to the bathroom. . . . He
knelt down—she could see him doing it—*and put
the gun under the bed.*

That's where it was.

These two would have been standing by the bed
or sitting on it listening as she talked to Wayne and
then her mother, seven-thirty this morning. They
didn't notice it because the phone was on the night
table on her side of the bed and the gun was under
Wayne's side. She wondered if he might have

brought it downstairs later. But she didn't remember seeing it downstairs before they left and if he did they would have found it.

No, the shotgun was still under the bed, loaded.

Richie said, "What's wrong with our little bunny?"

Armand didn't say anything.

Richie said, "Hey, what's wrong with you? You scared or what?"

Carmen raised her eyes from the table. "Of course, I'm scared."

Richie acted surprised. "There's no reason to be. Old Wayne gets home, all we're gonna do is have a talk with him. Isn't that right, Bird?"

Armand, hunched over his plate, looked up at her with dull eyes, indifferent. He said, "That's right."

Carmen didn't speak. There was nothing to say that would mean anything. Richie seemed dumb enough to think she might believe him and Armand was telling her he didn't care if she believed it or not or care what Richie said. Richie could do whatever he wanted. Armand would watch. What she had to do, soon, was think of a way to get around the table past them, run upstairs to the bedroom, lock the door and pray to God the shotgun was under the bed and she'd have time to pick it up before they came busting in.

*   *   *

When the phone rang Richie said, "That must be old Mom, huh? Let's tell her you can't make it today, you're sick." He took Carmen by the arm into the kitchen, giving her instructions on the way. If it was Wayne, tell him to hurry. If it was anybody else, tell them she couldn't talk now, she had to get to her mom's. She reached for the phone and he said, "Wait now," and felt her jump as he slipped cold metal into the rear end of her panties, nosing the barrel of the nickelplate down to rest against her tailbone. He said, "Don't be dumb now and get your bummie shot off. I want it in one piece for after. Okay, make it quick."

Richie moved in close to listen and smell her hair. Heard the mom say, "Well, where *are* you?" Tough old broad. Carmen told her she was sorry but she couldn't make it. Richie poked her with the nickelplate. She said, "I'm sick." Her mom asked what was wrong. Carmen said she didn't know, she just didn't feel good. The mom said it must've been something she ate on the road and that's why she didn't travel, the food being terrible out there. The mom said, "Well, you don't sound too bad." The mom wanted her to come anyway on account of she was in awful pain and had called the doctor three times and he still hadn't called back, he let her sit by the phone for hours while he was busy

making money. Richie agreed with her. Doctors he
had known in the joint all had a superior attitude.
He got a surprise then when Carmen said all of a
sudden, "Can't you stop thinking of yourself for
one minute and listen?" Uh-oh. "I'm sick. Do you
understand that? You've had your turn, now it's
mine." Her mom didn't like that one bit. She said,
"Well, thank you very much—after all I've done
for you," and hung up.

Taking her back to the table Richie said, "You
ought to be ashamed of yourself, talking to your
mom like that."

Armand had the container of lasagna in front of
him now eating from it, taking his time; it was
pretty good, still warm. Richie had gone to the
toilet and Carmen in that undershirt was looking
at Richie's Model 27 Smith & Wesson lying on the
table. He said to her, "You ever shot one of
those?"

It caught her by surprise. She looked at him a
moment before shaking her head.

"Good," Armand said. Their eyes held for another moment and he was sorry he had spoken to
her.

Richie came in from the hall zipping up his
pants, a magazine under his arm. He said, "Jesus
Christ, Bird, you still eating?" The punk chewing

his gum. "Man, I already showed you what you're gonna look like."

Armand stopped eating, pushed the lasagna away from him and leaned on the table, his arms flat along the edge, one hand hanging, feeling his belly through his tie. He watched Richie, seated now, the magazine open, showing Carmen the picture of the twelve-hundred-pound man lying in bed, his little head peeking out from that tremendous body.

"Bird," Richie said, never shutting up, "listen to what the guy eats. For breakfast, two pounds of bacon, a dozen eggs and some rolls. Lunch, four Big Macs, four double cheeseburgers, eight boxes of fries, six little pies and six quarts of soda. Am I making you hungry?"

Keep talking, Armand thought, watching Richie blow a bubble and pop it.

"For supper he'll have three ham steaks, six sweet potatoes, six or seven regular potatoes and stuffing. Bird, can you imagine this guy taking a dump? Jesus Christ." Richie shook his head, studying the picture in the magazine. When he looked up he was starting to smile. "You know who could cook for this guy? Old Donna. Be like cooking for a whole fucking cellblock."

Armand watched Richie turn to Carmen.

"Donna Mulry's the Bird's sweetheart."

And was surprised when Carmen looked at him and said, "Why does he call you the Bird?"

Armand liked her asking him that. It reminded him of who he was. Or who he had been. He said, "I'm called the Blackbird," and almost smiled at her.

"Him and Donna are going to Memphis," Richie said, cracking his gum, "so they can visit Graceland, hold hands looking at all that Elvis Presley shit. Isn't that right, Bird?"

Look at the punk chewing away. "I think so," Armand said.

"Donna's this dried-up old broad use to be a corrections officer," Richie said to Carmen. "Man, did she love corrections. I can tell you why, too, if you want to know." Richie paused, he had plenty of time, and got a bubble going. A big one.

Armand's right hand came out of his coat holding the Browning auto. Richie wasn't looking. Armand racked the slide to put one in the chamber. Now he was looking, his eyes big peeking over that bubble. Armand the Blackbird said, "You get one, Richie, like everybody else," extended the Browning and shot him in the center of that pink bubble. The sound of it so loud—as Richie's head snapped back and came forward to hit the magazine lying on the table—always louder than Armand expected.

*   *   *

Carmen heard him say, "There," and heard him
blow out his breath even as she felt her head ringing, the room filled with the sound. She was holding herself rigid, but didn't realize it until the
sound faded to silence and she watched Armand
get up and move to the end of the table, watched
him lay his gun next to Richie's, lift Wayne's jacket
from the back of Richie's chair and use it to cover
Richie's head and shoulders. Carmen thought of
stopping him. Don't, that's my husband's. But kept
quiet, trying to feel Wayne close by, the way she
had felt him before and used him to get mad and
hold on. If he was with her now, he wasn't saying a
word. She stared at his jacket, at IRONWORKERS
BUILD AMERICA, blue on silver, and beyond it a
splash of color on the wall, deep red.

"You know what he did?" Armand said.

Carmen looked up. He was going toward the
kitchen.

"He called me Bird for the last time, that's what
he did." Armand walked into the kitchen and Carmen waited. She looked at the dull-metal automatic and the nickel-plated revolver on the table
next to the covered shape. Armand came out of the
kitchen with his bottle of whiskey saying, "I'm no
bird. All I know about that stuff was from my

grandmother. It was so long ago I don't even remember most of it."

Carmen watched him sit down at his place and
pour whiskey into his glass. He raised the glass to
her and took a sip.

"I'll tell you something else. I never saw her get
seagulls to shit on a car. Oh, they said she could do
it, but I never saw it. She was gonna turn me into
an owl one time. I said, 'I don't want to be no owl,
I want to be a blackbird.' She said okay. So I went
in the sweat lodge, I was in there hours. I come out
naked holding a blanket around me. She beats on
this little drum she's got and chants in Ojibway
awhile. She stops, she tells me to throw off the
blanket and fly away. I throw it off, raise my arms
up. Nothing happened. I feel my body, I said to
her, 'I'm no blackbird, I'm still me.' She says,
'When was the last time you bathed?' I said, 'You
mean washed myself? I took a bath yesterday.' She
says, 'Oh, you not suppose to bathe for a month.'
So I didn't become a blackbird." He raised his
glass to her, said, "That's my life story, whether
you understand it or not," and took a drink.

Carmen said, "Who wants to be a blackbird?"

He seemed to like that and came close to smiling. "If you could be any kind of bird there is,
what kind would you be?"

Carmen thought of birds and saw the bird prints

covering the walls of her mother's house. She said, "I wouldn't be a bird. I'd be something else."

He seemed to like that, too. "All right, what would you be?"

Carmen took a moment, breathed in, hesitated and breathed out through her mouth. She said, "Maybe a deer." She watched him nod, thinking about it. She said, "Although . . ." pulled the neck of the tank top away from her, lowered her head slightly and sniffed. "They smell awful."

He said, "We all smell at times."

She fanned the air in front of her. "Not this bad." She said, "That buck lure really smells." She said, "Could I get dressed?"

"If you want, sure. I'm not Richie, I'm not the same as him."

Carmen watched him raise his glass to the shape at the end of the table and take a drink.

She said, "I'll have to go upstairs."

There was a silence.

He said, "Well . . ."

She waited, expecting him to say, Didn't you bring clothes? Or, I'll go up with you. She watched him pour whiskey into his glass.

He said, "Okay, I'll give you one minute."

She didn't move.

"Go on."

Now she got up, walked around the table past him. When she was in the hall she heard him say,

"You don't want to be a bird, think of what you would be."

Carmen closed the bedroom door and locked it. She went to Wayne's side of the bed, dropped to her hands and knees and saw the Remington, right there, brought it out feeling the weight of it and smelling the oil smell. She went into the bathroom, closed the door and pumped the gun. There would be a cartridge in the chamber now if the gun was loaded. She pumped it again and a three-inch magnum slug ejected. It was loaded. She picked up the slug from the floor and shoved it into the magazine. Now, go do it. And thought, I can't. And told herself, Don't think. But at the bedroom door, her hand on the old-fashioned key sticking out of the lock, she started thinking again, she couldn't help it.

There was a George Jones song Armand had liked called "The Last Thing I gave Her Was the Bird," until he got sick and tired of Richie and then he didn't care for it anymore. That fucking Richie, he was like something stuck to the bottom of your shoe you couldn't get rid of, like his chewing gum. That wasn't a bad idea, though, take Donna down there to see Graceland. Why not? She was a stupid woman, but that was okay, he was tired of being alone in hotel rooms, bars, motels—take her on a trip, play some Yahtzee . . . One moment he felt relieved, a weight lifted off him, looking at the ironworker's jacket covering the punk. The next moment he didn't feel so good.

She could wait for him to come up. Get down behind the side of the bed with the gun aimed at the door. He walks in . . . But if he came upstairs he'd be ready, he'd have his gun in his hand he killed a man with, nothing to it, so easy for him, or he'd have a shotgun. Or he could wait, her nerves bad enough, and she wouldn't know where he was. Or she could listen for the stairs to squeak . . . And heard Wayne say to her, For Christ sake, if you're gonna do it, do it. Wayne took her that far, gave her the loaded gun. Now she had to hear herself say it, in her own words, and after that stop thinking.

You have to kill him.

There wasn't a sound in the house.

You have to go downstairs and kill him.

Carmen turned the key to unlock the door.

He was sorry now he had started talking to her. It was the same with the old man in the hotel room, he was sorry after they had talked; though he didn't feel sorry for the girl who ordered breakfast from room service and hardly touched it, wasting the old man's money. He had never talked to a person he was going to kill before he talked to the old man and now he had talked to this woman Carmen. He was thinking he'd better not talk to her anymore . . . and heard the stairs creak and heard her steps coming down to the front hall. Looking at his watch Armand said, "You're ten seconds late." Talking to her again, saying that without thinking because she was easy to talk to. He took a drink, waiting to see her come in, and held the glass, listening. When no sound came to him he said to himself, Man, you're getting old, you know it? He sat waiting. There was no way she could sneak up on him, but she was trying something. It got his mind working again. This woman had nerve. Putting the glass down he laid the palms of his hands flat on the table and turned his head enough to see his Browning close to Richie's .38, where he had laid it when he covered the punk with the jacket. He could reach it if he leaned over and stretched—pick it up with his left hand.

"So you don't like the idea of a bird," Armand said. "What do you want to be?"

No answer.

She was there, but she wasn't talking.

* * *

Carmen had the stock of the Remington against her bare shoulder, the barrel aimed at his face, his profile, twelve to fifteen feet away, close; though she was back far enough that she could see everything at the table: the covered shape, the two guns, Richie's bright one and Armand's dull-metal automatic, his head turned that way, and on the other side of him, to his right, the shotgun leaning against the table. She saw the light from the window shining on the crown of his black hair, above the slug barrel's front sight, her mind telling her, You have to kill him. But saw Richie killed as she heard that word, shot through the head, some of him coming out red to smear against the wall. And she lowered the sight to a point between Armand's shoulder blades, a thick solid shape in the black suit. *Do it* . . . Or she could shoot him through the cane back of the chair framed in dark wood. She raised her face from the gunmetal smell to look at him quick and make up her mind to shoot high or low but for God's sake shoot . . .

Just as he said, "Where are you, Miss?" and half-turned, brought the chair sideways to the table to sit looking at her over his shoulder.

Standing there in those nice little underpants with the shotgun. She knew it was here all the time, tricked him.

Armand said, "You found it, 'ey?" and squinted at that black hole pointing at him. "It looks like the same one you had that other time. Yeah, with the slug barrel." Wanting her to understand he didn't give a shit about it. "Let me ask you something. Is it loaded?"

"It's loaded."

Her voice sounded calm, but that didn't mean she wasn't scared. "You sure now. You not bullshitting me."

She said it again. "It's loaded."

Maybe she was afraid to say anything else, give away how nervous she was inside her nice underwear. He was thinking he had never gone to bed with a woman as slim and beautifully shaped as this one. He could see the points of her breasts in the undershirt, but couldn't see her dark place through the white panties. The ironworker's little wife surprised him then.

She came into the room, moving sideways to keep the 12-gauge pointed at him, and went to the end of the table to stand by the two handguns. He thought she was going to do something with them, get them out of the way. No, what she did was put the stock of the 12-gauge under her arm to hold it with one hand and with the other lifted the ironworker's jacket, uncovering the dead punk. It amazed him. To look at Richie? No, to fold the jacket against her body one-handed and lay it on the other corner of the table. Her husband's, taking care of it for him. This was the kind of woman to have. Live in the city and take her places, but not the Silver Dollar. He could take Donna Mulry to the Silver Dollar or Memphis, Tennessee. He felt tired and wouldn't mind lying down a while. Then pushed that from his head thinking, Man, what are you doing? Take the fucking gun away from her and use your own, one shot, get it done.

Armand got up from the chair. He heard wind rattle the windows, glanced over that way, picked up his glass and put it down, nothing in it, moving just a small step closer to her.

"Look at him, Miss," Armand said, nodding at the punk, wanting her to see the mess his bullet had made of Richie's head, his hair matted and dyed black now, some of what little brains he had shot out of him.

But she wouldn't look.

"See? You can't do it, you're a nice lady. You don't shoot people, you won't even look at dead ones. I'll tell you something, that slug gun would make a bigger hole than the one there." He inched one foot along the rag carpeting to take the next step, the big one.

"Miss, you don't want to put a hole in me."

Saying it to that slug barrel. She had both eyes open but they didn't tell him anything, the gun aimed at his chest. He was sure he couldn't talk her into putting it down. Maybe, if he hadn't shot Richie in front of her; but knew he would do it again, so forget it. He noticed the barrel waver a little. The gun became heavy holding it like that for so long. She had to be scared. Her nerves could make her pull the trigger when she didn't want to. Though it looked like she did.

Armand said to her, "You're not gonna shoot me. You know why?" He raised his left hand slowly and extended it, pointing a finger. "You see that little button? . . . You got the safety on."

He had her.

Saw her eyes change. Saw her finger come out of the trigger guard to feel for the catch, that push button. Armand grabbed the barrel, no problem, got both hands on it and gave it a twist, the gun was his. He took a moment to check the safety. It was off. She got nervous, didn't remember. Now she wouldn't need this thing. He threw the 12-gauge across the table to skid and land on the floor, over on the other side, turned back to her and said, "Oh, shit."

She had his Browning.

That fast, Christ, she had it aimed at him, holding it in both hands with her eyes wide open—not scared-to-death open, just open, staring at him.

He raised his hands to show her, Look, I'm unarmed, and stepped back saying, "Okay, take it easy, Miss," trying to think of a story to tell her . . . And she shot him. Fired his own gun at him and it was like the sound of it punched him in the belly, made him grunt and double over. He put his hand on the table to straighten up, said, "Wait now," and she shot him again, socked him in the chest with it so hard he went back against the chair and sat down. She was still pointing his gun at him. He told her, "Jesus Christ, you shot me." She didn't say anything to him. He was holding himself and had to take one hand from his body to lay his arm on the table and lean against the edge to keep from falling. She was holding the gun in two hands, her eyes the same as before, still not telling him anything. He was thinking, Never stick them in a bathroom like that nurse and say she didn't see you good. Never talk to them before. Never let them get hold of a gun you didn't know was there. He couldn't believe it, a woman in her fucking underwear had shot him and he was going to die.

Armand told her that. "You shot me." Like saying to her, Look what you've done. Wanting her to feel sorry for him. He said, "Don't you know you've killed me?" and saw her lower the gun. Now she spoke. What? Said something about her house. He couldn't hear too good and was slipping in the chair and had to hold on to the table. He said, "What?" and she spoke again, this time loud enough for him to hear.

She said, "You walked in my house!"

Mad. He thought, Yeah . . . ?

She wanted to hit him because he was dead and wouldn't listen to her. The son of a bitch. The feeling lasted a few moments. The only thing left to say to him was, "Goddamn you," for making her do it. She phoned the detective with the Michigan State Police and went outside to wait. They had better not ask her if she had an attitude problem.

Hours later, after they'd gone, she cleaned the kitchen, threw out all the food that was left, the candy, the gum she found in a drawer, the plastic tablecloth, and washed the wall in the dining room. She couldn't stay in the house. She put on her navy coat, turned the porch light on and went outside to walk in the field and wait for her husband. The wind had died to a cool breeze. Carmen would raise her face to it, her eyes closed.

"I got stopped," Wayne said, "goddamn it. I figured the shortest way would be take Fifty-seven up to Seventy, cut across to Indianapolis, catch Sixtynine, take it up to Ninety-four and follow Ninetyfour home. Is that the way you came?"

Carmen shook her head, standing with him in

the porch light, at the foot of the steps. "I took Fifty-seven all the way to Ninety-four."

"How's your mom?"

"The same."

"You go see her?"

"Not yet. I spoke to her—"

"I should've done that, stayed on Fifty-seven," Wayne said. "What happened, I missed the turn in Indianapolis, had to keep on Seventy all the way to Ohio and get on Seventy-five north. Well, you know what happened. Shit. I'm almost to Findlay and see the gumballs closing on me fast. . . . You call that cop?"

"I called," Carmen said, nodding, and could keep talking now if she wanted to, but paused.

"So the trooper comes up to the car, has the hat on. 'Sir, you know you were going seventy-eight in a posted sixty-five zone?' I tell him the reason I'm in a hurry there's an emergency at home."

Carmen listened.

"The guy never changes his expression. 'Sir, would you follow me, please?' What're you gonna say, no? They take your goddamn registration and driver's license. So I got to see beautiful Findlay, Ohio, and it only cost me fifty bucks."

Carmen watched her husband look out at the dark mass of woods, his woods, giving him time . . . maybe giving herself time. What was the hurry? They were home.

"Less than two weeks to deer season," Wayne said. "I can hardly wait."

She felt his arm come around her shoulders to hold her close, both of them looking out at the woods now as he said, "You want to try it this year?" Gave her shoulders a squeeze and said, "Hey, it's something we could do together."

Coming Up . . .

A sneak preview of

TISHOMINGO BLUES

by Elmore Leonard

"America's greatest living crime writer."
The New York Times

Available now at a bookseller near you

DENNIS LENAHAN THE HIGH DIVER would tell people that if you put a fifty-cent piece on the floor and looked down at it, that's what the tank looked like from the top of that eighty-foot steel ladder. The tank itself was twenty-two feet across and the water in it never more than nine feet deep. Dennis said from that high up you want to come out of your dive to enter the water feet first, your hands at the last moment protecting your privates and your butt squeezed tight, or it was like getting a 40,000-gallon enema.

When he told this to girls who hung out at amusement parks they'd put a cute look of pain on their faces and say what he did was awesome. But wasn't it like really dangerous? Dennis would tell them you could break your back if you didn't kill yourself, but the rush you got was worth it. These summertime girls loved daredevils, even ones twice their age. It kept Dennis going off that perch eighty feet in the air and going out for beers after to tell stories. Once in a while he'd fall in love for the summer, or part of it.

The past few years Dennis had been putting on one-man shows during the week. Then for Saturday and Sunday he'd bring in a couple of young divers when he could to join him in a repertoire of comedy dives they called "dillies," the three of them acting nutty as they went off from different levels and hit the water at the same time. It meant dirt-cheap motel rooms during the summer and sleeping in the setup truck between gigs, a way of life Dennis the high diver had to accept if he wanted to perform. What he couldn't take anymore, finally, were the amusement parks, the tiresome pizzazz, the smells, the colored lights, rides going round and round to that calliope sound forever.

What he did as a plan of escape was call resort hotels in South Florida and tell whoever would listen he was Dennis Lenahan, a professional exhibition diver who had performed in major diving shows all over the world, including the cliffs of Acapulco. What he proposed was that he'd dive into their swimming pool from the top of the hotel or off his eighty-foot ladder twice a day as a special attraction.

They'd say, "Leave your number" and never call back.

They'd say, "Yeah, right" and hang up.

One of them told him, "The pool's only five feet deep," and Dennis said, no problem, he knew a guy in New Orleans went off from twenty-nine feet into twelve inches of water. A pool five feet deep? Dennis was sure they could work something out.

No, they couldn't.

He happened to see a brochure that advertised Tunica, Mississippi, as "The Casino Capital of the South" with photos of the hotels located along the Mississippi River. One of them caught his eye, the Tishomingo Lodge & Casino. Dennis recognized the manager's name, Billy Darwin, and made the call.

"Mr. Darwin, this is Dennis Lenahan, world champion high diver. We met one time in Atlantic City."

Billy Darwin said, "We did?"

"I remember I thought at first you were Robert Redford, only you're a lot younger. You were running the sports book at Spade's." Dennis waited. When there was no response he said, "How high is your hotel?"

This Billy Darwin was quick. He said, "You want to dive off the roof?"

"Into your swimming pool," Dennis said, "twice a day as a special attraction."

"We go up seven floors."

"That sounds just right."

"But the pool's about a hundred feet away. You'd have to take a good running start, wouldn't you?"

Right there, Dennis knew he could work something out with this Billy Darwin. "I could set my tank right next to the hotel, dive from the roof into nine feet of water. Do a matinee performance and one at night with spotlights on me, seven days a week."

"How much you want?"

Dennis spoke right up, talking to a man who dealt with high rollers. "Five hundred a day."

"How long a run?"

"The rest of the season. Say eight weeks."

"You're worth twenty-eight grand?"

That quick, off the top of his head.

"I have setup expenses—hire a rigger and put in a system to filter the water in the tank. It stands more than a few days it gets scummy."

"You don't perform all year?"

"If I can work six months I'm doing good."

"Then what?"

"I've been a ski instructor, a bartender . . ."

Billy Darwin's quiet voice asked him, "Where are you?"

In a room at the Fiesta Motel, Panama City, Florida, Dennis told him, performing every evening at the Miracle Strip amusement park. "My contract'll keep me here till the end of the month," Dennis said, "but that's it. I've reached the point . . . Actually I don't think I can do another amusement park all summer."

There was a silence on the line, Billy Darwin maybe wondering why but not curious enough to ask.

"Mr. Darwin?"

He said, "Can you get away before you finish up there?"

"If I can get back the same night, before showtime."

Something the man would like to hear.

He said, "Fly into Memphis. Take Sixty-one due south and in thirty minutes you're in Tunica, Mississippi."

Dennis said, "Is it a nice town?"

But got no answer. The man had hung up.

This trip Dennis never did see Tunica or even the Mighty Mississippi. He came south through farmland until he began to spot hotels in the distance rising out of fields of soybeans. He came to signs at crossroads pointing off to Harrah's, Bally's, Sam's Town, the Isle of Capri. A serious-looking Indian on a billboard aimed his bow and arrow down a road that took Dennis to the Tishomingo Lodge & Casino. It featured a tepee-like structure rising a good three stories above the entrance, a precast, concrete tepee with neon tubes running up and around it. Or was it a wigwam?

The place wasn't open yet. They were still landscaping the grounds, putting in shrubs, laying sod on both sides of a stream that ran to a mound of boulders and became a waterfall. Dennis parked his rental among trucks loaded with plants and young trees, got out, and spotted Billy Darwin right away talking to a contractor. Dennis recognized the Robert Redford hair that made him appear younger than his forty or so years, about the same age as Dennis, the same slight build, tan and trim, a couple of cool guys in their sunglasses. One difference, Dennis's hair was dark and longer, almost to his shoulders. Darwin was turning, starting his way as Dennis said, "Mr. Darwin?"

He paused, but only a moment. "You're the diver."

"Yes sir, Dennis Lenahan."

Darwin said, "You've been at it a while, uh?" with sort of a smile, Dennis wasn't sure.

"I turned pro in '79," Dennis said. "The next year I won the world cliff-diving championship in Switzerland, a place called Ticino. You go off from eighty-five feet into the river."

The man didn't seem impressed or in any hurry.

"You ever get hurt?"

"You can crash, enter the water just a speck out

of line, it can hurt like hell. The audience thinks it was a rip, perfect."

"You carry insurance?"

"I sign a release. I break my neck it won't cost you anything. I've only been injured, I mean where I needed attention, was my first time at Acapulco. I broke my nose."

Dennis felt Billy Darwin studying him, showing just a faint smile as he said, "You like to live on the edge, uh?"

"Some of the teams I've performed with I was always the edge guy," Dennis said, feeling he could talk to this man. "I've got eighty dives from different heights and most of 'em I can do hungover, like a flying reverse somersault, your standard high dive. But I don't know what I'm gonna do till I'm up there. It depends on the crowd, how the show's going. But I'll tell you something, you stand on the perch looking down eighty feet to the water, you know you're alive."

Darwin was nodding. "The girls watching you . . ."

"That's part of it. The crowd holding its breath."

"Come out of the water with your hair slicked back . . ."

Where was he going with this?

"I can see why you do it. But for how long? What will you do after to show off?"

Billy Darwin the man here, confident, saying anything he wanted.

Dennis said, "You think I worry about it?"

"You're not desperate," Darwin said, "but I'll bet you're looking around." He turned saying, "Come on."

Dennis followed him into the hotel, through the lobby where they were laying carpet, and into the casino, gaming tables on one side of the main aisle, a couple of thousand slot machines on the other, like every casino Dennis had ever been in. He said to Darwin's back, "I went to dealer's school in Atlantic City. Got a job at Spade's the same time you were there." It didn't draw a comment. "I didn't like how I had to dress," Dennis said, "so I quit."

Darwin paused, turning enough to look at Dennis.

"But you like to gamble."

"Now and then."

"There's a fella works here as a host," Darwin said. "Charlie Hoke. Chickasaw Charlie, he claims to be part Indian. Spent eighteen years in organized baseball, pitched for Detroit in the '84 World Series. I told Charlie about your call and he said, 'Sign him up.' He said a man that likes high risk is gonna leave his paycheck on one of these tables."

Dennis said, "Chickasaw Charlie, huh? Never heard of him."

They came out back of the hotel to the patio bar

and swimming pool landscaped to look like a pond sitting there among big leafy plants and boulders. Dennis looked up at the hotel, balconies on every floor to the top, saying as his gaze came to the sky, "You're right, I'd have to get shot out of a cannon." He looked at the pool again. "It's not deep enough anyway. What I can do, place the tank fairly close to the building and dive straight down."

Now Darwin looked up at the hotel. "You'd want to miss the balconies."

"I'd go off there at the corner."

"What's the tank look like?"

"The Fourth of July, it's white with red and blue stars. What I could do," Dennis said, deadpan, "paint the tank to look like birchbark and hang animal skins around the rim."

Darwin gave him a look and swung his gaze out across the sweep of lawn that reached to the Mississippi, the river out of sight beyond a low rise. He didn't say anything staring out there, so Dennis prompted him.

"That's the spot for an eighty-foot ladder. Plenty of room for the guy wires. You rig four to every ten-foot section of ladder. It still sways a little when you're up there." He waited for Darwin.

"Thirty-two wires?"

"Nobody's looking at the wires. They're a twelve-gauge soft wire. You barely notice them."

"You bring everything yourself, the tank, the ladder?"

"Everything. I got a Chevy truck with a big van body and a hundred and twenty thousand miles on it."

"How long's it take you to set up?"

"Three days or so, if I can find a rigger."

Dennis told him how you put the tank together first, steel rods connecting the sections, Dennis said, the way you hang a door. Once the tank's put together you wrap a cable around it, tight. Next you spread ten or so bales of hay on the ground inside for a soft floor, then tape your plastic liner to the walls and add water. The water holds the liner in place. Dennis said he'd pump it out of the river. "May as well, it's right there."

Darwin asked him where he was from.

"New Orleans, originally. Some family and my ex-wife's still there. Virginia. We got married too young and I was away most of the time." It was how he always told it. "We're still friends though . . . sorta."

Dennis waited. No more questions, so he continued explaining how you set up. How you put up your ladder, fit the ten-foot sections on to one another and tie each one off with the guy wires as you go up. You use what's called a gin pole you hook on, it's rigged with a pulley and that's how you haul up the sections one after another. Fit them on to each other and tie off with the guy wires before you do the next one.

"What do you call what you dive off from?"

"You mean the perch."

"It's at the top of the highest ladder?"

"It hooks on the fifth rung of the ladder, so you have something to hang on to."

"Then you're actually going off from seventy-five feet," Darwin said, "not eighty."

"But when you're standing on the perch," Dennis said, "your head's above eighty feet, and that's where you are, believe me, in your head. You're no longer thinking about the girl in the thong bikini you were talking to, you're thinking of nothing but the dive. You want to see it in your head before you go off, so you don't have to think and make adjustments when you're dropping thirty-two feet a second."

A breeze came up and Darwin turned to face it, running his hand through his thick hair. Dennis let his blow.

"Do you hit the bottom?"

"Your entry," Dennis said, "is the critical point of the dive. You want your body in the correct attitude, what we call a scoop position, like you're sitting down with your legs extended and it levels you off. Do it clean, that's a rip entry." Dennis was going to add color but saw Darwin about to speak.

"I'll give you two hundred a day for two weeks

guaranteed and we'll see how it goes. I'll pay your rigger and the cost of setting up. How's that sound?"

Dennis dug into the pocket of his jeans for the Kennedy half-dollar he kept there and dropped it on the polished brick surface of the patio. Darwin looked down at it and Dennis said, "That's what the tank looks like from the top of an eighty-foot ladder." He told the rest of it, up to what you did to avoid the 40,000-gallon enema, and said, "How about three hundred a day for the two weeks' trial?"

Billy Darwin, finally raising his gaze from the half-dollar shining in the sun, gave Dennis a nod and said, "Why not."

Nearly two months went by before Dennis got back and had his show set up.

He had to finish the gig in Florida. He had to take the ladder and tank apart, load all the equipment just right to fit in the truck. He had to stop off in Birmingham, Alabama, to pick up another 1,800 feet of soft wire. And when the goddamn truck broke down as he was getting on the Interstate, Dennis had to wait there over a week while they sent for parts and finally did the job. He said to Billy Darwin the last time he called him from the road, "You know it's major work when they have to pull the head off the engine."

Darwin didn't ask what was wrong with it. All he said was "So the life of a daredevil isn't all cute girls and getting laid."

Sounding like a nice guy while putting you in your place, looking down at what you did for a living.

Dennis had never said anything about getting laid. What he should do was ask Billy Darwin if he'd like to climb the ladder. See if he had the nerve to look down from up there.